Even the phlegmatic Kruger showed some interest in the large and very elegant Edwardian mansion that suddenly came into view. Fronting the mansion, and facing south to take advantage of the view across the valley, was a broad, paved terrace guarded by a slate block retaining wall whose balustrade was capped with more of the decorative stone balls. There were even stone balls along the parapets of the huge dormer-windowed hall itself; whoever had built the mansion obviously had a strong liking for stone balls.

There were some more men on the terrace. They were wearing shapeless uniforms, and were gathered around garden tables playing cards. They too stopped to stare at the new arrivals.

Fleming followed the drive round to a cobbled courtyard at the rear of the mansion and stopped the car. He switched off the engine and gave Kruger an amiable smile.

'Welcome to Grizedale Hall, Otto. Number One Prisoner of War Camp for captured officers. This is now your home until the war's over.'

James Follett trained to be a marine engineer, and also spent some time hunting for underwater treasure, filming sharks, designing powerboats, and writing technical material for the Ministry of Defence before becoming a full-time writer. He is the author of numerous radio plays and television dramas, as well as fifteen novels including *The Tiptoe Boys*, *Churchill's Gold*, *Dominator*, *Swift* and *Trojan*. He lives in Surrey.

*Also by James Follett
and available in Mandarin*

Trojan
Dominator
Swift
Ice
Mirage
Churchill's Gold
The Doomsday Ultimatum
U700
Torus
Savant

James Follett

A CAGE OF
EAGLES

Mandarin

A Mandarin Paperback
A CAGE OF EAGLES

First published in Great Britain 1990
by Mandarin Paperbacks
This edition published 1993
by Mandarin Paperbacks
an imprint of Reed Consumer Books Ltd
Michelin House, 81 Fulham Road, London SW3 6RB
and Auckland, Melbourne, Singapore and Toronto

Copyright © James Follett 1989

A CIP catalogue record for this title
is available from the British Library
ISBN 0 7493 0036 1

Printed and bound by Firmin-Didot (France),
Group Herissey. No d'impression : 31569.
Reprinted 1995.

FOREWORD

In 1979 I wrote a novel, *U-700* (US title: *The Wotan Warhead*), which was based on the circumstances surrounding the surrender to the RAF in 1941 of a German U-boat and the subsequent 'trial' of the U-boat's first officer by his fellow prisoner of war officers at Grizedale Hall in the Lake District. Research for the book produced an astonishing flood of accounts from former POWs, guards, and even London 'Cage' interrogators. The useful material was very useful indeed, but it was outweighed by a mass of fascinating material that had no bearing on the incident I was concerned with.

Stumbling on such a motherlode of exciting material and not being able to use it rankled considerably. I had prospected for emeralds – and found them, but I had also stumbled upon gold. For example: try as hard as I could, there was no logical way that I could work into *U-700* the amazing story of the two escaping *Luftwaffe* officers who stole an RAF aircraft. It simply refused to fit. Nor could I use any of the material relating to the remarkable lengths that the senior German officer at Grizedale Hall went to in his attempts to warn the German High Command of the existence of 'Huff Duff' – seaborne high-frequency radio direction finding.

The obvious solution was to write another book.

This novel is not a sequel to *U-700*, although there are

unavoidable parallels with that earlier novel simply because the settings and some characters are the same. In *U-700* I described the 'trial' of a U-boat officer by his fellow POWs for cowardice. A similar kangaroo court-martial is covered in this book. Both events took place; both ended in a tragedy that still haunts those involved to this day.

I am indebted to the many individuals who provided such a wealth of material but particular thanks are due to Alan Graydon for supplying me with a detailed account of the time when, to use his own words, he 'gave' two *Luftwaffe* escapees an RAF trainer.

Having lived with the story of Grizedale Hall for so many years, I was also most grateful for being allowed to pick over the sad ruins of the hall (it was demolished by the Forestry Commission in 1957) so that I could build some of its slate blocks into the walls of my house. Strange to think that part of the original fabric of the 'Cage of Eagles' is now standing in a Surrey village.

James Follett
November 1987

Part One

ARRIVAL

The *Luftwaffe* had been busy over London.

In contrast with the devastation wrought by the bombers, Commander Ian Lancaster Fleming looked immaculate in his expertly cut Royal Navy Volunteer Reserve uniform. He was well aware of the admiring glances of office girls on their way to work as he motored his Bentley tourer into Seacole Lane off Fleet Street.

He was sorry to see that Pallisters had taken a direct hit: no more leisurely evenings whiled away before a roaring log fire under mellow oaken beams. The curious blast patterns from Goering's 1000-pound bombs had left a number of neighbouring buildings unharmed apart from shattered windows – now staring out on London like the eyeless sockets of a blind man. In other cases entire internal walls of four-storey buildings were exposed – each wall on each floor contributing to a clashing mosaic of coloured distemper, patterned wallpapers, and the tiled surfaces of what had once been bathrooms and kitchens. A fireplace, two floors up, even had a clock sitting unconcerned on its mantelpiece. Fleming's keen powers of observation, which would later stand him in good stead as a thriller writer, were such that he noticed the clock was showing the right time.

Fleming drove slowly down Seacole Lane, threading his way past hastily erected barriers around partly demolished buildings that council workers and Air Raid Precautions wardens were shoring up with baulks of timber. He was relieved to see that Louis Bros tailors' shop was still standing, albeit minus a few windows. Max, the surviving partner, was re-rolling a bolt of cloth that had been blown into the street. He was a distinguished-looking man in his early fifties, a man who took great care with whatever he was doing. So intent was he on re-rolling the cloth that he did not hear the Bentley sidle up to the kerb like a docking ship.

'Morning, Max,' said Fleming cheerily, stepping down from the Bentley's running board. 'Looks like I'm going to end up having to pay your bill after all if the Jerries keep missing you every night.'

Max looked up and gave a broad beam of genuine pleasure while at the same time running a critical eye over the cut of Fleming's uniform. 'Commander Fleming! Delighted to see you. Josie will put the kettle on while I see to that right shoulder pad.'

Fleming chuckled and held up his hand. 'Sorry, Max, old boy, but it'll have to wait. Can't stop.'

'But it needs trimming, commander,' Max protested. 'A simple alteration. It will only take five minutes.'

Fleming knew all about Max's idea of simple alterations that would take only five minutes. He shook his head regretfully. 'Later, Max. Meanwhile I've got a little job for you. Go and fetch your tape measure and tell Josie to cancel your appointments.'

Max looked puzzled, 'Now, commander?'

Fleming climbed behind the steering wheel of the giant car and reached across to open the passenger door. 'Right now, please, Max, old son. I've got a very important new client for you.'

After a twenty-minute drive in which Fleming talked animatedly about his schooldays in Switzerland, Max followed the naval officer into the hallway of a large, nondescript, Edwardian mansion standing in its own grounds in a cul de sac off the Bayswater Road. A man in civilian dress was sitting at a desk. He examined Fleming's blue Admiralty pass, gave Max a cursory glance, and nodded to the broad staircase.

'He's just had breakfast, sir.'

'Excellent,' said Fleming. 'Let's hope he's in a good mood this time.'

Max accompanied Fleming to the first floor, where an armed corporal was lounging against the wall outside a door. He snapped to attention when he saw Fleming and gave a crisp salute. Max caught a whiff of pungent cigar smoke. Fleming smelt it too; his aristocratic nostrils twitched. He frowned and said to the corporal, 'It would seem that our friend has got hold of some more of those infernal cigars.'

'Smells like it, sir,' said the corporal. 'Gawd only knows how he can stand them at this time of the morning.'

'Or indeed at any time,' Fleming murmured, rapping on the door.

There was a silence. Fleming rapped again.

A man's voice answered, 'Come!'

The single word was correctly pronounced but there was a curious clipped quality about it. Max was certain that the speaker wasn't English. He followed Fleming into a sparsely furnished sitting-room. The acrid smell of cigar fumes stung his eyes. He wiped them and saw a man sitting in an armchair, partially hidden by a copy of the *Daily Telegraph*.

'Morning, old boy,' said Fleming breezily. 'I've brought you the promised visitor.'

The man slowly lowered the newspaper without speaking and rose to his feet. He was in his mid-thirties and was tall – at least six foot three inches. He was wearing a badly stained shirt and ill-fitting trousers that did nothing to ease the sudden feeling of dread that Max experienced. It was the man's eyes – the hard, unwavering, hypnotic stare – that held the Jewish tailor's entire consciousness in a compelling, irresistible grip which seemed to bore straight into his soul, probing its innermost recesses for concealed guilt and hidden secrets.

'Good morning, Commander Fleming,' said the man stiffly, not taking his eyes off Max for an instant.

Max's stomach performed a double somersault and tried to crawl into his bowels. He had heard a whisper that Fleming was involved in 'hush-hush work'. If so, was this Fleming's method of arresting suspects? Was he about to be interrogated about the gossip he had overheard from his influential clients?

'Meet your first U-boat "ace", Max,' said Fleming affably. 'This is Korvetten Kommander Otto Kruger – commanding officer of *U-112*. Or, rather, he was until two days ago. Your job is to run him up a new uniform. We can't have him meeting the press in his present state, can we?'

Admiral Godfrey, the Director of Navy Intelligence, and his assistant, Ian Fleming, watched the newsreel in silence. The wailing air-raid alert sirens howling across London could be heard faintly by the two men sitting in the private cinema because the sound track of the *Movietone* newsreel rush they were watching was not ready.

The darkened room, with its deep, comfortable chairs for an audience of ten, was the same as that used by Winston Churchill when he wished to unwind by watching a favourite film such as *Gone with the Wind* or Chaplin's *The Great Dictator*.

The five-minute monochrome clip that the two men were watching with close interest showed Commander Otto Kruger disembarking down a ship's gangway in the company of two armed marines. His haughty, aristocratic features were fixed in an expression of sardonic inscrutability. Beside Kruger, the well-scrubbed marines guarding him looked decidedly scruffy; the captured U-boat commander was wearing a beautifully cut *Kreigsmarine* greatcoat, unbuttoned at the front to reveal his double-breasted uniform jacket and knife-edge-creased trousers. His Knight's Cross and Oakleaves, awarded by a grateful Hitler to his top-scoring U-boat 'ace', gleamed dully at his throat. Every detail of Kruger's uniform was correct – right down to the white cap-cover that U-boat commanders wore so that they could be distinguished by other members of the U-boat's crew at night.

Kruger disdainfully ignored the camera and the reception committee of two NCOs by pausing at the foot of the gangway to light a cheroot. The camera moved in for a close-up of the hawk-like, impassive features. The German officer's brooding eyes regarded the camera in contempt for a few seconds and then, as if to underline his disdain, he exhaled a cloud of cigar smoke straight at the lens.

The brief newsreel insert ended with Kruger exchanging crisp, very correct salutes with an army officer and entering the back seat of a Humber staff car.

The lights came on. Fleming languidly stubbed out his cigarette and consulted his notes. He chuckled and said to Admiral Godfrey: 'The commentary will run something along the lines, "Well may you strut and preen, Herr Kruger; well may you sneer and try to look proud, but you're not so proud now, are you, you Nazi rat? Not with your U-boat two and a half miles down on the floor of the Atlantic. But don't worry, Herr Kommander – it isn't alone because our brave boys on the high seas are sending it plenty of your Fuehrer's submarines to keep it company and there'll be plenty of company for you with all your U-boat cronies at your prisoner of war camp somewhere in England."'

'Good grief,' Admiral Godfrey muttered.

Fleming grinned. 'I think I could do better, sir.'

'I don't doubt it for one moment,' the admiral murmured drily.

'Actually, sir, Kruger isn't a Nazi. He has no interest in politics and appears to hold all politicians in contempt.'

'And the British, of course.'

'I don't think so, sir. He did admit to me that his loyalties are to the Fatherland, his flag officer – Admiral Doenitz, and his crew.'

'How about his family?'

Fleming shook his head. 'He refused to discuss it.'

'A wife or girlfriend?'

'He gave us two names and addresses for his Red Cross notifications. A secretary, Alice Kramer – a girl in his home town of Bremen, and Doenitz himself.'

Admiral Godfrey gave Fleming a shrewd glance. 'Why was he kitted out with a new uniform?'

'Major Charleston at the Ministry of Propaganda agreed with me that it would look more effective that way.'

'I see. And whose budget has the cost dropped on? Ours or theirs?'

'Ours, sir. I thought it might be useful if they owed us a few favours.'

Admiral Godfrey sighed. 'How much?'

Fleming looked uncomfortable. 'The clothing depot at Didcot provided the material. It's not a perfect match but it's near enough.'

'I didn't ask where the material came from.'

'Three hundred guineas, sir.'

Admiral Godfrey's eyes opened wide. 'For a uniform?' His voice was deceptively mild.

Fleming fiddled sheepishly with his briefcase. 'Kruger refused to be filmed unless he was provided with a complete wardrobe, sir. Shoes, socks, shirts, greatcoat, gloves, ties – everything.'

'We could have filmed with or without his permission,' Admiral Godfrey pointed out.

'Yes, sir. But I thought it would be a good idea if audiences saw a top German at his best so that they'd realize that appearances alone don't make them invulnerable.'

Admiral Godfrey grunted. 'And all we've got out of it is a scowl at the camera. Fleming, has it occurred to you that Kruger may be using you rather than the other way round?'

'I'll get more than a scowl out of him before I'm through, sir,' said Fleming smoothly.

Admiral Godfrey looked unconvinced. 'Well, we don't appear to have got anything out of him yet,' he remarked testily. 'I've not seen a report from you.'

'I haven't really interrogated him, sir, if that's what you mean.'

The admiral looked sharply at his subordinate. 'After two weeks? Why not? I put you on to him because you speak fluent German – not so you could take your time.'

'Kruger's a unique prisoner, sir. My guess is that he's one of the few U-boat commanders to be issued with the new magnetic torpedo. He's sunk more shipping than any naval commander in history. He's shrewd and he's cunning. Orthodox interrogation methods won't work.'

'The magnetic torpedo isn't the only thing we're interested in right now,' Admiral Godfrey interrupted caustically.

Fleming looked surprised. 'But I thought –'

'The G7e torpedo will be issued to an increasing number of U-boats as it goes into full production,' said Admiral Godfrey. 'It's only a matter of time before we get our hands on a talkative torpedo officer or, better still, we manage to get a boarding party on to a U-boat before it's scuttled. The information we need from Kruger is much more vital than that.'

'What information, sir?'

The admiral regarded Fleming thoughtfully. 'Is it true that you met Kruger before the balloon went up?'

'Yes, sir. During the Coronation Spithead Review in

1937. The *Admiral Graf Spee* was lying alongside the *Hood*. Kruger was a lieutenant then. He was amongst a party of German officers who were invited on to the *Victory* for a drink by the C-in-C of the Home Fleet.' Fleming smiled diffidently. 'Actually Kruger and I got on somewhat famously together. He spent his weekend in London at my flat.'

Admiral Godfrey nodded. He unbuckled his briefcase and handed Fleming a folder marked 'Most Secret'. 'Two reports for you to read, Fleming. The first one is from our naval attaché in Montevideo. One of his staff managed to get aboard the *Graf Spee*'s hulk in the River Plate and climb its wireless mast. The sketches he supplied of what was left of its radio aerials have convinced the PM's scientific advisors that the Germans have developed a method of radio ranging for gunnery control. Do you know what radio ranging and location is?'

Fleming had heard the expression mentioned in the Admiralty but he prudently shook his head.

'Well, I'm no boffin,' said the admiral. 'Everything you need to know is in the reports. Basically, radio ranging is a method of using the echoes from beamed wireless transmissions to plot the position of an enemy ship over a distance of twenty miles – maybe more.'

Fleming was silent for a few seconds as the full import of what the admiral had said sunk in.

'I hope we're working on something similar, sir.'

'I expect we are,' said the admiral noncommittally. 'The second report details some of the extremely sketchy information we have on radio ranging research that the Germans carried out during the thirties. There was a committee set up in Berlin in 1934 to co-ordinate research. Around 1937, when the German U-boat arm was re-established, a special *Kriegsmarine* subcommittee was set up to develop radio ranging and location equipment that was small enough to be installed in U-boats.' Admiral

Godfrey paused. 'It's one thing to build several tons of cumbersome gear for installation in a battleship – quite another to make it small enough to fit in a U-boat. And if it can be built to go in U-boats, then it can be installed in aircraft. I don't have to spell out what that would mean.'

Fleming nodded. 'Did they succeed?' he asked.

'In 1938 the U-boat subcommittee authorized the production of an equipment called *Drehturm Gerat*,' Godfrey replied.

'Revolving turret apparatus,' Fleming translated.

'Something like that. Anyway, it was fitted into several U-boats. How many – we don't know. How effective it was – we don't know. Nor do we know which company made it – probably Siemens in Berlin – or what frequency it operated on.'

'What has all this got to do with Kruger, sir?'

Admiral Godfrey stood. While Fleming was helping him into his overcoat he said, 'What we do know is that a certain Otto Kruger was on both *Kriegsmarine* committees.' He gave Fleming a hard look. 'It's my guess that Kruger's presence on the *Graf Spee* before this lot started had something to do with his knowledge of radio ranging and location. He must know a hell of a lot about this *Drehturm Gerat* equipment. There's also the possibility that it was fitted to his U-boat, which would account for his uncanny ability to track down convoys – either that or it was sheer good luck.' The admiral moved to the door and gave Fleming another hard stare. 'As far as the War Cabinet is concerned, Kruger is the most important prisoner to fall into our hands so far. The *Graf Spee* equipment was installed over two years ago and therefore must be out of date by now. Therefore it's imperative that we discover just how advanced the Germans are now with their radio ranging and location equipment. You've got to know Kruger, Fleming. That's why, as from now, you're being

17

given a free hand to find out all you can from him and other prisoners about *Drehturm Gerat*.'

Fleming looked alarmed. 'Kruger's no fool, sir. It won't be a simple matter of asking a few quest –'

'You're the one who's always advocating subtle and unorthodox interrogation methods,' Admiral Godfrey interrupted testily. 'Well, now's your chance to practise what you've been preaching. I'm having you posted to Kruger's POW camp as a special intelligence officer.'

Fleming looked aghast. 'You mean that I'm being posted away from London?'

'The experience of the Shap Well Hotel camp is that the prisoners are not on their guard once they're no longer being interrogated. The intelligence officer there has picked up a great deal of information. You must do the same. And, as I said, you have a free hand. Thank you for the film show. It was most interesting, although I'm not sure treating Kruger like that has served any useful purpose. The Prime Minister is taking a personal interest in this matter. I've told him that my best operator is dealing with the problem and that he will have some concrete information by the end of the month, and regular monthly reports thereafter. Straight, factual reports, please. And try to keep the melodramatic cloak and dagger content to within reason. You will be writing reports, not thriller novels. Good day to you, Fleming.'

The senior intelligence officer strode out of the private cinema leaving an appalled Ian Fleming gaping after him.

The wind howling round the windscreen and the shrill scream of the Amerhurst-Villiers supercharger, sounding as though it was about to blow itself into a thousand pieces, made ordinary human speech in Fleming's Bentley tourer an impossibility, especially when the throttle pedal seemed to spend most of the journey in Fleming's favourite position: hard on the floor. The only variation in his driving technique was when the brake pedal was hard on the floor.

Even if talk had been possible, Fleming guessed that Kruger would have spent most of the eight-hour drive north in a stoic, brooding silence. Over lunch in a Preston restaurant that specialized in drab food and shining prices, Kruger had unbent slightly to recount his days as a cadet on the *Kriegsmarine*'s sail training ship, *Gorch Fock*. He had made no mention of when or how he had joined the U-boat arm, and Fleming, biding his time, had not pressed him on the matter. Fleming, in turn, was a little surprised that the U-boat ace had shown no interest in where he was being taken.

It had been a magnificent day with a blazing May sun traversing a clear blue sky and promising that the summer of 1941 was going to match the glorious summer of 1940.

By 4 pm the car was skirting the panoramic sweep of Morecambe Bay at a modest forty miles per hour. Fleming waved a languid arm at the vast expanse of sand where the sea was a band of molten light, barely visible on the horizon. He remarked in German, 'In the spring and autumn the tidal bore comes in at thirty miles an hour. In the last century the stage-coaches would chop about twenty miles off their journey by risking a short-cut across the sands. A lot of them were never seen again. If the quicksand didn't get them, the tide did.'

'Interesting, Commander Fleming,' answered Kruger in his clipped but perfect English. He lit a cheroot and looked as bored as a caged eagle on a hot afternoon.

Fleming grinned at his passenger. 'Any idea where we are, Otto?' He had started using Kruger's first name during the journey.

Kruger inhaled on his cigar and glanced across at the dashboard in front of Fleming. 'We've driven three hundred miles due north from London – nearly five hundred kilometres. The sun's on our left, therefore we are on the western coast of northern England, nearly into Scotland. This must be Morecambe Bay near the Lake District. Correct, commander?'

It was the longest sentence that the aloof U-boat ace had uttered so far; Fleming was delighted. 'Spot on, Otto,' he answered in English.

Kruger gave a ghost of a smile at the Englishman's capitulation. 'Why are there no road signs? When I was studying at Exeter University there were many road signs.'

'Ah. That's to confuse the invader.'

'I see. You believe that the German army will have to depend on road signs when they arrive?'

Fleming wasted one of his disarming grins on Kruger whilst making a mental note to check up on the period of time that Kruger had spent at Exeter. That he had studied in England was a new piece of information which might be worth following up. 'Well,' he replied cheerfully, 'I daresay we've been judging the map-reading ability of the German army by the map-reading ability of the British army, Otto.'

Kruger did not respond to Fleming's jibe at his own countrymen. Instead he studied the scenery intently as though he were imprinting it on his mind.

Fleming swung the car inland and followed a winding main road that took them through the craggy splendour of the granite-scarred Cumberland fells. He cut the super-charger and trickled the tourer along at a steady twenty miles per hour, occasionally reducing speed to pass fell walkers togged out in full hiking kit despite the hot afternoon. Sheep browsed on the rolling green slopes; hedge sparrows intent on nesting fought among themselves over wisps of wool that the sheep had left on the ragged dry-stone walls that snaked over the hills like grey varicose veins, and an invisible skylark, high up in the cloudless sky, presided over the spring awakening with a sweet, continuous song.

'Makes you wonder why we're bothering to fight a war, eh, Otto?' said Fleming, wondering what the impassive German officer was thinking.

'I don't need magnificent countryside to make me think that, commander,' was the curt reply.

Despite Fleming's debonair, easy-going nature, his armour against such barbs was exceptionally resilient. He chuckled and made no reply.

As they motored deeper into the mountains and away from the coast, Kruger noticed that the British enthusiasm for removing signposts appeared to have waned: the little town of Newby Bridge, with its neat houses and shops built of blue slate from the nearby quarries at Coniston, was clearly marked, and so was the bridge across the River Leven that the town was named after. It was as they were crossing the river that Kruger caught his first glimpse of an English lake.

'Windermere,' said Fleming in answer to Kruger's question. 'Over ten miles long and the largest lake in the Lake District. The smaller ones are called tarns.'

The scenery changed dramatically fifteen minutes later when the winding country lane Fleming was following plunged into the deep valley of Grizedale Forest. The pleasant views across broad fields gave way to thickly wooded, sombre hills which were completely hidden by countless acres of spruce and Douglas fir. The pines stood tall and silent in their regimented rows, as if well aware that they were out of character with the surrounding countryside. So closely planted were they that there was no natural light to sustain ground cover; the straight trunks grew out of bare soil that had been poisoned by generations of pine needles. There was little insect life and therefore the birdsong was conspicuous by its absence.

Fleming pulled up outside a magnificent pair of wrought-iron gates set into a high slate wall. The gates' piers were crowned with large, decorative, stone balls. A soldier emerged from a wooden guardhouse and carefully examined the documents that Fleming showed him. Satisfied, the soldier nodded to a second guard, who grudgingly unlocked the gates and waved the Bentley through.

The car swept up a curving drive and skirted an unkempt lawn that covered several acres. A whooping mob of about thirty men, all wearing shabby, unrecognizable uniforms, were storming across the grass. They were laughing and cheering themselves hoarse. The object of their adulation was a good-looking young man with blond hair who was being carried in shoulder-high triumph by two of the men. Someone shouted and pointed to the car. The mob fell silent and gazed in astonishment at the sight of an immaculately dressed *Kriegsmarine* officer riding as a passenger in an open-tourer Bentley.

Even the phlegmatic Kruger showed some interest in the large and very elegant Edwardian mansion that suddenly came into view. Fronting the mansion, and facing south to take advantage of the view across the valley, was a broad, paved terrace guarded by a slate block retaining wall whose balustrade was capped with more of the decorative stone balls. There were even stone balls along the parapets of the huge dormer-windowed hall itself; whoever had built the mansion obviously had a strong liking for stone balls.

There were some more men on the terrace. They were wearing shapeless, unrecognizable uniforms, and were gathered around garden tables playing cards. They too stopped to stare at the new arrivals.

Fleming followed the drive round to a cobbled courtyard at the rear of the mansion and stopped the car. He switched off the engine and gave Kruger an amiable smile.

'Welcome to Grizedale Hall, Otto. Number One Prisoner of War Camp for captured officers. This is now your home until the war's over.'

*

Leutnant Willi Hartmann was a plump, balding Bavarian whose taste for bribery, graft and a spot of corruption here and there was a sharp contrast to his strong aversion to any form of physical exercise other than counting money.

Willi had shrewdly joined in the riotous celebration of Dieter von Hassel's release from twenty-eight days' solitary confinement following his latest escape bid, because the revellers' ringleader was Hauptmann Paul Ulbrick, the camp's senior officer. That was the only reason; the perspiring little Bavarian felt that galloping around the grounds on a hot afternoon was an enterprise that was definitely very low on fun and non-existent on profitability. He fervently hoped that von Hassel's inevitable next escape bid – his sixth – would be more successful.

Willi wiped the sweat from his moon-like face with a grimy handkerchief and jogged gamely into the courtyard with his fellow officer POWs. They stopped a respectful distance from the car and stared bug-eyed at the apparition of a resplendent *Kriegsmarine* commander stepping down from the tourer and exchanging salutes with Major James Reynolds, Grizedale Hall's commanding officer.

Willi blinked several times. Maybe the mixture of a prison diet and American chocolate bars was affecting his eyesight. But there was no doubt about it: the German officer was wearing a greatcoat made of best-quality worsted wool, top-quality black leather shoes polished to perfection, kid gloves, and, as a final touch, the Knight's Cross and Oakleaves pinned to his black tie. To round off the image, the new arrival was smoking a cigar.

'My God,' breathed Ulbrick. 'Maybe we've won the war and the *tommies* haven't had the guts to tell us?'

The two prisoners carrying von Hassel on their shoulders allowed him to slide to the ground. The flamboyant young *Luftwaffe* pilot looked slightly aggrieved at no longer being the centre of attention.

'We've not won anything,' said a U-boat officer despairingly. 'That's none other than Otto Kruger of the First U-boat Flotilla.'

The news was greeted with a buzz of comment.

'What's he like?' asked Ulbrick, noticing that he was outranked by the new arrival.

'There was a joke at Lorient that there was a plan to have him pulled down and a human being built instead.'

A *Luftwaffe* officer gave a loud groan. 'He's a commander, Paul – that means he'll be taking over as the senior officer.'

Willi gazed in mounting alarm at Kruger as he accompanied Fleming and Reynolds to the administration block adjoining the kitchens and converted garages on the far side of the courtyard. Kruger's hard, sardonic expression and hawk-like features suggested that the relatively easy days at Grizedale Hall under Hauptmann Paul Ulbrick were over.

Kruger's inscrutability was put to the test. He put down his cup of coffee on Reynolds' desk and stared incredulously at the Canadian officer. 'A holiday camp?' he echoed. 'You mean to tell me that the British are housing us POWs in a *holiday camp*?'

Major James Reynolds, Canadian Army Corps, DSO, adjusted his black eye-patch to cover his embarrassment. He found Kruger's piercing gaze as disconcerting as his perfect English.

Reynolds had lost his left eye at Dunkirk the year before and had been ruled unfit for further active service. He had been offered early retirement, a pension, and a free, army-issue, pink eye-patch. He had declined all three: the early retirement because he was only thirty-three, and the pink eye-patch because he thought that his black one gave him Douglas Fairbanks' swashbuckling air. He glanced irritably at Fleming, who was doing his best not to laugh.

Avoiding the German officer's hard stare, he replied, 'Well, hardly a holiday camp, Commander Kruger. Grizedale Hall was built in 1905 for Harold Brocklebank, a shipping millionaire. He died in 1936. The Holiday Fellowship used it until last year – 1940 – when it was requisitioned by the War Office.'

'Who's the senior German officer at the moment?' inquired Kruger, lighting a cheroot.

'Hauptmann Paul Ulbrick of the *Luftwaffe*,' Reynolds replied. 'You outrank him, of course, therefore you are now the senior officer.'

'Has he maintained good discipline?'

Reynolds scowled. 'Hardly. He's a close friend of Dieter von Hassel – our dedicated escapee who has spent most of his time here in solitary confinement for his hare-brained bids. He's tried five times now with Ulbrick's connivance. As the senior officer, he should know better.'

'Isn't it a POW's duty to escape, old boy?' inquired Fleming.

'It's one thing to escape from Grizedale Hall, Commander Fleming,' Reynolds replied testily, wondering whose side Fleming was on, 'but it's quite another to escape from the fells.' He turned to Kruger. 'I'm sure you must have noticed on your drive here just how remote we are. The pikes may look beautiful but you'd be surprised at the number of walkers who've died on them.'

'Pikes?' Kruger queried. 'I am sorry – it is a new word.'

'The local name for the mountains,' said Reynolds curtly. 'I'm from Montreal and I thought I knew everything there was to know about hard winters, but here they can be really something. Last January a German officer died of exposure on Heron Pike. He'd spent two days in a blizzard wandering in circles. And if the pikes don't get you, the bogs and tarns most certainly will. Another thing – the Home Guard and War Reserve Constables here are all

25

local lads who know the fells like the backs of their hands. It never takes them long to pick prisoners up. Incidentally, tunnelling is out of the question because Grizedale Hall is built on rock – there's only a few inches of topsoil.'

Kruger exhaled boredly on his cheroot and regarded Reynolds steadily through a cloud of curling smoke.

'There're one or two other things we need to get straight,' Reynolds continued. 'Firstly this is a "white" camp for non-Nazi officers. The borderline cases go to the "grey" camps, and the hard-liners go to the "black" camps run by the Free Polish in a manner the War Office turn a blind eye to. Any suggestion of Nazi bullying – indoctrination – anything like that – and the prisoner concerned is sent immediately to a "black" camp.' Reynolds paused and gestured to the window. 'Secondly, as you've seen, Grizedale Hall is a magnificent stately home, one of the finest in the country, and I aim to keep it that way. After the war the War Office will have to hand it back to its owners in its original condition. If it comes to any harm, we'll be only too happy to rehouse you in huts. The prisoners have freedom of movement in the hall and grounds during the day and they're locked in the hall between sunset and sunrise. How they organize their accommodation is up to their senior officer. He's reponsible for internal discipline – we look after security. It's a simple system and it works. There's a Queen Alexander's Royal Army Nursing Corps sister, Brenda Hobson, who has a sickbay next to the downstairs shower rooms. She works here twenty hours a week and looks after the medical records of all eighty-two prisoners. All prisoners are required to help out in the kitchens. Organizing the rota is your job. There's a daily roll-call in the courtyard at 0800. Snap roll-calls can be called at any time. Any questions?'

Kruger shook his head.

'Sergeant Finch!'

The camp adjutant poked his head around the door from

the adjoining office. He was a stocky, belligerent-looking little man who, with his toothbrush moustache, bore a striking resemblance to Hitler. He was a shrewd man, a clear thinker with a capacity for cunning that belied his somewhat absurd appearance. He glowered resentfully at Kruger. It wasn't a case of hate at first sight because Sergeant Finch hated all Germans even before he saw them.

'Saar?'

'Show Commander Kruger around the hall please, sergeant, and see that he is supplied with a list of all the prisoners.'

'Yes, saar!' The NCO glared at Fleming. He wasn't over-fond of the Royal Navy either. 'Excuse me, saar. But how much longer is that car going to be parked outside? Only the Jerries are showing a lot of interest in it so I've had to post two men on it.'

'Commander Fleming will be leaving shortly,' said Reynolds irritably.

When the two men had left, Reynolds said to Fleming, 'It's unusual for a prisoner to be delivered here personally, commander.'

Fleming grinned. 'As I was coming up anyway, I thought it would be a chance to get to know him. I presume you've been told about my posting here?'

'I received a letter last week.'

'Don't worry, I won't be here full-time. Just flitting in and out as the mood takes me.'

'I don't mean to sound rude, commander, but just what the hell is going on?' Fleming's casual tone had irritated the Canadian.

'It's all to do with obtaining intelligence from POWs after they've been placed in their camp. Can you provide me with an office please, old boy? Nothing pretentious.'

Reynolds referred to the letter that Fleming had given him. 'I guess so.'

'I take it you have no objection to me having access to your prisoners?'

'Do I have any choice?'

'Not really, old boy. Just observing a few courtesies.' Fleming grinned broadly. 'Incidentally, our friend Kruger is believed to be a mine of useful information, so please don't lose him.'

'My prisoners don't escape. Well, not for more than forty-eight hours.'

'Oh? What about our missing torpedo officer – Leutnant Herbert Shultz?'

Reynolds looked uncomfortable. Leutnant Herbert Shultz was his least favourite topic of conversation. 'What about him?'

'He's now been missing since last October. Six months.'

'He escaped before I took over.'

'Oh really?' said Fleming innocently. 'I thought it was a week after. A pity he's not around. I looked at his inter-rogation transcript the other day. It was bungled. If he was questioned properly, he might provide some useful gen on the latest German torpedoes. Everyone seemed to be too obsessed by the fact that he was a vet in civilian life.'

Reynolds groaned inwardly. First it was War Office busybodies poking their noses into the affair of Leutnant zur See Herbert Shultz, now it was the Admiralty. He decided to change the subject. 'Will you be staying around here, commander?'

'You must call me Ian,' said Fleming affably. 'And I'll call you James. Yes, I daresay I'll be staying here on and off. The Eagle's Head at Satterthwaite looks comfortable.'

Reynolds cursed his misfortune. Satterthwaite was the neighbouring village whereas most London visitors opted for the comfortable hotels of Ambleside ten miles to the north.

Fleming looked at his gold wristwatch. 'I don't suppose they'd thank me for turning up at this time of the afternoon,

James. My inner man is screaming for attention so I don't suppose your mess could fix me up with a bite, could they?'

'Yes,' Reynolds muttered, standing up. 'I'll join you.'

As the two men moved to the door, Fleming noticed some fishing tackle standing in a corner. 'Is the trout fishing any good around here?' he inquired.

'It's great,' said Reynolds, warming to his favourite subject. 'Mrs Standish lets me fish in her tarns.'

'Mrs Standish?'

'One of the local landowners. She actually owns most of the Grizedale Estate – that is, the bits that the Forestry Commission didn't want. She's very rich and very widowed.'

'Ah. Think she might let me join you one afternoon?'

'I guess she might,' said Reynolds heavily, thinking what a rotten war it was turning out to be.

In the courtyard a group of prisoners were admiring Fleming's Bentley under the watchful eyes of two guards. The leading admirer was Leutnant Dieter von Hassel.

'A magnificent car, commander,' the young flier remarked to Fleming as he and Reynolds walked past.

Fleming paused and replied in fluent German: 'The finest in the world, leutnant. Perhaps, when the war is over, we'll see some more duels between Bentleys and Auto Unions at Brooklands?'

At first Hassel was nonplussed by Fleming's command of German but he recovered quickly and smiled. 'With the Auto Unions winning as usual, of course,' he replied. He knelt down and pointed to the wide gap between the cobbles and the tourer's running board. 'That's the trouble with the Bentleys, commander, they're too high off the ground. The centre of gravity is wrong. The banking at Brooklands was built especially for Bentleys but our Auto Unions do not need it.'

'I'm sure you're right,' agreed Fleming, not wishing to be drawn into an argument.

*

Fleming and Reynolds left the camp by a guarded side gate set into the perimeter wall and crossed the narrow lane to the converted outhouses that served as the guards' quarters.

Dieter von Hassel, deep in thought, continued to study the Bentley. While watching the two guards every bit as carefully as they were watching him, he ran his hand lovingly along the graceful bonnet. Suddenly he had an idea that he considered nothing short of brilliant.

Willi was sitting in the open doorway of the common room's French windows that opened on to the terrace when he spotted Kruger mounting the terrace steps that led from the garden. He started whistling – the signal to the other prisoners on the terrace and in the common room that a guard was approaching.

Willi suddenly felt somewhat foolish: although Kruger wasn't a guard, the U-boat commander's sinister demeanour had triggered Willi's in-built alarm system which had developed as a result of being a prisoner of war for a year.

Kruger paused on the steps and stared contemptuously at Willi and then at the prisoners playing cards. 'Your name, please?'

Willi was pleasantly surprised by the unexpected friendly tone in Kruger's voice. He scrambled to his feet and gave Kruger a hurried salute. 'Leutnant Willi Hartmann, commander,' he blurted out.

Kruger's gaze moved to the Army School of Motoring 'MS' insignia embroidered on Willi's grubby shoulder marks. 'What are you doing in a prisoner of war camp, leutnant?'

'I was shot down, commander.'

'You're a motor transport officer?'

'Yes, commander.'

'What vehicle do you normally drive?'

'A Benz truck, commander.'

'You were shot down in a Benz truck?'

'No, commander.'

'So what were you shot down in?'

'A Heinkel bomber, commander.'

Willi flinched away from the hard stare.

'What were you doing in a Heinkel?'

It was a question that Willi had been dreading. 'My unit had been posted to Chartres in France where there was a Heinkel bomber group,' he replied, trying hard not to look embarrassed. 'I scrounged a flight as an observer on a daylight raid on the Isle of Wight.'

'Why?'

'I wanted to see England, commander.'

Kruger gave a ghost of a smile and glanced at the panoramic view south down the valley. 'Well, you're seeing a lot of England now, aren't you, leutnant?'

'Yes, commander,' said Willi miserably.

'Are you ever bored?'

'Sometimes, commander.'

'You won't be for much longer. The British NCO, Sergeant Finch, told me that the short fat one knows everything that's going on here. His words were that you can scrounge anything and that you've got your thieving, pudgy little fingers into every pie and that one day he's going to break them off one by one. I presume he meant you?'

'Yes, commander.'

'Excellent, Willi,' said Kruger. 'As from now you're my executive officer. I've found two suitable rooms on the top floor for my office and bedroom, which I shall require you to furnish, but first I want you to pass the word that all officers are to assemble in the common room in thirty minutes.' Kruger looked at his watch. 'At 3.30 pm precisely.'

While Willi was wearily trudging around the four acres of Grizedale Hall's grounds, passing on Kruger's message, a group of twelve prisoners entered the courtyard at the rear of the hall and started a lively game of football. They used a goal that had already been chalked on the slate buttressing wall at the northern end of the courtyard. The two guards standing boredly by Fleming's Bentley were only too glad to have something to watch. They didn't notice Dieter von Hassel and Peter Ulbrick emerge from the laundry room and lean casually against a wall.

Play stopped after five minutes over a hotly disputed goal. The claim by the *Luftwaffe* team that they had scored was met with hoots of derision from the defending *Kriegsmarine* side.

Von Hassel and Ulbrick became very tense and braced themselves against the wall.

In the absence of a referee, the argument developed into an all-out row. A U-boatman suddenly swung a vicious punch at a fighter pilot and within seconds all hell broke loose with fists flailing and boots seeking targets that were not the football. The two guards cursed roundly and ran across the courtyard. They waded into the midst of the brawl, blowing their whistles and hauling the combatants clear of the battle zone by their arms and legs.

Ulbrick and von Hassel moved as one despite their lack of rehearsal. They raced forward, threw themselves down on the cobbles and rolled under the Bentley in one neat, well-co-ordinated movement. Ulbrick yanked several leather laundry hamper straps from under his jacket while von Hassel hooked his legs over the car's rear axle and pushed himself off the ground by his hands. Working quickly and silently, Ulbrick passed three straps around von Hassel's body and lashed the ends securely to the vehicle's chassis. He did the same with the young flier's arms and legs, leaving a hand free so that von Hassel could cut the straps with a knife.

'Okay, Dieter,' Ulbrick whispered. 'You can let go.'

Von Hassel relaxed his grip on the underside of the car. The makeshift leather harness held his body six inches clear of the ground. 'How do I look?' he grunted, trying to ease his cheek away from the rough surface of a cross-member.

'Like a trussed chicken.'

The clatter of guards' boots and yelled orders in English announced the arrival of reinforcements.

'See you when you come out of the cooler,' chaffed Ulbrick, grinning.

'This time I'm not coming back, Peter.'

'That's the sixth time I've heard that from you.'

'I mean it, Peter. This time I'm going home.' The *Luftwaffe* officer's voice was deadly serious.

Ulbrick grinned at his friend. 'Don't forget to write,' he said, pushing a sheathed kitchen knife into the front of von Hassel's jacket where it could be reached easily.

Von Hassel grinned. 'Good luck with the new senior officer.'

Ulbrick made no reply. Instead he grasped von Hassel's free hand briefly and peered across the cobbles to where the fight was dying down. Gauging the right moment, he rolled out from under the car, crawled towards the wall and stood. He propped himself against the wall with his hands thrust casually into his pockets.

Sergeant Finch pounded into the courtyard like a demented walrus. He didn't join the tangle of prisoners and guards but braked to a standstill some paces away, his eyes darting everywhere and missing nothing.

'Stop!' he bellowed.

All activity ceased. Prisoners and guards alike gaped apprehensively at the puce-faced apparition confronting them.

'What's going on here?'

'A fight, sarge.'

Sergeant Finch moved his face to within a fraction of an

inch of the hapless guard who had spoken. 'What have I always said about diversions, Corporal White?'

The guard pointed to a *Luftwaffe* officer who was nursing a split lip and a U-boatman in charge of what held the early promise of turning into a Technicolor eye. 'It was too serious to be a diversion, sarge.'

Finch glared suspiciously at the Germans. 'Okay, you lot. The party's over.' He gave a slow, malicious grin. 'In more ways than one, I fancy. Your new commanding officer wants to meet you all in the common room in twenty minutes.'

Of the eighty-one expectant faces filing into the ornate, oak-panelled common room that had been Harold Brocklebank's drawing room, the dozen faces that belonged to the two football teams looked in need of urgent repair.

Kruger stood with his back to the magnificent white marble mantelpiece and consulted the list that Sergeant Finch had given him. Willi took his place at a small writing desk and waited, pen and paper at the ready.

'You may all be seated, gentlemen,' said Kruger, glancing up at the prisoners and returning to a detailed study of the list.

Some of the Germans dropped into the large, easy chairs while others distributed themselves on the floor or on the carved staircase that led to the gallery. Two posted themselves near the French windows and one stood guard near the main doorway. All were silent, waiting for Kruger to speak.

The U-boat ace cleared his throat. 'I take it there's a system for ensuring that we're not overheard?'

'Yes, commander,' said one of the officers by the open French windows.

Kruger nodded. 'Good afternoon, gentlemen,' he said in a clear voice. 'Firstly, I will introduce myself. I'm Otto

Kruger, the former commander of *U-112* and, whether you like it or not, I'm taking over from Hauptmann Ulbrick as senior officer until we're liberated.'

The blunt opening produced an exchange of glances.

'I propose,' Kruger continued, 'to run this camp along the same lines that I ran *U-112* – that is, at maximum efficiency. Therefore there are going to be a number of changes. Within a week I will have Grizedale Hall running like clockwork. To achieve that, every man will have a task to perform and there will be monthly rotas so that no one need ever get bored.'

'Are you suggesting that we do menial work?' queried Ulbrick from the back of the hall.

Kruger turned a cold stare on Ulbrick. 'Your name?'

'Hauptmann Peter Ulbrick.'

The U-boat ace gazed steadily at Ulbrick. 'No, Hauptmann Ulbrick, I'm not *suggesting* that you do menial work. I shall be ordering you to do so – because that's the only work there is. If I could put you on to something useful such as building Heinkels or U-boats, I would do so.'

Kruger's rare approach to what might be termed a joke was rewarded by chuckles; it effectively discouraged Ulbrick from further argument.

'As I call out your names,' said Kruger, tapping his list, 'I want you to stand up so that I can see who you are. But first, can anyone tell me why Leutnant Herbert Shultz's name has a question mark against it on the roll?'

'He escaped, commander,' said Ulbrick.

'When?'

'October 1940.'

Kruger arched his eyebrows. 'It's now May 1941. Has he reached home?'

Ulbrick shrugged. 'We would have heard by now if he had. The British won't admit that he has escaped. Every morning at roll call, Finch yells out his name, and every morning he doesn't answer.'

'Have you tried to find out what has happened to him?'

'From whom?'

Kruger lit a cigar and snapped the spent match in two with his thumbnail. The U-boatmen who knew Kruger from their days at Lorient recognized the danger signal. 'From the Red Cross, Hauptmann Ulbrick,' said Kruger icily. 'As the senior officer at the time, it was your duty to find out.'

'Well, it's now your duty, commander.'

Kruger realized that a face was missing. 'Where is our habitual escapee?'

'Von Hassel is sleeping,' Ulbrick replied promptly, deliberately omitting Kruger's rank.

'I passed the word that all officers were to muster in here,' said Kruger mildly.

'Be reasonable,' said Ulbrick. 'He's just been released from twenty-eight days in the cooler. This is the first time in a month that he's been able to sleep in a decent bed.'

Kruger considered for a moment and appeared to come to a decision. He glanced down at his list. 'Very well. The first name is Aisne, Hubert R. Hauptmann Aisne, will you please stand.'

While von Hassel was waiting patiently, trussed like a potato peeler blade to its handle beneath Fleming's Bentley, the weather set about doing something that it was exceptionally good at doing in the Lake District: it started raining. It was proper Lake District rain that went sideways, lashing itself to a fine spray with the ferocity of a thousand demented bullwhips.

Von Hassel heard some shouted 'goodbyes' followed by running footsteps. He twisted his head slightly and saw Fleming's polished shoes dancing around the car as their owner pulled the Bentley's hood up. The driver's door opened and closed. The finely tuned engine fired on the first crank of the self-starter. A linkage moved near von

Hassel's hand as the handbrake was released. The car swung in a circle, drove out of the courtyard and down the uneven drive to the main gates. The jolting caused the leather straps supporting von Hassel to bite painfully into his body. He managed to twist his leg away from the rapidly heating exhaust pipe. Water thrown up by the huge wheels drenched him; it ran along the underside of the vehicle and trickled down his neck. He realized that he was in for the most uncomfortable ear ride of his life.

The car stopped at the main gate in the middle of a large puddle. Hassel twisted his head round and his heart nearly stopped when he saw the reflection in the puddle of his right leg under the Bentley's running board. A guard had merely to glance down at the puddle when checking the car and it would be another twenty-eight days in the cooler for Dieter von Hassel.

'Thank you, gentlemen,' said Kruger when the last prisoner had identified himself. 'It will take me a week to remember all your names. Willi Hartmann will be issuing my work rosters within the next seven days. Who are the members of the escape committee?'

'There isn't one,' said Ulbrick. 'I didn't see the point of one. If a man came up with an idea, then it was up to him to carry it out if he wished.'

Kruger nodded. 'Perhaps that's just as well because from now on, my express orders are that escapes are strictly forbidden unless the would-be escapee can convince me that every detail has been thought out, including plans for getting home.'

The guard's boots splashed through the puddle, breaking up the reflection of Hassel's leg, but splattering the escapee's face with muddy water.

'All okay, sir,' the guard called out.

The wrought-iron gates squealed open. Fleming drove

out of the camp. Von Hassel offered up a silent prayer of thanks when he heard the gates clank shut. The next minute he was grimly trying to lift his body as high as possible as Fleming accelerated along the winding country lane.

In the driving rain, Fleming missed the Satterthwaite fork and only realized his mistake after ten minutes motoring along a lane that had degenerated into little more than a rough track. He turned the car around in the entrance to a field and drove back the way he had come. He wiped the inside of the windscreen clear of condensation while trying to peer through the torrential rain. He passed a farmhouse that he hadn't seen before and realized that he was hopelessly lost. He had no choice but to continue down the hill because the lane, with its high banks, was too narrow to turn the car around.

Fleming swore roundly and braked hard. The Bentley's wheels locked and brought the big car to a standstill at the edge of a ford that crossed a wide stream. From underneath the car, von Hassel couldn't see the stream but he could hear broken water surging past rocks.

Fleming wiped the inside of the windscreen again and tried to assess the depth of the ford. From the way the water danced over small rocks, he guessed that it couldn't be more than a few inches deep and would therefore be no problem for the Bentley with its high ground clearance. Also the road on the far side was in good condition and looked as if it might go somewhere. He revved up the engine, engaged first gear, and released the handbrake.

Contact with the icy mountain water made von Hassel gasp with shock. He put his free hand down and touched the gravel-strewn bed of the stream. Although the water was shallow and therefore he wasn't in danger, he decided that now, with the car moving slowly, was a good time to cut himself free. He pulled the knife from its sheath and was about to cut the first strap when the Bentley's rear wheel slipped off a small boulder and dropped the car six inches.

The sudden jolt caused the knife to slip from his fingers. It dropped into the water. He tried to snatch it from the bed of the stream but the forward movement of the car put it out of reach.

Suddenly the Bentley's rear wheels were spinning impotently and von Hassel could hear Fleming's faint curses above the roar of the engine. The wheels stopped and went into reverse, churning up muddy water that swirled over Hassel's thighs.

After four attempts in forward and reverse which only served to bog the car down even more in the mud, Fleming decided that he would have to walk back to the farmhouse to fetch help. Cursing his misfortune, he removed his shoes and socks, rolled up his neatly pressed trousers, and stepped down in the water.

Von Hassel waited for a minute after the British officer had left and set to work with his fingers to untie the nearest knot in the leather straps.

After tearing his fingernails and lacerating his skin for five minutes, he realized that the water was causing the leather straps to tighten. He started sawing the strap back and forth on the rough edge of a chassis member. A crumb of comfort was that at least the water was supporting his weight to some extent so that the straps weren't cutting into him so much. It was then that he experienced the same sensation of raw fear that he had felt the previous year when the Hurricane's machine-gun shells had raked his Me109 and set fire to his fuel tanks: the reason the water was supporting his weight was because the level of the stream was rising. And it was rising fast.

He frantically renewed his efforts to saw through the strap. If only he could cut one strap, he might be able to wriggle free.

The surging water crept up to his face which he then had to press hard against the underside of the Bentley in order to breath. He could no longer see what he was doing and the rising water deadened the diminishing effort that his aching arms muscles could put into the hopeless task of sawing through the unyielding strap.

Suddenly the water was over his chin. He began desperately tearing at the strap with terror-induced strength but to no avail. He started choking on a mouthful of water. In that moment, Dieter von Hassel did something that he had never done before: he panicked but there was no one to hear his sobbing cries.

'But you can't ban escapes!' Ulbrick protested. 'Not in the spring when the escape season's just started!'

'I didn't say I was banning them,' said Kruger, addressing all the prisoners and not just Ulbrick. 'I said that I would not permit any escape that had not been properly prepared or thought out. If someone comes up with a sound scheme, then it is likely that I will approve it. In due course, I will set up a new escape committee with myself as chairman to vet all plans placed before it. For the time being, anyone with an escape idea can forget it unless it is a first-class idea. That is all, gentlemen. The meeting is closed.'

Cathy Standish was a forty-year-old widow who knew how to wear her sexuality like most women knew how to wear slippers. Her horse knew it and so did Fleming but neither did much about it: the horse was too busy hauling Fleming's Bentley out of the swollen stream, and Fleming was in no mood for dalliance – not even with someone as dalliable with as Cathy Standish.

'Come on, Brutus. Come on,' said Cathy, giving the Suffolk Punch an encouraging slap on the rump when the car got stuck again. 'That's my boy. Heave ho.'

The horse threw its weight on the collar. The rope tightened, squeezing water from its fibres, and the Bentley lurched out of the swollen stream. Water streamed off its running boards which had been partly submerged by the time Fleming had returned with Cathy and Brutus.

'Mrs Standish,' said Fleming gratefully, bending down to untie the rope from his car's front axle. 'I don't know how to thank you.'

Cathy placed her hands on her hips and laughed. The rain enhanced her voluptuousness by causing her denim trousers and blouse to cling to her body like wet wallpaper to a pillow. 'You can start by calling me Cathy, commander. Do you think she'll start?'

'Only one way to find out,' Fleming replied as he climbed behind the wheel.

After ten attempts, Fleming ended up with a flat battery and a flooded, silent engine.

'Water in the petrol I expect,' Cathy diagnosed. 'Hitch the rope up again, commander, and we'll haul you back to Grizedale Hall. Some of the prisoners there are mechanical geniuses.' She gave Fleming a mischievous smile. 'Or we could tow it back to the farmhouse to try out your skills.'

Fleming grinned amiably. With water streaming down his face, he said. 'Perhaps I could take a rain cheque on that kind offer, Mrs Standish?'

Ulbrick was playing table tennis in the billiard room when word reached him that Fleming and the Bentley had returned on the end of a towrope attached to one of Cathy Standish's horses.

It had stopped raining when he strolled casually into the courtyard. His mind raced when he saw the Bentley. Had there been enough time before the breakdown occurred, or whatever had happened, for von Hassel to have cut himself free? Was he still strapped under the car?

Major Reynolds was listening sympathetically to Fleming as the naval officer related his catalogue of misfortunes. Cathy Standish was nearby holding Brutus by his reins.

Ulbrick moved nearer the car and combed his hair. He deliberately dropped the comb and stooped to pick it up, glancing towards the Bentley as he did so. He saw a lifeless hand resting on the cobbles.

Suddenly Ulbrick wanted to be violently sick.

All of the prisoners had seen the guards removing von Hassel's lifeless form from beneath the Bentley, and the supper that evening at long trestle tables in the common room was an unusually subdued affair. The blond, happy-go-lucky flier had been one of the most popular men in the camp. Ulbrick had spent the entire meal staring with unseeing eyes at his untouched plate of sausage and mashed potatoes. There was very little conversation to die away when Kruger stood and rapped his spoon for silence.

His speech was short and to the point. 'In view of today's events, I am imposing a total ban on all escape attempts until further notice. Any prisoner who disobeys me will be court-martialled at the first opportunity after our liberation.'

'What will happen to von Hassel, commander?' asked a fighter pilot.

'His body is to be sent home,' Kruger replied dispassionately. 'I suppose it can be said that at least von Hassel will have finally achieved his objective.'

Part Two

HUFF DUFF

Willi broke the War Office censor's seal on his letter and read the typewritten contents in some dismay. It was the third warning he had received from the Feldgendarmerie at Chartres. The oberst in charge of investigations regarding the disappearance of certain motor spares from Willi's old depot and their reappearance on the black market was not interested in the feeble excuses that Willi kept trotting out. Unless Leutnant Willi Hartmann presented himself to the Feldgendarmerie within twenty-eight days, he would be summarily arrested, no matter where he was, and taken back to Chartres by armed escort.

The War Office censor had scribbled in German at the foot of the letter a somewhat gleeful 'Bad Luck, Leutnant Hartmann'.

Willi sighed and broke the seal on the envelope with the Bremen postmark that was addressed to Kruger. The woman's handwriting and her scented envelopes were familiar; he was groping in his drawer for his magnifying glass even before unfolding the letter.

Alice's letters to Kruger were long, verbose affairs, full of gossip about the goings on in her solicitors' office. Who was sleeping with whom; who had been sacked, and so on. The closing paragraphs were couched in affectionate terms and always ended with a string of 'Xs'.

Willi studied the epistle through the magnifying glass and found the first tiny break between one letter and the next almost immediately. He wrote down the letter preceding the break on a separate piece of scrap paper. His magnifying glass continued tracking along the line and stopped when it came to the second break. That letter too was written down.

After ten minutes Willi had a brief message for Kruger from Admiral Doenitz. The simple letter code, which Kruger had shown Willi how to operate, had been devised by Doenitz in collaboration with all his U-boat commanders so that in the event of capture, they could continue to send intelligence back home.

A distant whistling of the opening bar of Beethoven's Fifth warned Willi that Kruger was approaching.

'Willi,' said Kruger, marching into the room. 'If you insist that I should have a signature tune, please find someone who can whistle in the right key.' He spotted the letter that Willi had decoded. 'What has the admiral got to say this time?'

'He wishes you a happy birthday,' said Willi boredly.

Beatrix Potter, or Mrs Heelis as she preferred to be called, was a formidable seventy-five-year-old Lake District landowner. She was dressed in grimy, ill-fitting tweeds, a moth-eaten bonnet and several layers of old cardigans – the few remaining buttons of which were fastened to the wrong buttonholes.

As she chatted animatedly to Reynolds on their tour of Grizedale Hall's grounds, the Canadian officer couldn't help thinking that she looked exactly like Mrs Tiggy Winkle, the character that she had created many years before. Unlike Mrs Tiggy Winkle, Beatrix Potter was a phenomenally rich woman, thanks to the royalties that her children's books continued to earn, even though she had given up serious writing many years before. The great interests that now dominated her cloistered life were her Lake District estates, her herds of prize-winning Herdwick sheep, and the National Trust of which she was a founding member and one of its principal benefactors.

It was this latter interest that had brought her to Grizedale Hall in a chauffeur-driven car from her farm at the neighbouring village of Near Sawrey.

'Of course, I never knew Harold Brocklebank personally, Major Reynolds,' she said when they paused on the eastern side of the estate, near the overgrown vegetable gardens which a party of prisoners were clearing. The men stopped work to gape at the unlikely couple. 'But I do remember Grizedale Hall being built. My late husband was involved in some of the legal work you know.'

Reynolds didn't know. 'About Commander Kruger's suggestion –' he began for the third time.

'Of course, it was the Ainslie family that owned the original estate.' She gestured to a hill to the west which had always puzzled Reynolds by its symmetrical shape. 'That mound is artificial. Brocklebank had it built because he couldn't stand the sight of the Ainslies' house. He was an eccentric, you know.'

My God, thought Reynolds. That's rich coming from you. 'Miss Potter –' he began.

'What's that monstrosity?' Mrs Heelis interrupted, pointing an accusing finger south at a crude tower made from pine trunks that was rearing above the shrubbery.

'It was a Forestry Commission firewatchers' tower,' Reynolds explained. 'I requisitioned it and had it moved to the corner of the barbed wire fence to serve as a watchtower for my guards.'

Mrs Heelis grunted. 'It's a disgrace the way the Forestry Commission and War Office seem to be able to do exactly as they please without consulting the National Trust. Planting ugly pines everywhere, turning people's homes into concentration camps.' She waved an imperious hand at the working party. 'At least you've got some gardeners in. High time too. The place was going to rack and ruin.'

47

'They're German POWs, Mrs Heelis,' said Reynolds patiently, wondering if it would ever be possible to bring the conversation around to the subject of her visit. He also wanted to ask her endless questions about Peter Rabbit, Tom Kitten, Ginger and Pickles, and all the other characters he had read about during his Montreal childhood.

'At least they're working,' said Mrs Heelis, running an approving eye over the acre of land that had been cleared.

Reynolds saw an opportunity and seized it. 'They're extremely hard-working, thanks to their new commanding officer, Miss Potter. He believes in keeping them busy. The War Office say that his suggestion is a great idea, so if –'

Mrs Heelis pounced on a chocolate wrapper. 'A Hershey bar,' she cried indignantly. 'You see? Even the Americans leave their litter everywhere.'

'A prisoner must've dropped it.'

'Where would he have got a Hershey bar from?'

'Miss Potter, this camp is flooded with food parcels from pro-German sympathizers in the United States. You wouldn't believe the amount of chocolate they receive.'

'Anyway,' said Mrs Heelis abruptly. 'I think your German's idea is an excellent one, major. Matters are a disgrace around the popular spots. Whenever I complain, people throw up their hands in despair and say that there's a war on. I shall suggest at the next National Trust meeting that the trustees fully support the scheme.'

Reynolds managed to conceal his sigh of relief.

Willi loved a good argument provided he was present but not involved. Very often choice pieces of gossip were let slip when tempers got frayed. Back home in Munich, during his motorcar double-dealing days, he had run a nice little blackmail sideline based on information gleaned from eavesdropping on rows.

The row that finally erupted between Kruger and Ulbrick a month after Kruger's arrival fulfilled both Willi's requirements. The only trouble was that it was a bit one-sided: nothing that Ulbrick said elicited a flicker of response from Kruger. The U-boat commander sat impassively at his desk, inhaling occasionally on a cheroot and staring at Ulbrick while the angry *Luftwaffe* officer took advantage of Kruger's permission to speak freely by delivering a harangue concerning Kruger's changes, which were, in Ulbrick's opinion, making it easy for the British to administer the camp.

'Examples, please,' Kruger requested when Ulbrick paused for breath.

'This business of us all having to work the vegetable gardens.'

'Don't you like fresh vegetables?'

'That's not the point. The more food we provide for ourselves, the more we make available for British mouths.'

Kruger shook his head. 'The agreement I entered into with Major Reynolds was that whatever extra food we grow will not affect our rations. Also, the work is good for the men and it eases the boredom.'

'With the American food parcels, it's not as if we're short of food.'

'We don't get sent fresh vegetables.'

Ulbrick realized that he was losing the argument. 'It's undignified for officers to do labouring work while watched by British conscripts,' he stated.

Kruger shrugged. 'Boredom is even more undignified, Ulbrick.'

'They wouldn't be bored if they were allowed to plan escapes.'

Kruger nodded to Willi. 'Show him the survey, Willi.'

Willi opened his desk drawer and passed a handwritten sheet of paper to Ulbrick.

'A survey I've carried out of every escape since the camp was established,' said Kruger. 'Ninety per cent of them weren't planned. They were a matter of opportunities being seized as they arose: a guard's back turned for an instant on an exercise walk, that sort of thing. The ten per cent that were planned weren't planned properly. The escapees had little or no money, inadequate travel and identification documents, and no proper clothing.'

Ulbrick was unimpressed. 'The object of escaping is to tie down enemy resources,' he said. 'The more soldiers there are guarding us or searching for us, then the less soldiers the British have to fight us.'

Kruger carefully tapped the ash off his cheroot. 'The object of escaping is to get home and rejoin one's comrades in the fight. Also, I doubt if searching for escaping prisoners does tie down British resources. The British use volunteers to a greater extent than we do: Home Guard, War Reserve Constables and so on. Read the British newspapers and you will learn about the thousands of girls who've left service to work in the factories and how former ladies of leisure have mobilized themselves into volunteer organizations – nursing, bandage-making, driving ambulances, fund-raising – a whole host of activities that we would never allow our women to join in.'

There was a low whistle from the corridor. Willi moved with astonishing speed despite his bulk. He crossed to the window and released the sash lock which enabled him to slide back a section of the wooden windowsill from its frame. Beneath the sill was a cavity filled with documents. He snatched the survey from Ulbrick, dropped it into the cavity, slid the sill back into place and locked it with the sash catch. He was back behind his desk by the time the door was thrown open by Sergeant Finch, accompanied by Corporal White and Private Jones.

The sergeant's suspicious glare at the three German officers was completely ruined by the acrid fumes from Kruger's cheroot which made his eyes smart and water. He made a mental note to check the next consignment of food parcels to find out who was sending Kruger the poisonous weeds.

'I have a message from Major Reynolds,' the British NCO announced, wiping his eyes on the sleeve of his battledress.

'And *I* have a message for Major Reynolds,' said Kruger coldly, rising to his feet and fixing Finch with an icy stare. 'Inform him that I am organizing a series of instruction courses in various subjects for the men in my charge. If he would like me to include a course of lessons in manners for his NCOs, then I will be happy to do so. The first lesson will be on the correct way to enter a room.'

Finch was unmoved. 'My apologies, sir,' he said crisply. 'Major Reynolds says that the National Trust are in favour of your suggestion to use POW working parties to clear litter from picnic sites.'

Ulbrick looked dazed. 'Clearing picnic sites?' he echoed.

'Before agreeing,' Finch continued, 'Major Reynolds will require a parol from you – a binding promise – that there will be no escape attempts from the working parties.'

'He shall have my word on it,' Kruger promised.

Ulbrick stared at Kruger in frank disbelief. 'Clearing picnic sites?' he repeated. 'I'm sorry, commander, but have you gone completely insane?'

Leutnant Hans Schnee stared at the questionnaire. The form had been handwritten: all the questions were printed in pencil in Willi's neat block capitals.

'This is lunacy,' he protested. 'Do I have to answer every question?'

'Every one,' Willi affirmed. 'Every new prisoner has to fill in the form. Commander Kruger's orders.'

Schnee turned the sheet of paper over. 'But there's at least thirty questions. Service details, special skills, civilian occupations, special training, hobbies. Everything.'

'Well, how do you think I feel?' Willi complained. 'I've

51

had to draw up over a hundred of those forms, so don't you go messing it up.'

'But I'll have to give information that I refused to give the British when they interrogated me.'

'Just answer the questions please,' Willi pleaded.

'Supposing this form fell into British hands?'

'It won't.'

Schnee read carefully through every question. He was a well-scrubbed, fresh-faced U-boat 2nd Watch Officer barely out of his teens. He looked up at Willi. 'Supposing Kruger decides from my answers that I'm not eligible to be a POW? Will he send me home?'

Willi groaned.

'Anyway,' said Schnee emphatically. 'I'm not going to write down anything about my capture. If Commander Kruger wants to find out, then he'll have to question me himself.'

Kruger was lost in silence for some seconds, staring with unseeing eyes out of his office window as he brooded on the loss of *U-100*. The U-boat had been from the 1st U-boat Flotilla based at Lorient: the same flotilla as his *U-112*. Its commander, Joachim Schepke, had been one of his few close friends. He turned round to face Schnee and relit his cheroot.

For once Willi was not present. Nettled at being told by Kruger to make himself scarce, he had crept into the next room, a disused boxroom, and was listening to the conversation with the aid of a tumbler purloined from the kitchens. He was holding it sandwiched between the adjoining wall and his ear.

'I'm very sorry to hear about Schepke,' said Kruger, sitting at his desk. 'He was a fine U-boat commander.'

Schnee nodded and remained silent.

'Are you sure that the destroyer came straight at you out of the darkness?'

Schnee nodded again. 'Yes, commander.'

'What was *U-100* doing when the destroyer rammed you?'

'We were shadowing a convoy that was under attack. We had expended all our torpedoes. Commander Schepke hoped that there might be a chance to pick off stragglers with our 88-millimetre.'

'How far astern of the convoy were you?'

'About six miles.'

'And a warship broke away from the battle to attack you?'

'Yes, commander.'

Kruger was baffled. Schnee's story tallied with accounts from other recently captured U-boatmen who told of convoy escorts that had left their station and 'came straight at us from out of the darkness'.

The deadly 'wolf pack' tactics that Admiral Doenitz had insisted on his U-boats adopting after the decimation of Convoy SC7 the previous October depended on a surfaced U-boat, when sighting a convoy, to shadow it while radioing frequent reports on its course and to speed back to headquarters, which would then direct other U-boats to the target for a massed, surface attack. The advantage of the surface attack was that a U-boat could use its diesels, giving it a top speed of 18 knots as opposed to a submerged speed of 5 knots on its electric motors. Also, a surfaced U-boat was difficult to spot, especially in heavy seas and driving rain; and under-water detection equipment such as ASDIC was rendered impotent. Additionally, a surfaced U-boat was highly manoeuvrable, so its commander could use one torpedo per ship instead of the wasteful submerged attack technique of firing a fan of four torpedoes across the bows of a single ship.

But the recent spate of British successes against shadowing U-boats suggested that the enemy had developed an efficient method of detecting a surfaced U-boat at night, at a distance of several miles, regardless of the weather conditions.

From the experiments he had been involved with before the war, Kruger knew that radio location using impulses reflected from a target was useless in mid-ocean against a U-boat's low profile because the top of a U-boat's conning tower was invariably below the level of the swell.

'What was the weather like when you were rammed?' Kruger asked.

'Filthy, commander. Force Seven and we were shipping it green down the bridge hatch.'

'So why did you refuse to enter the circumstances of your capture on my form?'

Schnee hesitated and said guardedly, 'I didn't want to write anything down because I know that the British have got some sort of equipment for plotting the position of surfaced U-boats.'

Kruger stubbed out his cheroot and lit another one. 'Why do you think that, leutnant?'

'I was on the bridge with Commander Schepke and the lookouts when we were rammed. Visibility was less than four hundred metres and yet that destroyer was dead on course for us when she appeared out of the squall. She hit us square on the bridge. I was thrown into the water and was picked up by the destroyer about thirty minutes later with six other members of the crew.

'At daybreak we were transferred to an armed merchant-man, the *Farnham Castle*. It was crammed to the bulwarks with survivors of the convoy battle. Dutch, Poles, Lascars – the lot.' Schnee gave a wry smile. 'Conditions were chaotic below decks. We were wearing these overalls – none of us were in uniform – so we thought it best if they didn't discover that they had some U-boatmen among them. We kept quiet and stayed out of the way.

'The next day I found a paint scraper and a wire brush and discovered that I could move about the ship without being challenged. I overheard two officers talking about a "Huff Duff" fix on a U-boat.'

'A what fix?'

'"Huff Duff",' Schnee repeated.

Kruger pushed a pencil and paper across his desk. 'Spell it,' he ordered.

Schnee thought for a moment and wrote 'HUF DUF' in block capitals. 'It sounded like that, commander.'

Kruger frowned at the two meaningless words.

'I decided to find out what "Huff Duff" meant,' Schnee continued, 'so I started cleaning the paint off the companionway ladder that led to the radio shack. The door was open. A radio operator was sitting in front of an ordinary wireless set but there was another apparatus that was like no other set that I'd seen before. The radio operator heard me. He turned round and told me to clear off.'

'Can you describe the apparatus?'

'I can do better than that,' Schnee replied. 'I can draw it. I memorized everything I could. I wasn't close enough to read what the controls were for and my English isn't that good anyway.'

'Could it have been nothing more than a new type of ordinary wireless set?'

'I suppose so, commander. But there was a queer-looking antenna array above the radio shack. I can draw that as well. I've got a rough idea of its size because someone was working on it.'

Kruger considered for a few moments. 'What do you think the apparatus was?'

'A radio direction-finding system?' Schnee ventured.

Kruger looked faintly contemptuous. 'Direction-finding at sea, leutnant? Firstly, accurate direction-finding requires large, steerable aerials operating from at least two land bases. Secondly, the stations have to be over four hundred kilometres apart in order to obtain reliable triangulation fixes on a radio transmitter operating in the mid-Atlantic.

And thirdly, the radio transmitter you're trying to get a fix on has to operate for long periods. As you well know, U-boat transmissions rarely last longer than thirty seconds.'

Schnee looked suitably crushed. Kruger moderated his tone and added, 'I think it's safe to assume that the apparatus you saw was nothing more than a new type of communications wireless set.'

'I suppose so, commander,' Schnee admitted, although he didn't sound convinced.

A week later Fleming arrived at Grizedale Hall in the company of a man in civilian dress. Schnee was in a small working party that was clearing the drive when the Bentley hooted. The prisoners stood to one side to allow the vehicle past. Schnee stared in astonishment at the man dressed in a British Merchant Navy uniform who was sitting beside Fleming. The young U-boat officer made a hurried excuse to his comrades and went looking for Kruger. He found him in the common room leafing through a consignment of National Geographic magazines that had just arrived from America.

'I'm sorry to disturb you, commander, but the radio operator who saw me in the *Farnham Castle*'s radio shack has just arrived here.'

Reynolds frowned and glanced at Fleming and the Merchant Navy officer in turn. 'An identity parade?' he queried. 'May I ask why, gentlemen?'

'Sorry to mess up your routine, old boy,' said Fleming blandly. 'But we're scooting all over the place checking the survivors that were brought into Liverpool on the *Farnham Castle* last month. One of them may have seen something on the wretched boat that he should not have seen.' He opened his briefcase and handed Reynolds a list of four names. 'Those are the four Jerries you're sitting on who were on the *Farnham Castle*. I'd like this gentleman to take a look at them to see if he recognizes one of them.'

Reynolds looked none the wiser.

'I'm sorry about this, Major Reynolds,' said the Merchant Navy officer. 'But the man who looked into my radio shack was doing some maintenance work on the ship at the time. I told him to go away and thought nothing more about it until I mentioned it to the bosun. He told me that he hadn't given orders to any member of the crew to do any work around the radio shack.'

'So whoever it was,' murmured Fleming, 'we aim to find him. Wheel out those four Jerries please, old boy.'

The Merchant Navy officer stood in front of the four prisoners who were lined up in Reynolds office and stared hard at each man in turn. He seemed to hesitate when he studied Schnee's face and then he shook his head.

'Alright, sergeant,' said Reynolds to Finch. 'Wheel them out.'

'The trouble is,' said the Merchant Navy officer as he climbed into the Bentley, 'I only got a glimpse of the blighter's face as I turned round. And he was standing against the light.'

'Next stop is the POW camp at the Shap Fell Hotel,' said Fleming, starting the Bentley's engine. 'They're looking after a couple of U-boat NCOs who were on your ship.'

Kruger examined the two sketches that Schnee had drawn. One was of the apparatus that the U-boat officer had seen in the *Farnham Castle*'s radio shack and the other was of the antenna array. Both drawings were neatly inscribed with estimated dimensions and were captioned 'HUF DUF'.

Kruger lit one of his evil-smelling black cheroots and inhaled on it while gazing across his desk at Schnee. The young naval officer fidgeted uncomfortably.

'Alright,' said Kruger at length. 'It's obvious that you

57

saw something important in the ship's radio shack and that the British are very jumpy about it. The question is: what is it that you saw?'

Schnee was still convinced it was a radio direction apparatus but Kruger had already demolished that argument so the junior officer was reluctant to bring it up again. Instead he shook his head.

There was a silence while Kruger absentmindedly doodled on the sketches by pencilling-in the letter 'u' in 'HUF' and in 'DUF'.

'Perhaps it was radio ranging and location apparatus?' Schnee ventured.

Kruger made no reply: he was staring at his handiwork. His normally impassive expression was one of surprise. The two words amended by his doodling now spelt 'HF DF'.

The letters 'DF' were familiar to Kruger. In English they stood for 'direction finding'. But 'HF'?

Schnee sensed that something was amiss but was wholly unprepared for what happened next. Kruger suddenly thumped his desk and exclaimed: 'My God! "Huff Duff"! High Frequency Direction Finding!'

Schnee goggled anxiously at his senior officer, wondering what he had done wrong. 'Commander?'

'Schnee,' Kruger declared. 'I owe you an apology. The British *have* developed a seaborne direction-finding system.'

Willi looked at Schnee's sketches of the 'Huff Duff' apparatus and its antenna array and shook his head doubtfully. 'I'm sorry, commander, but it would take weeks of coded letter writing to convey this information to Admiral Doenitz. And they'd probably get it wrong even then.'

'Yes, I agree, Willi,' Kruger conceded. 'And yet it's vital that we get the information home somehow.'

'I suppose it could be done,' said Willi, anxious to please. 'But it would involve such long, rambling letters – full of

58

numbers. The War Office censors would be certain to stop them.'

The same thought had already occurred to Kruger. 'I can't take that risk and we don't have the time,' he murmured.

'Why is it so important, commander?'

Kruger inhaled thoughtfully on his cheroot. 'The U-boat arm was sinking half a million tonnes of allied shipping a month when I was captured. Our only hope of defeating the British by the end of the year is by maintaining that figure.' He tapped the sketches. 'If this equipment is as good as I suspect it is, it may turn the tables against us.'

Willi could think of nothing constructive to say.

Kruger was lost in thought for a moment. And then he appeared to come to a decision. 'A pencil and paper, Willi. I want to dictate a draft letter to "Alice". After that I want you to look through the questionnaires to find out if any of the prisoners were once tailors.'

Willi found a pencil and paper.

'And Willi.'

'Commander?'

'Not a word about this to anyone or I'll have you court-martialled.'

If Hauptmann Dietrich Berg had existed in fiction he would have served an aspiring writer well as a mad scientist, although he was neither mad nor a scientist. He was an extremely clever, eager to please young technician who happened to be accident-prone on a scale best described as monumental.

He first blew himself up at the age of six with the aid of a children's chemistry set that its makers had guaranteed was harmless. At school he decimated a chemical laboratory in addition to losing two fingers during his first attempt at building a perpetual motion machine. His three years at university were punctuated by an assortment of minor explosions and a number of major ones. He became obsessed with geology and took up pothole exploring in the Hartz Mountains because they were rich in minerals. His experiments with underground explosions in order to open up new galleries led to him spending a week underground, trapped in a very new gallery that was the fruit of one of his experiments.

When asked by the army for a reference, his university authorities had recommended that Berg should be posted to a department dealing with some form of research, possibly explosives. The German army, with its remarkable ability to put square pegs in round holes – a talent it shared with the British army – sent Berg to an infantry regiment as a wireless operator because they discovered that he had been an amateur radio enthusiast until Hitler had revoked all 'ham' radio licences in 1936 on the day after Berg had been issued with his.

After that Berg had to content himself with blowing up the odd radio valve here and there, although he did succeed in shooting off his big toe during rifle drill. The injury left him with a slight limp that contributed to his capture at Dunkirk and later being run over by a Post Office van at Euston railway station while in the company of two guards who were quicker on their feet than he was.

Despite the loss of two fingers, he was an accomplished engineer. The alarm system he rigged up in his workshop at Grizedale Hall consisted of a cocoa tin cum electric gong operated by a strategically placed prisoner on lookout duty. It worked perfectly; nothing incriminating was in sight by the time Kruger strode into the workshop. The dozen or so prisoners present were intent on the wooden cuckoo clocks they were making under Berg's guidance.

The two officers exchanged salutes.

'Any luck with the wire-cutters?' inquired Kruger.

Berg went to his cupboard and produced two lengths of flat spring steel from underneath a heap of rock samples.

He showed them to Kruger. 'These are just the job, commander,' he said enthusiastically. 'We'll drill a pivot hole at each end and file a notch in each cutting edge. They're long enough to provide the leverage needed to cut through a ten-millimetre iron bar.'

'Just so long as they can cut through barbed wire,' said Kruger acidly. 'I'll want them by Wednesday evening.'

'Two days? They'll be ready,' Berg promised.

Kruger fingered the two pieces of steel. 'Where did you get these from, hauptmann?'

Berg grinned. 'Sergeant Finch will insist on parking his Austin near the laundry room. We removed a leaf spring from each side of his rear axle.'

'Is his car safe to drive?'

'No, commander.'

Kruger gave a ghost of a smile. 'Unfortunate.'

Berg hesitated. 'Er – may I ask who will be escaping, commander?'

Kruger's smile froze. 'No,' he said curtly. He turned on his heel and went off to look for Willi. He found him in the common room. 'Willi, what sort of pressure can you put on the guards?'

The little Bavarian looked baffled. 'Pressure, commander?'

'Blackmail,' said Kruger bluntly.

'I would never dream of blackmailing anyone,' Willi protested indignantly.

'Of course you don't dream about doing it – you actually do it. I need one of those flashlights that the guards are issued with.'

Willi looked relieved. 'Oh, I won't have to blackmail anyone for one of those, commander. Just a little bribery: two bars of chocolate ought to be enough.'

Sergeant Finch levered his bulk behind the wheel of his baby Austin. His head pressed against the soft canvas roof and he wondered for the hundredth time whether or not he should have bought the larger Wolseley. But the insurance money his mother had left him had just been enough to buy the Austin outright. And besides, he was in love with the tiny car even though it didn't have enough power to pull the skin off a rice pudding.

He drove it down the drive. A bumpy ride because the narrow wheels hopped from one rut to the next regardless of what the steering wheel told them to do.

He simmered with impatience at the main gate while Corporal White made a great show of examining his pass and peering underneath the vehicle.

'Going to get a new flint for it, sarge?' inquired Chalky, opening the gates.

Finch scowled, revved up the engine and shot forward into the lane. The front wheels took the pothole in their stride but disaster struck when it was the turn of the rear wheels. There was a loud crash and a deafening scream of metal on asphalt caused by the Austin's body hitting the ground where it had parted company from the rear axle. The tremendous jolt punched Sergeant Finch's head through the car's canvas roof and trapped it by the neck.

Chalky gaped in amazement at the sight of his NCO's head jammed through the car's roof like a hog's head on a platter and then he doubled-up over his rifle in helpless laughter, tears streaming down his cheeks.

'Corporal White!' snarled Finch, twisting his head round in its new collar. 'You're on a charge!'

Oberleutnant Max Kluge, foot-sore and half dead on his feet, toiled wearily up the gloomy back stairs that led to Kruger's office. He had the sort of backache that could be framed and put on display in an osteopath's waiting room.

Max and a party of nine fellow prisoners had spent the day walking the entire length of Cunsey Beck, picking up litter under the watching eyes of three guards on horseback. They had cleared the southern bank in the morning and the northern bank in the afternoon – working in the opposite direction. Cunsey Beck was a pretty little mountain stream near Grizedale Hall that discharged into the western shore of Lake Windermere. Max couldn't imagine why the beck was so popular with walkers because it seemed to flow uphill in both directions. But popular it was, as was evidenced by the number of sacks that his team had filled with litter.

He tapped on Kruger's door and entered when bidden. The office stank of cigar fumes. Max exchanged polite greetings with Kruger while wondering where the seemingly inexhaustible supply of the lethal cheroots was coming from.

'Anything of interest, oberleutnant?' inquired Kruger.

Max was too tired to answer. He had just about enough strength left to empty his specially deepened trouser pockets on to Kruger's desk. The U-boat officer's eyes widened very slightly at the cascade of miscellaneous items that tumbled out: bus tickets, letters, bills, receipts, nail scissors, combs, a full packet of English cigarettes, a box of used Swan Vestas matches and another box that looked half used. The packet of Durex condoms was definitely unused, and there was even a hiker's compass – all litter that somehow had not ended up in the sacks loaned for the occasion by Windermere Urban District Council.

'Well done, oberleutnant,' said Kruger, examining the compass. 'This is a remarkable find.'

Max sat down without being invited. 'The *pièce de résistance*,' he grunted, producing a wallet from beneath his blouse and handing it to Kruger.

Kruger opened the wallet. Inside were four pounds in banknotes, an identity card, a driving licence, and a 'Ramblers' Association' membership card. All were made out to a Mr Ian Proctor of Liverpool.

'This is fantastic, oberleutnant,' said Kruger in genuine

astonishment. 'Absolutely amazing. I had no idea your first sortie would produce such results. Don't forget to draw the maps while the details are still fresh in your mind.'

Max's answer was a deep snore.

The news was a bombshell. Schnee gaped bug-eyed at Kruger. 'I'm to do what?' he stuttered.

'You're to escape,' Kruger repeated with a flash of irritation. 'You're in possession of valuable information which we can only get to the OKM if you escape. What's the matter? Don't you want to go home?'

Schnee collected his reeling thoughts. 'Well, yes, commander. But how? When?'

'Through the wire. Tonight,' answered Kruger cryptically. 'Escaping from Grizedale Hall is not difficult. Staying escaped is impossible unless proper plans have been made – which they have in your case. Any questions?'

Schnee had a thousand and one questions.

The game that the prisoners played in the courtyard that afternoon was rough, and one that the guards hadn't seen before. Two teams of ten men each, one man carrying a team mate on his shoulders, squared up to each other. Battle commenced on a blast from Kruger's whistle. The teams charged into each other. The object of the game was for the men being held aloft to topple a rival from an opponent's shoulders.

The pitched battle surged unsteadily back and forth across the courtyard. Men went crashing down amid loud cheers from onlooking prisoners and guards, and there was some brisk wagering with cigarettes.

One team got the upper hand and drove the opposition under the high granite archway of Grizedale Hall's rear entrance.

The mêlée of wrestling, yelling prisoners provided a screen for Berg while he unscrewed the fusebox cover. The

64

guards, sensing that the battle of the archway was a diversion, obligingly looked in the opposite direction. It took Berg less than thirty seconds to wind a length of coat-hanger wire across the terminals of the main fuse and to replace the cover.

The game ended when Kruger blew his whistle. He walked over to Berg. 'Everything alright, hauptmann?'

Berg looked very pleased with himself. 'Yes, commander. I've uprated the hall's main fuse from a hundred amperes to about five hundred amperes. The floodlighting fuse is now certain to be the weak link in the hall's entire circuit.'

'Let us hope so,' Kruger murmured.

As usual, the floodlights that illuminated Grizedale Hall like a granite ballerina came on an hour before dusk.

At 9 pm, after the prisoners had been locked in the hall, an expectant group of them gathered around Berg in one of the dormitories to witness his latest piece of insanity.

All had unlit cigarettes in their mouth and all watched in silence as Berg, wearing gloves, picked up a sharpened pencil in each hand. The lead graphite core at the end of each pencil had been exposed and connected to lengths of cable whose ends had been inserted into an electric power socket. The reason why the crude arrangement looked lethal was because it was.

Berg glanced at his watch – one minute to go.

Three floors below, Kruger and Schnee were crouched by a window that opened on to the terrace. The junior U-boat officer was wearing a heavy woollen jersey and denim trousers. On his back was a small hiker's rucksack that had been made from a *Kriegsmarine* haversack. If a guard chose to patrol along the terrace, Schnee was certain that his pounding heart would be heard.

*

'The pencils will work on the same principle as the carbon arc lamps in cinema projectors,' Berg explained enthusiastically to his sceptical audience. 'When the guards come to see what has happened, I will explain that I was merely creating a continuous spark to light our cigarettes because we'd run out of matches.'

Berg gave a boyish grin and brought the pencil points closer together so that there was a twelve-inch gap between them. 'All right. Who wants to light their cigarette?'

Berg was not exactly overwhelmed by eager volunteers.

'Oh, come on, fellows. It's perfectly safe.'

'Okay,' said a prisoner, moving forward and offering his cigarette gingerly in the direction of the makeshift electrodes. He closed his eyes tightly. 'I'll try it.'

'What you must appreciate,' said Berg, bringing the pencil points even closer together, 'is that I've never actually done this before.' He chuckled. 'I'll probably get seven days in the cooler.'

The points were less than half an inch apart when he finished speaking. Nothing happened.

Berg looked disappointed. 'It doesn't look as if it's going to work,' he commented.

Suddenly there was a tremendous bang and a blinding blue flash in the dormitory, followed by the sound of a distant explosion, followed by all the lights going out, including the floodlights, leaving Grizedale Hall plunged into total darkness.

An aroma of charred wood and burnt human hair filled the pitch-black dormitory. There was a silence and then a respectful voice in the darkness said, 'Berg?'

There was a long pause before Berg answered. 'Yes?'

'I think you'll definitely get your seven days.'

The instant the floodlights went out, Kruger opened the window and shook hands hurriedly with Schnee. The young U-boat officer tightened his grip on Berg's homemade wire cutters and jumped out on to the terrace. He leapt over the balustrade and dropped the eight feet to the lawn. It took him less than forty seconds to cover the three hundred yards down the slope of the lawn and across the vegetable plots. He weaved through the shrubbery, threw himself flat on the ground in front of the barbed wire fence and started cutting his way through. The strands weren't difficult to cut but they parted with loud cracks that Schnee was certain could be heard by the two guards perched in the nearby firewatchers' tower. There was a sudden uproar of pounding boots and shouted orders from the direction of the hall as a company of guards turned out to investigate the power failure.

Schnee cut through the final strand and gingerly twisted the severed ends of wire to one side. Before crawling through the hole, he buried the wirecutters in a pre-arranged spot so that they could be recovered for future use. He wriggled through the wire and raced towards the cover offered by the pines. Once safe in the shadows, he rested for a few minutes to allow his thumping heart to return to its normal rhythm. Curiously, there was no feeling of elation at being free; perhaps it was the thought of the daunting twenty-kilometre cross-country walk to Grange-over-Sands on Morecambe Bay that lay ahead of him that night.

He checked his bearings with the aid of the compass and a hand-drawn map, and struck out due south, threading his way through the dark, brooding pines of Grizedale Forest.

The lights had been back on five minutes when Reynolds, wearing pyjamas and dressing gown, examined the charred remains of the two pencils that Sergeant Finch had placed on his desk. He poked at the two lengths of cable.

'All right, sergeant. I'll ban all games in the courtyard. But what do you think of Berg's story?'

'Well, it's possible, sir. They don't receive that many

matches in their parcels – plenty of cigarettes, yes – but no one seems to think about matches.'

Reynolds was suddenly reminded of something. 'Who sends Kruger those lousy cigars?'

'No one, sir,' Finch reluctantly admitted. 'I don't know where he's getting them from.'

'Okay. We'll look into it another time. I guess we'd better let Berg have the benefit of the doubt but I'm giving him seven days for damaging government property. That ought to be long enough for him to grow new eyebrows.'

A weak moon broke through the clouds a few minutes after midnight just as Schnee was crossing the lonely little bridge over River Leven at Backbarrow near the southern tip of Lake Windermere. He left the deserted road and crouched beneath a hedgerow to check his position against the map.

He worked out that he had just crossed the Lakeside and Haverthwaite Railway, which meant that the main road nearby had to be the A590 to Grange-over-Sands. Apart from the occasional call of a nightjar and the barking of dogs in distant farmyards, the night-shrouded countryside was still and silent. He decided to stick to the main road; he could always jump over one of the low dry-stone walls into a field if he heard anything suspicious.

He made good time walking on the metalled surface. Twenty minutes later, after skirting the village of High Newton, he saw the moonlight gleaming on the sea in Morecambe Bay. He stared for some seconds, hardly believing his luck and, after picking out his objective – the Humphrey Head peninsula – he started walking again with renewed vigour.

From now on the sketch map was vague, but by swinging south-west across the fields, he was able to keep the Humphrey Head in sight. The route took him west of the tidy little Victorian resort town of Grange-over-Sands. He crossed the Furness railway line and came to a bank of sand dunes. He paused at the top of the dunes and saw with dismay that what he thought was the sea was in fact a vast expanse of wet sand. There was no sign of the sea nor was there any sign of the barbed wire entanglements defending the coast that Kruger had warned him to expect near the town. Obviously the British didn't think it likely that the invasion would take place in Morecambe Bay, a useful snippet of intelligence to take home.

Schnee checked his watch. 3.05 am. In forty minutes he would be among his own countrymen and on his way home. His feet sank alarmingly into the sand. It was far softer than he had anticipated. Also, the beach was absolutely flat – there was no slope to indicate in which direction the sea lay. He assumed that he would eventually reach the water's edge if he walked with his back to the land.

Schnee trudged on for fifteen minutes and paused for a rest. It was hard going through the soft, clinging sand, and his ankles were beginning to ache. No wonder the British weren't expecting an invasion force to land in Morecambe Bay: anything heavier than a lawnmower attempting a landing from the sea would be bogged down. But where the hell was the sea? He battled on for another ten minutes and decided that it was time to send the prearranged recognition signal. He aimed the flashlight due south and sent four dashes and a dot. He waited a minute and signalled again, this time sending a dot and four dashes. To his joy, the U-boat responded immediately with four dots and a dash. The signal was barely discernible which meant that either the U-boat was using a low intensity lamp or it was standing off a long way from the shore.

He took a few steps forward and immediately sank up to his knees in the half-mud, half-sand. From then onwards forward progress became a tedious, ankle-wrenching business of having to haul his feet out of the clinging quicksand with every step. Suddenly he sank up to his waist. He cursed out loud and threw himself forward. By pushing down on outspread hands he was able to lift one leg clear, only to have his arms sink up to the elbows. His struggles to free himself from the glutinous ooze caused his body to sink until he was trapped up to his chest. Every movement of his body produced obscene sucking noises as though the quicksand was a living creature. He stopped struggling because he thought he heard a strange hissing noise like a distant waterfall. Maybe it was his imagination. He was about to curse again but the expletive died on his lips and his eyes widened in horror. Straight ahead, shining clearly in the moonlight, was a line of white water that stretched into the distance on either side for as far as he could see. The hissing noise grew steadily louder as the menacing tidal bore hurtled towards him at what seemed to be the speed of an express train.

Schnee cried out in terror and renewed his futile struggles to escape the grip of the treacherous ooze. The three-foot high wall of charging water was one hundred yards from him when he began to scream out and claw dementedly at the engulfing sand.

'Seawater and sand in the lungs. It'll be death by misadventure on the report,' said the green-overalled pathologist, marching ahead of his two visitors through the gloomy, marble-lined corridor at the Barrow-in-Furness mortuary.

The pathologist showed Fleming and the Merchant Navy officer into a high-ceilinged room where the naked body of Leutnant Hans Schnee lay on a dissecting table. The three men approached the table and regarded the body of the young man in silence.

'We get several drownings every year,' complained the pathologist. 'People simply won't read the warning signs. The sands look innocent enough but they're lethal. And at this time of year, the tidal bore comes in at thirty miles an hour. Not even a horse can out-gallop it.'

'Well?' Fleming asked the Merchant Navy officer.

There was a silence. The officer studied Schnee's face carefully for a few moments before looking up at Fleming. He nodded. 'Yes,' he said. 'It *was* him. I'm certain of it now.'

'If he ever had an identity disc, he'd lost it,' said the pathologist. 'So who was he? A serviceman on holiday?'

'Something like that,' murmured Fleming, moving to the door.

Part Three

RADIO GRIZEDALE

After two months under Kruger's leadership, the prisoners' morale was remarkably high, and the rift between Kruger and Ulbrick had largely healed. Ulbrick's initial hostility to Kruger's many changes had been gradually replaced by the realization that demanding work rotas were eliminating the corrosive effect that boredom had on the men's minds and souls. Where work didn't exist, Kruger created it. He persuaded Reynolds to allow those prisoners with catering skills to take over in the kitchens for one day a week. Following the success of the experiment, this was later increased to two days. Another concession he won – despite opposition from Sergeant Finch – was to assume responsibility for the distribution of the prisoners' mail and food parcels. Even the prisoners' leisure time was occupied with compulsory attendance on any two of the ten or so instruction courses that were now running every day. The most popular, after Kruger's English language classes, was Hauptmann Dietrich Berg's clock and model-making course.

As Berg climbed the stairs to Kruger's office, his most fervent wish was to be left alone in his workshop. He cursed his willingness to try to please as many people as possible, especially Kruger. If only he could learn to say 'no' now and then, he would not have these problems.

His face was lined with anxiety as he knocked apprehensively on Kruger's door. He was so preoccupied rehearsing a string of excuses regarding his failure to produce a satisfactory pocket compass that he forgot to wait outside the door until summoned. He was sent scurrying out of the office by a blast of invective from Willi and a blistering scowl from Kruger.

Berg re-entered correctly. His apologies were silenced by a gesture from Kruger, who indicated the chair in front of his desk. Willi sat with pencil poised ready to take notes while Berg perched nervously on the edge of the chair. Kruger took his time reading carefully through a form which Berg recognized as the questionnaire he had completed upon his arrival at Grizedale Hall. Kruger opened his box of cheroots and hesitated before selecting one. Willi noticed the uncertainty. He had already noticed that Kruger was smoking less than usual. Obviously the mysterious supply was not inexhaustible after all. Willi decided to carry out a thorough search of Kruger's quarters when the senior officer was on one of his inspection tours. Willi hated mysteries.

'Good afternoon, hauptmann,' said Kruger, lighting a cheroot and regarding Berg through a cloud of smoke.

'Good afternoon, commander. Commander, I'm extremely sorry about the delay in producing a pocket compass. I'm doing my best but –'

'I'm not interested in compasses at the moment,' Kruger interrupted. He tapped Berg's questionnaire. 'You say here that you were once a licensed amateur radio operator?'

'Only for one day, commander. I got my licence on a Wednesday and they were all revoked on the Thursday.'

'But you passed the examinations?'

'Yes, commander,' said Berg, wondering what all this was leading up to.

'And you were a radio operator in the army?'

'Yes, commander. But only for six months before my capture.'

Kruger steepled his fingers and stared at Berg. 'Haupt-mann Berg. Could you build a radio transmitter?'

Berg goggled in alarm. 'What – here, commander?'

'Where else do you think I mean?'

The young army officer was lost for words. He was always eager to help and he had a measure of self-confidence that frequently led him to attempt anything. But building a radio transmitter? He resolved to say 'no' and risked a sideways glance at Willi as a possible source of support. The chubby little Bavarian was pretending to be busy writing.

Berg caught Kruger's eye and his resolve began to collapse. 'Well,' he said cautiously. 'I'm not sure, commander. It all depends.'

'On what?'

'Er – well, the frequency you want it to operate on for one thing.'

'15,460 kilocycles,' said Kruger succinctly. 'It's one of the standard U-boat frequencies.'

Berg swallowed. A thousand problems crowded into his fertile brain. 'And the power output, commander?'

'Enough for me to communicate with the headquarters of the 1st U-boat Flotilla at Lorient in western France.'

The young army officer looked as though he was about to faint. 'Commander, that would be extremely dangerous.'

'Why?'

'Sending directional signals south – down the entire length of England – they would be certain to be heard and bearings taken on their source.'

Kruger considered for a moment and nodded. 'Very well then, hauptmann. How about sending directional signals due west across to southern Ireland – which is neutral anyway – and out into the Atlantic?'

'Commander,' said Berg desperately. 'Even assuming I could build a transmitter and a directional aerial, who would hear such signals?'

'U-boats,' Kruger answered curtly. 'They operate in mid-Atlantic where the convoys have no air cover.'

Berg wanted to close his eyes and open them again to discover that the interview was really a particularly bad nightmare. 'Mid-Atlantic?' he croaked. 'A distance of about three thousand kilometres?'

'About that,' Kruger agreed. 'The transmitter will require a power output of at least fifty watts.'

By now Berg's eyes were permanently glazed with shock. 'Fifty watts? But ten watts would be adequate.'

'I have a considerable amount of text to send,' said Kruger. 'Repeating the signals three or four times would be dangerous because the British monitor the U-boat frequencies. One powerful transmission will ensure that HQ will be able to piece together the entire signal from the logs of several U-boats. Could you build a fifty-watt transmitter?'

Bracing himself for the worst, Berg said, 'I'm very sorry, commander, but I have to be honest with you. No.'

'Why not?'

'There are so many components I would need – valves, condensers, resistors, potentiometers, wire and solder, *and* a soldering iron. The list is endless. To build just a receiver would be difficult enough, but a transmitter will be impossible.'

Kruger inhaled on his cheroot without saying a word.

'I'm very sorry, commander,' Berg repeated, feeling foolish. 'But it is impossible.'

Kruger broke the silence that followed. 'Hauptmann Berg, have you noticed anything unusual about the thirty or so new prisoners who've joined us this month?'

Berg looked puzzled. 'No, commander.'

'Most of them are U-boat officers,' said Kruger coldly. 'The reason for that is because the British have developed a new equipment that enables them to pinpoint the position of surfaced U-boats. Last week, Leutnant Schnee gave his life attempting to get valuable information home concerning this new equipment. We owe it to our country, our U-boat crews, and to the memory of Leutnant Schnee to get the information home somehow. It's too complicated and too long to be incorporated in coded letters, so I intend transmitting it by radio.' The U-boat ace paused and fixed the unfortunate Berg with a hard, unblinking stare. 'Therefore, Hauptmann Berg, you will build a suitable transmitter-receiver to communicate with U-boats and you will have it working within two weeks from today. All the talents we have in the camp and all its limited resources are at your disposal. Brief me on your progress every morning immediately after roll-call.'

'Yes, commander,' Berg muttered.

'And, hauptmann.'

'Commander?'

'Good luck.'

Standing exactly five feet in his bare feet when they were clean, radio officer Leutnant zur See Fritz Brunel, one of the *Bismarck*'s junior radio officers, was the smallest POW at Grizedale Hall.

He was also the most agile, which was why none of the guards watching over the litter-gathering party of perspiring POWs saw him execute a neat dive into the thick undergrowth at the edge of the picnic area. The other prisoners studiously avoided looking in his direction as he hopped over a dry-stone wall like a marauding dung beetle and catapulted himself into a ditch.

He ran, bent double, along the bottom of the dried-out ditch, vaulted another stone wall and worked his way across two fields. His objective was a row of holiday cottages about half a mile away. He was within a hundred yards of them when he saw that an end cottage had an aerial wire strung up the length of its garden. Had the woman dozing in a deckchair in the back garden opened her eyes, she would have seen Brunel dart through her open kitchen door and emerge a minute later clutching the family radio under his arm. But she didn't open her eyes and Brunel was able to race, unchallenged, in the direction he had come. He reached a spot where the working party was moving towards him through the undergrowth and went to work on the radio receiver with a screwdriver. He removed the component-encrusted chassis from its cabinet, eased the valves from their sockets and laid them carefully in the long grass. He also removed other bulky components such as the tuning condenser and spread them around on the ground. Small, detachable items such as control knobs went into his pockets. He scratched a hole in the thick peat beneath the trees and buried the unwanted wooden cabinet.

A litter-gathering prisoner approached and, without a word to Brunel, started putting the various components and the chassis into his sack. Brunel stood up and helped him.

None of the guards noticed that Brunel had been absent.

Berg carefully and methodically dismantled the fourth domestic wireless receiver that had come into his possession during the week. As always, he had started by un-soldering the resistors and reading their coloured rings to determine their resistive value before placing them in appropriately marked matchboxes. His soldering iron consisted of a brass bit mounted on a steel shank thrust into a file handle. Occasionally he reheated the bit by holding it in the flame of a home-made Bunsen burner. The short lengths of wire that he removed from the set were tied into neat bundles according to their colour.

When all the components had been removed, he turned his attention to the largest one of all: an aluminium-encased electrolytic condenser the size of a hand grenade. The other characteristic that such condensers shared with a hand grenade was a tendency to explode when overloaded.

Berg decided that a protective shield for the condenser would be a good idea. He wrapped a strip of aluminium around the condenser and tried to hold the assembly in place while he bored the holes for the clamping screws. The awl slipped and punched right through the condenser's casing, releasing toxic aluminium borate on to his workbench. It wasn't a disaster because of an identical spare condenser removed from another stolen radio. But it was the only one, so maybe trying to make a shield wasn't such a good idea.

He carefully cleaned the poisonous chemical off his bench and shook it out of the window.

Suddenly the cocoa tin electric alarm rattled as though a stag beetle with St Vitus' Dance was trapped inside. Berg picked up the false top to his workbench, opened the door of a large, unfinished, wall-mounted cuckoo clock, and tipped the incriminating items into the clock's base. The half-dismantled radio set disappeared under a floorboard that had to be slid, not lifted. He failed to notice a resistor that rolled on to the floor.

By the time Sergeant Finch strode into the workshop with two guards in tow, Berg was quietly tempering a piece of the cuckoo clock's escapement mechanism in the Bunsen burner flame.

Finch sat down and lit a cigarette while the two privates carried out a snap search of Berg's workroom. The POW was well-liked by the guards, so they refrained from ransacking the place. They checked his cupboard containing finished and unfinished cuckoo clocks without harming the contents and prodded his collection of rock samples to see if they were hollow.

'Good afternoon, Corporal Finch,' said Berg in the best English he could manage.

Finch scowled ungraciously. 'It's *Sergeant* Finch, jerry.'

Berg shrugged and continued with his work while Finch

81

called out occasional orders to the two guards, telling them where to search. He picked up the chunk of Coniston granite that Berg used as a paperweight.

'Can't imagine why anyone would want to collect lumps of rock,' Finch observed, juggling several of Berg's prized geological samples.

'Always I wanted to be geologist,' Berg explained.

'Nothing, sarge,' reported one of the guards.

Finch grunted. As he stood and turned to leave, Berg spotted the resistor on the floor where it was about to be trodden on by the sergeant.

'Sergeant Finch!'

Finch gave Berg a suspicious look. 'What?'

Berg's mind raced. 'Sergeant Finch. You would like a cuckoo clock, yes?'

'A cuckoo clock?'

'I have a fine clock. Just made. Wait please.' As Berg brushed past Finch, he managed to kick the offending resistor under his bench. He took a small, neatly carved clock from the cupboard and returned holding it out with a beguiling smile on his face. It was his first and therefore least successful attempt at making cuckoo clocks.

'Look, you will see that it works.'

Berg proudly held the clock up and tripped its mechanism. A tiny door flew open and out popped a creature that resembled a raped, one-eyed sparrow. It managed a strangled 'Uck yoo' and disappeared.

Berg held the strange timepiece out to Finch. 'It is yours. I am sorry that it has one eye only. They are difficult to make.'

Finch accepted the clock with a muttered 'thanks'. To cover his embarrassment at Berg's gesture, he barked an order at the guards and marched out of the workshop with the clock tucked under his arm.

'This was in today's post,' said Willi, handing 'Alice's' latest decoded message to Kruger when the senior officer entered his office.

Kruger took the slip of scrap paper and read it through twice.

BDU TO U112. CONTENTS YOUR 12/41 AGREED. URGENT YOU CONVEY FULLEST DESCRIPTION OF HFDF. IN PARTICULAR OKW REQUIRE DIMENSIONS OF AERIAL ARRAY. U-BOATS IN OPERATIONAL AREA WILL MAINTAIN DAILY 1155 TO 1230 LISTENING WATCH FOR YOUR CALL SIGN.

'Did you also arrange a radio call-sign with Admiral Doenitz?' asked Willi curiously.

'It cost nothing, Willi,' Kruger murmured enigmatically. He lit a cheroot and burned the slip of paper in his tin lid that served as an ashtray. 'So – it would seem that I'm going to have to write a long signal for Brunel to transmit.'

'Still no sign of Leutnant Herbert Shultz, old boy,' murmured Fleming, inexpertly casting a fly into the centre of the tarn.

Reynolds' cast was equally abysmal. He swore. 'You know something, Ian? Before I lost the sight of one eye, I could drop a fly within a couple of inches of a fish.'

'About Leutnant Herbert Shultz,' Fleming reminded him.

Reynolds scowled. 'After all this time, the guy's dead,' he said, trying to hide his irritation at the question. 'He has to be.'

'But no body, James.'

Reynolds spooled in his slack line. 'The summer visitors are starting to flock into the Lake District. His body will turn up on a pike or somewhere.'

'Good afternoon, gentlemen.'

Both men turned round and called out greetings to Cathy

Standish, who was urging her horse along the track to where they were fishing in her lake. Her riding companion a youngish man dressed in neat tweeds, allowed his horse to graze some two hundred yards away. Reynolds returned his wave.

Cathy reined in and jumped down from her saddle. She was wearing a tight-fitting gingham blouse and even tighter jodhpurs. She gave the two men the special smile that she reserved for men in uniform, even though Fleming and Reynolds were dressed in old clothes. 'Commander Fleming. Major Reynolds,' she said breezily, shaking hands with the two men. 'Had any luck?'

Fleming shook his head. 'We've only been here a few minutes, Mrs Standish.'

Cathy gave Fleming an impish smile. 'Commander, if you wish to drop your rod in my tarn I have a right to insist that you call me Cathy.'

'Hey, ma'am,' joked Reynolds. 'Does that go for me as well?'

'Certainly not,' said Cathy with a severity that was diminished by the laughter in her eyes. 'Not so long as you let your prisoners go roaming all over the Lake District stealing wireless sets. Mine's now disappeared.'

Fleming was immediately intrigued. 'Stealing what?'

'There's been a spate of break-ins round here,' Reynolds intervened. 'Radios and valuables disappearing from houses. The police are satisfied that it's not the prisoners because the break-ins always occur at least a mile away from where they're working.'

'Interesting,' Fleming observed.

Reynolds didn't share Fleming's view. The visits by the police had made the issue a sensitive one as far as he was concerned. 'Windermere CID think that it's a gypsy who operates near a POW working party in the hope that the prisoners will be blamed. Anyway, if the POWs wanted a radio, they'd steal one set, not four.'

'Five,' Cathy corrected, chuckling mischievously. She swung a not unshapely leg over the saddle. 'I daresay they've got a home-made crystal set hidden somewhere in that vast hall.'

'No, they haven't,' said Reynolds defensively.

'Well, if you find it, let me have it. There's not a wireless set to be had in any of the shops in Windermere or Ambleside.'

'Cathy,' said Fleming quickly. 'I'm returning to London tomorrow. If you'd like me to look out for a wireless for you, I shall be happy to do so.'

'Super, Ian,' she replied, matching his smile. 'You bring me one back and I'll lay on a special wireless-warming party just for you.' Her smile became decidedly mischievous. 'And you've yet to cash that rain cheque, Ian . . . Must go now. Bye.'

'Rain cheque?' Reynolds queried as the two men watched Cathy riding away. 'What did she mean by that?'

'Heaven only knows,' Fleming murmured sagely.

'Her parties are really something,' said Reynolds, reeling in his line. He added hastily: 'So I've heard say.'

It was after midnight when Kruger entered the linen storage cupboard in the labyrinth of Grizedale Hall's attics. He rapped on the back of the cupboard. The thin plywood panelling that had been made into an inward opening door was opened by Brunel. The tiny naval leutnant saluted Kruger and ushered him into the cavernous, elongated space under Grizedale's steeply pitched slate roof which ran the entire east-west length of the hall. The gloomy space, lit by a string of naked, low-wattage light bulbs, was broken at ten-foot intervals by fans of timber trusses supporting the weight of the roof.

Brunel indicated a taut, inclined wire that appeared to be stretched the length of the roof space. 'Mind your head on the aerial wire, commander,' he said, leading the way along narrow catwalk planks laid across the ceiling joists to where Berg was working at a bench he had built over the main water tank.

The reluctant radio engineer looked up from the tangle of valves and wiring he had assembled on the chassis of the largest of the stolen radio receivers. His attempt at a salute resulted in him cracking his hand painfully on a roof truss.

'Good evening, commander.'

Kruger nodded and ran his eye over the radio that was lying on its side. It had no enclosing cabinet. Despite all the problems Berg had, the results of his labours looked remarkably professional: the radio's wiring was neatly routed around the various components and the soldered joints were smooth and gleaming. Even the mahogany baseboard on which the home-made morse key was mounted had been french polished with a concoction that Berg had made from pine resin and methylated spirits.

'It all looks very smart,' said Kruger with less ice in his voice than usual.

Berg's anxious expression cleared slightly. He gave a nervous smile. 'I've been lucky, commander. One of my biggest worries at first was finding a suitable solder. I tried some lead from the roof but its melting point was too high. Then I realized that the bulges in the lead pipes in the shower rooms were wiped solder joints. I scraped some of the metal off and found that it worked perfectly. For flux I used some pine resin that a litter clearing party brought back – the stuff oozes out of the trees around here.'

'Does the radio work?' Kruger inquired.

Berg, warming to his subject, turned the radio upright and pointed to an identical pair of valves that were mounted side by side. 'They're the main RF power valves, commander. I was able to match a pair from two receivers. The only way to get their power output up is to have them working together in a push-pull circuit.'

Kruger wasn't interested in the technicalities. 'Does the radio work?' he repeated in some irritation.

Berg hesitated. 'Er – well – yes.'

'What's that supposed to mean?'

'I think the output's about half a watt.'

Kruger regarded Berg steadily. 'You only think?'

Berg looked embarrassed. 'I'm sorry, commander – I don't have a power meter. I can only guess at the power output by the temperature the dummy load reaches when the morse key is operated.'

'The chances of a U-boat hearing a half-watt signal are almost nil, Berg. I ordered you to provide fifty watts.'

'Well, I can't,' said the army officer showing uncharacteristic spirit. He had worked virtually day and night for a week to get the transmitter to its present state, and precious little thanks he was getting. He gestured to the radio. 'Maybe those valves could pump out fifty watts for a short period before they blew up, but there's no hope of that without a suitable power supply.'

'So build a power supply,' Kruger ordered dispassionately.

Berg looked despairingly at Brunel who was hovering in the background. He showed Kruger the disembowelled remains of the stolen radios. 'Look, commander. These radios had power supplies designed to provide one watt of audio output – a nice, comfortable volume for listening in a small living room. What we need is the sort of power supply that you find in public address system amplifiers. When we're liberated, you can have me arrested, court-martialled, stood up in front of a firing squad – whatever you like – because there is no way that I make this thing deliver more than one watt.'

Surprising himself with his own courage, Berg met Kruger's piercing gaze without flinching.

'I've got an idea,' said Brunel brightly.

*

As soon as it was dark, Brunel crawled out of an attic window and on to the highest point of Grizedale Hall's roof. Fortunately, the floodlights had been arranged so that their beams were concentrated on the façades of the building. A prisoner passed him a roll of stair carpeting and a coil of rope that was attached to a grapnel made from the business end of a gardening fork.

Brunel ran along the ridge towards the eastern end of the hall and slithered down the tiled slope to the eaves. He braced himself, launched himself into space, and landed lightly astride the ridged roof of the kitchen outhouses which ended under the overhang of the hill.

Brunel whirled the grapnel around and sent it sailing up to hook on to the barbed wire fence. The fence, tucked into the cliffside overhang, was over thirty feet above ground level but it was only five feet high because the British never expected any prisoner to attempt an escape by the cliff route.

Brunel lashed the roll of carpet across his shoulders and shinned up the rope hand over hand. He clung to a fencing post, untied the short roll of carpet and managed to fling it over the barbed wire so that it provided a safe route for him across the vicious entanglement.

Fifteen minutes later, after a difficult climb up the precipitous hillside, he was loping along the lonely road towards Ambleside seven miles to the north. Owing to his fitness, he wasn't out of breath and nor would he be, even if he maintained his present pace all the way.

On occasions, when he neared pedestrians, or when vehicles approached him, he slowed to a casual saunter, but for most of the way he was able to travel at an easy jog.

His luck held. In the blacked-out streets on the outskirts of Ambleside he even asked a woman the way to the cinema. As Kruger had rightly guessed, his accent aroused no suspicions because the little lakeside town was a popular centre where Free French, Poles and Dutch servicemen spent their leave. The woman directed him along Kelsick Road to the market place and even told Brunel that he would just catch the main film if he ran.

He found the cinema near the old Salutation Hotel without trouble, purchased a shilling ticket in the stalls from the five shillings that Kruger had given him, and settled down in the packed, darkened auditorium to watch the pre-war film *Band Wagon* about a gang of comedians running a pirate television station. He found the antics of the comics as incomprehensible as the plot but the audience enjoyed it hugely.

Before the end of the programme, he disappeared into the toilets and folded his tiny frame into a cleaners' cupboard. The national anthem was played and a few men used the urinal. After that there was silence apart from the final check by the cinema manager to make sure that everyone had left.

He waited an hour, surrounded by buckets and mops, slowly getting cramp, before cautiously emerging from his hiding place. The auditorium was pitch black and deserted. He lit a candle and made his way to the back of the cinema. A door marked 'Private' took him to his objective – the projection room. The projector used for the final reel was still warm to the touch as Brunel began his search. His luck continued to hold: the cinema had a standby sound amplifier concealed behind a dusty stack of film cans. He dragged the heavy, steel-cased instrument from its hiding place and examined the maker's label. It was exactly what Berg needed: a 100-watt cinema amplifier manufactured by Western Electric. Brunel swung it on to his shoulder. It weighed at least seventy pounds.

Despite his superb physical condition, getting the unwieldy amplifier back to the camp was a nightmare: the blackout proved a blessing in the back streets of Ambleside because he was able to hide whenever he heard approaching footsteps, but the seven-mile trudge along the country lanes – having to crouch behind dry-stone walls or hedges at the slightest sound – quickly developed into a back-breaking murderous slog.

The eastern sky was tinged with the dawn by the time he was dragging the amplifier over the carpet-covered barbed wire fence. A prisoner helped him lug it across the out-house rooftop, and a third prisoner dropped a rope down so that it could be hoisted on to the roof of the hall.

Ten minutes later it was safely on Berg's bench.

Berg removed the amplifier's outer casing and examined the huge rectifier valves. 'Marvellous,' he breathed to Kruger. 'Marvellous. I'll have the transmitter working by tomorrow, commander. *And* it will be delivering at least sixty watts.'

Kruger turned to Brunel. The diminutive officer was grinning from ear to ear. 'Brunel, as soon as we're liberated I shall recommend that you receive the Knight's Cross.'

Two days later, at 11.40 am, Berg and Brunel finished checking the fencing wire aerial. The single strand of taut steel was stretched the entire length of the roof. It was anchored as high as possible at the western end of the roof and sloped down to the ceiling joists at the eastern end. In places Brunel had sawn niches in the timber roof trusses so that no part of the aerial's forty-metre length was earthed.

'Why isn't the wire horizontal?' asked Kruger.

'So that the eastward signal shoots into the sky,' Berg explained, sitting at the bench to check the connections to the morse key. 'It means that there's less radiation for any monitoring stations to pick up.' He pointed up at the wire. 'Actually, commander, a wire aerial like that – two wavelengths long – is very directional; most of our signal will be going due west in the direction that the aerial's pointing.'

'Will there be emissions to the north and south?'

'There's certain to be some, commander,' Berg replied,

inspecting the wiring that linked the modified cinema amplifier to the transmitter. 'Without proper filtering, this transmitter will be splattering harmonics all over England.' He switched on the power and watched the transmitter's valves as they began glowing. 'But if any British monitoring stations to the south do pick us up, they'll probably think we're a U-boat off the Faroe Islands or somewhere.'

'Especially as we'll be using a weather station U-boat call sign,' Kruger remarked.

Berg made sure that the morse key was switched off. He stepped back to admire his handiwork. 'She's ready, commander.'

Kruger looked at his watch and glanced at Brunel. 'Have you practised on the morse key?'

'Yes, commander,' Brunel replied, sitting at the bench. 'It's a bit mushy but I've got the feel of it.'

Kruger pulled a sheaf of book flyleaves from his pocket and dropped them on the bench. Each sheet of paper was covered in neat, hand-printed text. 'That's the signal, Brunel. Start transmitting *en clair* at 1100 precisely at a speed of no more than ten words per minute. The message must be received in its entirety on the first transmission.'

Berg snatched up the signal. 'But all this is going to take at least ten minutes to send!'

'So?'

'But I thought you'd be transmitting for only a few seconds at a time!'

'Did I say anything about the length of the transmission?' inquired Kruger, his voice deceptively mild.

'Commander,' Berg beseeched, pointing at the transmitter. 'Those valves are going to be about three hundred per cent overloaded as it is. They won't stand a continuous transmission – they'll blow up!'

'I'll be the one that blows up if they do,' Kruger threatened softly, taking the papers from Berg and placing them in front of Brunel. 'They have only to last for the one transmission.' He nodded to Brunel. 'My call sign is "UBW58". Send it five times. The "standing by" acknowledgement from a U-boat will be the usual six "V"'s. Off you go.'

Brunel gave nervous smile and switched on the morse key.

Fifty miles to the south at the Royal Navy's Liverpool monitoring station, Wren Chief Petty Officer Jenny Linegar heard Brunel's 'UBW58' call sign in her headphones. She switched on the pen recorder and carefully adjusted the aerial selector knob on her 'Huff Duff' receiver until the pulsating ellipse of light on the set's cathode ray tube was tuned to hard line. The graticule around the edge of the circular screen showed that the signal bearing was due north. Switching on her recorder had illuminated a warning light above the huge wall map of the western approaches at the far end of the operations room. The duty officer left his rostrum and crossed to Jenny's console.

'A UBW weather station U-boat, sir,' Jenny reported. 'Bearing due north. Signal strength three.'

The lieutenant glanced at the pen recorder that was busily spiking the U-boat's morse on to a moving roll of paper. The pen stopped oscillating and drew a straight line while the transmitting U-boat awaited an acknowledgement. It came with a weaker string of 'V's that the pen faithfully reproduced.

'UBW58,' mused the lieutenant, reading the morse straight off the recorder when the U-boat started transmitting again. 'Have we heard him before?'

Jenny checked her log. 'No, sir.'

'Mm. Well, he looks out of harm's way. Probably up in the Arctic Circle. Chatty too. Who's east of us to give us a decent cross-bearing? Just to be on the safe side.'

'There's 90 Group's Baker Six, sir.'

The lieutenant groaned. 'Blasted army. Their trouble is

that they don't understand anything that's not on dry land. Oh well, let's give them a chance to shine.'

The lieutenant picked up a telephone.

Brunel frowned in concentration as he keyed out the long signal. The dull ache in his wrist brought home to him just how rusty his morse had become since his imprisonment.

The strange light illuminating the roof space prompted him to glance at the transmitter. What he saw almost caused his wrist to falter in the middle of a word: the transmitter's driver valves were glowing with an intense blue light and the energies building up inside the big electrolytic condenser were causing its maker's label to blister and flake. He could even feel the heat from the grossly overloaded components on his face.

Berg was staring at the condenser in alarm. He opened his mouth to protest but Kruger silenced him with an impatient gesture.

'Yes, well that's jolly interesting and all that, old boy,' said the lieutenant patiently, talking into the telephone and winking at Jenny. 'And I'm sure your D/F gear is spot on, but I'm afraid your cross-bearing puts our U-boat smack in the middle of Lake Windermere.'

There were accusing squawks from the receiver's earpiece. The lieutenant looked pained. 'Yes – I know a U-boat got into Scapa Flow, old boy. But Lake Windermere isn't the same as Scapa. . . . Look, I hate to be too dogmatic about this, but the only way that a U-boat could get into Lake Windermere would be to carry it overland on the backs of pink elephants.'

The unfriendly squawks coming from the earpiece became distinctly more hostile – to the navy in general and the lieutenant in particular.

'I daresay. I daresay,' said the lieutenant boredly. 'But I seem to recall that it was a lot of piddling little boats that brought a certain army back from Dunkirk last year.'

The squawks degenerated into expletives and then the line went dead.

'Strange creatures, soldiers,' the lieutenant remarked to Jenny. 'Never able to admit when they're wrong. Anyway, there's not much point in worrying just yet about a U-boat on a weather station billet.' He leaned forward, switched off Jenny's pen recorder and looked speculatively at her. She was definitely the most beautiful Wren in the place. 'Tell me, chief, are you doing anything special tonight?'

Jenny gave the naval officer a sweet smile. 'That all depends on what my husband has in mind, sir.'

Berg jerked his hand away from the burning condenser.

Brunel ignored him by turning to the second page of the signal with one hand and maintaining the staccato rhythm on the morse key with his other hand.

Berg watched the near-molten valves and the bulging condenser knowing full well that the transmitter had no more than a few seconds left to live.

'Commander,' he pleaded. 'You must –'

'Quiet!' Kruger snapped.

'But –'

'I said, quiet!'

'I'm halfway, commander,' muttered Brunel, not breaking his concentration.

Kruger glanced in some concern at the tortured transmitter. 'All right, hauptmann, you'd better put a screen or something over those valves.'

Berg picked up the metal case that had housed the cinema amplifier. He was about to lower it over the transmitter when the condenser suddenly split with a loud crack and blasted fragments of aluminum foil in his face. He cried out, dropped the heavy case on the valves – causing them to

94

implode, and fell back clutching his face and moaning in agony. Blood starting welling between his fingers.

It took Brenda Hobson nearly fifteen minutes to pick as many fragments of aluminum foil as she could out of Berg's face with her tweezers and drop them one by one into a sterile dish. She looked up at Reynolds as he walked into her sickbay and shook her head.

'I'm sorry, sir, but he needs hospitalization. I can't get all these bits of metal out from around his eyes because of the swelling, and I think some have gone in his eyes as well. What I don't understand is why the bits of foil, or whatever they are, are causing such inflammation. It doesn't make sense.'

'Has he said how it happened? Or what he was doing?'

'No, sir. I've asked him several times but he refuses to answer.'

'Goddamn stubborn jerry,' Reynolds muttered. 'Okay. I'll call an ambulance.'

'I've already called one,' said Brenda.

Kruger stood impassively to attention in front of Reynolds' desk, staring straight ahead at the wall as though Reynolds didn't exist. He had refused to answer any of Reynolds' opening questions.

The Canadian rose to his feet, walked round his desk and stood close to Kruger, their faces inches apart.

'Okay,' said Reynolds, staring Kruger straight in the eye. 'If you won't do any talking, I will. Some straight talking that you won't like. Firstly, the hospital Berg has been moved to is St George's Royal Eye Hospital. Secondly, the surgeons there think they may be able to save his eyesight if only they knew what the hell it is that's causing the infection. Thirdly, he won't tell us what he was doing when he had the accident, and fourthly, I've got a goddamn shrewd idea that you do know.'

Kruger's icy gaze went briefly to Reynolds and returned to the wall. 'If Berg refuses to speak, then I have nothing to say either.'

Reynolds stared at Kruger in contempt. 'Have you ever wondered how I got this eye-patch, commander?'

Kruger remained silent.

'No,' said Reynolds. 'I guess you haven't. Maybe I'm wrong but I've got a pretty shrewd idea that you don't give a damn about other people. I lost my eye at Dunkirk when a shell exploded nearby. I went through three weeks' hell in hospital wondering if I was going to go blind. I know exactly what Berg is going through now. My opinion of anyone who would deliberately put a comrade through that sort of torture doesn't bear repeating. Words such as coward and skunk come to mind plus a few others.'

Kruger's silence continued.

'Get out,' said Reynolds wearily. 'I don't want to see you in this office again. In future you will pass all messages through Sergeant Finch – at least he knew you for what you were from the moment he saw you. I'm only sorry that I've turned out to be such a lousy judge of character, but not as sorry as I am for that poor bastard lying in St George's.'

'I have only your word for it that Berg is in danger of going blind,' said Kruger calmly after a pause.

'For Chrissake!' Reynolds exploded. 'You saw his face! You saw the blood!'

Kruger's face remained expressionless.

'Anyway,' said Reynolds, calming down. 'At least I won't have the job of writing the letter home to his parents telling them what has happened to their son. Nor will I be the one who has his blindness on my conscience for the rest of my life.'

Kruger was lost in thought for some seconds. He met Reynolds' gaze for the first time and seemed to come to a decision. He felt in the pocket of his great-coat and placed the remains of the electrolytic condenser on Reynolds' desk.

'This was found by a litter clearing party and was given to Berg. He was doing something to it when it blew up in his face.'

Reynolds examined the remains of the condenser, turning it over in his hands. 'What in hell is it? I can't even read the maker's name on it.'

'It was made by the Telegraph Condenser Company,' informed Kruger. 'It's a radio component but I've no idea what was in it or what Berg was using it for.'

Reynolds picked up his telephone receiver and asked to be put through to St George's Hospital. He looked up at Kruger while he was waiting for the connection to be made and gave the German a wry smile. 'I guess I didn't misjudge you after all, commander.'

'Perhaps,' said Kruger. 'But I definitely misjudged you.'

The deputy director of the Telecommunications Research Establishment at Malvern gingerly pushed the wrecked condenser across his desk with his pencil. 'One electrolytic condenser that's been subjected to about a five hundred per cent overload, I'd say.'

'How?' asked Fleming.

'Too much juice pumped through it. Serves you right if the navy's started using domestic spec components in service equipment.'

Fleming looked depressed. 'So you definitely think it's been used in a transmitter?'

'No doubt about it,' said the scientist emphatically. 'A powerful one, too. That condenser was intended by TCC for use in domestic wireless receivers. There isn't, or rather, wasn't, a receiver on the market that could do that to an electrolytic.'

Fleming carefully folded the burst condenser into a handkerchief and returned it to his briefcase. He stood and shook hands with the scientist. 'Thank you, Mr Nicolson, you've been most helpful.'

'If you're staying overnight in Malvern, I can recommend the Foley Arms. Roast lamb on Tuesdays.'

Fleming's diffident smile concealed his concern at the scientist's opinion about the condenser. 'I have to be getting back to London today.'

The scientist grunted. He had hoped for dinner at the Navy's expense.

'So what did TRE have to say?' Admiral Godfrey wanted to know as soon as Fleming arrived back at the Admiralty.

'Definitely used in a transmitter, sir,' Fleming replied.

Godfrey sighed. 'And I suppose those blighters at Grizedale had time to concoct a story that they've all stuck to?'

'I'm afraid so, sir. I spent about four hours with every POW involved. I couldn't shake them. They're all sticking to their story that they were listening to a home-made receiver when the condenser blew up.'

'What about the one who's in hospital?'

'He's refusing to talk,' Fleming replied glumly.

Admiral Godfrey came to a decision. 'Very well, Fleming. We're damn certain that they transmitted. Probably on a U-boat frequency. So we must work on the assumption that the transmission was heard. I'll arrange for all recently-captured U-boat crews to pass through the London "Cage". Officers *and* ratings. You're to stay in London until you get results. I'm sure I don't have to remind you just how important it is that we find out what those blighters at Grizedale Hall know.'

Fleming thought wistfully about Cathy Standish's rain cheque that he had yet to cash but wisely remained silent.

Part Four

THOSE MAGNIFICENT MEN

Oberleutnant Harry Wappler and Leutnant Heinz Schnabel did things together: both belonged to the same *Luftwaffe* group; both were pilots; both had been shot down over Southern England and both had been interrogated at the London 'Cage'. To round off this achievement in comradeship, marred only by Heinz's inability to speak English as well as Harry, and a failure by Harry to share Heinz's passion for trains, both arrived at Grizedale Hall in the same truck.

The canvas-covered Bedford ground to a standstill in the courtyard. The three soldiers guarding Harry and Heinz vaulted over the tailboard and unlatched it with a loud crash.

'Out!' yelled the lance-corporal.

Harry and Heinz dutifully jumped down and hoisted their Red Cross issue kitbags on to their shoulders. They looked around in bewilderment. Guards were yelling orders, prisoners were piling out of the hall and forming up into neat lines, while other soldiers were running around the grounds, blowing whistles and shouting at prisoners tending the vegetable plots. From within the hall came the sounds of organized ransacking. To add to the confusion, the weekly laundry van, loaded with giant hampers of soiled linen, was pounced on by two privates under the command of Chalky, who overturned all the hampers, tipping their contents on to the courtyard like camels going berserk in an Arab bazaar. Three soldiers even crawled under the vehicle.

The truck that had delivered Harry and Heinz was searched before roaring away, leaving the two new arrivals standing in the midst of all this frenetic activity, puzzled and uncertain what to do next.

Harry was the taller of the two, a calm, methodical man with a droll sense of humour. By contrast, Heinz was a tortured, uncertain soul, torn between two conflicting desires. The first he shared with Harry: a craving to escape and rejoin his group. The second was his burning ambition to maintain his skin in one pristine piece throughout the war, which, like most German servicemen, he expected to be over by the end of 1941.

'What's going on?' Heinz asked a *Kriegsmarine* leutnant.

'Another blitz,' the naval officer replied, hardly glancing at the two men as he hurried by. 'Reynolds thinks we've still got a hidden radio. You'd better get in line.'

Harry and Heinz moved to the rear of the parade and joined the prisoners forming into lines. Harry nudged a major standing beside him. 'Who's the senior officer here?'

The major gave Harry a puzzled look. 'Commander Kruger, of course. Surely you've met him? He personally briefs all new prisoners.'

'We've not met anyone yet,' Harry replied.

The major pointed out Kruger and Reynolds, who were exchanging salutes at the head of the parade. He motioned Harry to silence as two British NCOs moved along the ranks counting the prisoners.

'One hundred and thirty-two, sir,' the first NCO reported to Reynolds.

Reynolds looked pained. 'Goddamn it,' he muttered. 'There should only be a hundred and thirty. Count them again.'

'One hundred and thirty-two prisoners, sir,' the NCO reported a few minutes later.

The news seemed to sadden Reynolds. 'Sergeant Finch!'

Sergeant Finch had heard the news, which he treated as a

personal insult. His face was thunder as he gripped his clipboard under one arm. He took two paces forward and crashed to attention. 'Saar!'

'We have two prisoners too many.'

'Yes, saar! I heard, saar!' He did an about turn and was about to bawl out an NCO when Reynolds quickly intervened.

'We'll have a normal roll-call, sergeant. Each prisoner to fall out when his name has been called.' He turned to Kruger. 'Will you translate please, commander.'

Kruger acknowledged and repeated Reynolds' order in German.

At the end of the roll-call, which included Leutnant Herbert Shultz's name being called out, Harry and Heinz were the only prisoners left in the courtyard, standing rigidly to attention and looking very worried about all the fuss. After much consultation of documents and poring over clipboards, the reason for their presence was discovered. They were marched off by a smouldering Sergeant Finch to Reynolds' office to face the Canadian officer's standard 'welcome to Grizedale and escape is impossible' spiel.

After lunch Willi ushered the airmen into Kruger's office. They stood to attention while the senior officer studied the questionnaires they had completed. He looked up at Harry while slowly lighting a cheroot. Willi watched the ritual with interest. He knew from his surreptitious searches of Kruger's quarters that the senior officer was down to three boxes of a hundred each of the poisonous weeds. The stock was definitely dwindling. Willi wondered gloomily what the senior officer's temper would be like when the supply was exhausted.

'Exactly how good is your English?'

Harry was taken back. The question had been asked in English.

'Please reply in English,' Kruger added.

'I've been told that my English is very good,' Harry answered in English, trying not to be intimidated by Kruger's hard stare and not succeeding.

'Did you tell the English during your interrogation that you spoke their language?'

'No, commander.'

'Why not?'

Harry shrugged. 'Why make it easy for them?'

Kruger gave a faint smile.

'Commander . . .' said Heinz tentatively, not having understood what had been going on.

Kruger raised a questioning eyebrow.

'How easy is it to get out of this camp?'

Kruger exhaled a cloud of cigar smoke. 'Very easy. All you have to do is join the morning cross-country exercise walks. Only thirty prisoners at a time, so you will have to wait some time before I include your names on the weekly rota.'

Heinz was at a loss. '*You* organize the walks, commander?'

'Yes. But the British like to supervise them. Understandable, of course.'

'Of course,' Heinz agreed.

'I take it you're thinking of escaping?'

Heinz nodded emphatically. 'Those wire fences looked easy enough to get past.'

'I'm sure they are,' said Kruger drily. 'However, I'm extremely difficult to get past. Listen to me, both of you. Despite what Major Reynolds may have told you, escaping from Grizedale Hall is not impossible. What *is* virtually impossible is escaping from these shores. And that's what you have to plan right down to the last detail if you wish to have an escape proposal approved by the escape committee. Bright ideas for getting out of the camp are not enough.'

Heinz looked disappointed. 'How many people on the committee do we have to convince?'

'Only one. The one with the vote. And that's me. It's a very democratic committee.' Kruger paused and nodded to Willi. 'Hauptmann Hartmann will show you to your quarters. Good day, gentlemen.'

'I can see that Kruger is going to be a problem,' Harry declared dolefully when he and Heinz were installed in the tiny bunk-bedded garret that they had been allocated. In Harold Brocklebank's day, the room would have been occupied by the most menial of his household staff. 'His aide – the little fat one – said that Kruger's never sanctioned an escape unless it was his idea.'

'Whose idea? The little fat one's?'

'No, Kruger.'

Heinz nodded and peered out of the grimy, south-facing window. In the distance he could just make out the silvery gleam of Lake Esthwaite Water. 'It's crazy, Harry. We could just walk out of this place. One watchtower that looks as if it's about to fall down, and a fence sheep could stroll through.'

'Sheep don't stroll. They gambol and frolic – but they don't stroll.'

The beginning of their argument was drowned by a formation of four single-engine light aircraft flying low over the hall. The two men pressed their noses against the window.

'Miles Magister trainers,' Heinz declared.

They watched wistfully as the little aircraft dwindled into the distance. As if mocking the captivity of the two men on the ground, the neat little formation broke up to perform a series of exuberant low-level aerobatics over the lake.

'We've *got* to get back,' said Harry resolutely. 'There'll be no more flying if we don't, and who's going to be at the bottom of the list when the decorations are handed out, eh? The ones sitting on their arses in POW camps when there's a peace settlement or an invasion.'

During the weeks that followed, Harry and Heinz slipped into the routine of life at Grizedale Hall. They tended the vegetable plot that they had been allocated, joined in Ulbrick's gruelling physical training sessions, and even did terms of duty as lookouts for Kruger's weekly meetings of the escape committee in the music room. The high spot of each month was the summons to Brenda Hobson's sickbay for the ritual routine with her weighing machine, the search for creatures in their hair, and the check on their fingernails for signs of dietary deficiency.

Although she was the only woman that the prisoners came into contact with, she knew enough about men to know that they rarely made passes if they were forced to stand naked in a chill, acorn-shrivelling draught.

On one occasion a sadistic dentist was present who insisted on filling one of Heinz's many neglected cavities. He used an ancient, foot-operated treadle drill and a bit that was blunt, and announced that he would fill another of Heinz's cavities the following month.

'We've got to escape before that damned dentist comes back,' said Heinz, examining his new filling in a shaving mirror. After two days his jaw was still aching abominably from its rough treatment.

'Your trouble is that you're a coward,' Harry observed unsympathetically, his lanky frame stretched out on his bunk where he was reading a British comic.

Heinz grunted. 'I'm not afraid of Spitfires or Hurricanes, but that dentist terrifies me.'

There was a knock on the door. Willi entered, a beaming smile on his moonlike face. 'Good news, gentlemen.'

'The dentist has been assassinated?'

'Nothing like that,' said Willi, who had also suffered at the hands of the dentist. 'Your names are now on Commander Kruger's list for inclusion in the cross-country exercise walks.'

*

'Right, you lot,' said Sergeant Finch on horseback, addressing the party of prisoners assembled outside the main gate. He glared down at Harry and Heinz. 'This is for the benefit of those of you who've never been on one of our little exercise walks before. Those of you who understand English can translate.' He gestured to the other four guards, who were also on horseback. 'Firstly, although there's thirty of you and only five of us, we're the ones who are armed. My lads are all local and they're all bloody good at shooting rabbits, which means that they won't have no trouble bringing down any of you lot who thinks he'll try making a run for it. You'll keep to the path we indicate, stay four abreast like you are now, and there'll be no singing. Understood?'

'*Jawohl, mein Führer*,' said a voice from the back of the column. The comment prompted sniggers.

Finch's face went puce. 'How many times do I have to tell you bloody Huns to speak to me in English!' He glowered down at the prisoners. 'Okay,' he ordered grudgingly. 'Open the gates.'

The wrought-iron gates swung open and the prisoners trooped out four abreast flanked by guards, with Finch at the head of the column. They turned south towards Satterthwaite, marching at a brisk pace. Finch kept the party in the centre of the road, with the guards evenly dispersed on each side so that there was no possibility of a man trying to dive unseen into a ditch or leap over a dry-stone wall.

After thirty minutes' hard slog up the steep, wooded slopes of Carron Crag, Harry and Heinz decided that walking was their least favourite form of travel. Heinz maintained that the best form of travel, after flying of course, was by rail. Indeed the high spot of his enforced stay in England had been the eight-hour journey from London to Lancaster in a train hauled by the *Coronation Scot*.

'Number 6223,' Heinz panted, toiling up the steep slope

behind Harry. 'A fantastic locomotive. I would have loved to have stayed on it for the climb up Shap Fell. Did I ever tell you that Shap Fell is the steepest –'

'Heinz,' Harry interrupted. 'Did I ever tell you that I'm not in the least bit interested in trains? Since meeting you, my lack of interest in trains has become a pathological hatred of them. Doesn't that make you feel just a little bit guilty – instilling this hatred of trains in a fellow human?'

'All right, you lot!' Sergeant Finch bellowed, reining in his horse. 'We'll take a five-minute rest.'

The party of weary prisoners sank gratefully to the ground. Harry and Heinz propped themselves against a rock and savoured the warmth of the late August sun on their faces. Harry pulled a bar of American chocolate from his pocket. He broke off a piece for Heinz and noticed Chalky and his horse looking enviously at him. He snapped a generous chunk off the bar and held it out.

'Please, you would like some?'

After a brief glance at Sergeant Finch, Chalky gratefully took the chocolate and bit into it with relish. 'Thanks, mate,' he said with his mouth full. 'Oh, bloody marvellous. Haven't had chocolate for months now. Here, boy . . .'

The horse disappeared the piece of chocolate off Chalky's outstretched palm with adroit promptness. It chomped noisily, baring its teeth in appreciation and dribbling threads of brown saliva.

'What's you name, corporal?'

'White. Alan White. Me mates call me Chalky.'

Harry nodded sagely. 'Ah, yes. Chalky White. We can call you Chalky – yes?'

Chalky nodded and took another bite out of his chocolate before his horse got it. 'Funny thing,' he mumbled. 'Here you are, prisoners and that, and yet you get all the sweets and everything you want from the Yanks, and we don't get nothing.'

'You get Lend-Lease tanks and destroyers and airplanes

from the Americans,' Harry pointed out. 'In a war such things are more useful than chocolate, I think.'

Four dots in the distant haze hardened into the droning outlines of Tiger Moth biplanes.

'RAF trainers,' Harry remarked in German to Heinz.

'Really, Harry? And to think I thought they were a squadron of heavy bombers.'

'Sometimes Magisters, sometimes Tiger Moths,' Harry observed, ignoring his comrade's sarcasm. He turned to Chalky. 'In such aircraft we learned to fly. Just like those.'

The guard nodded. 'Funny little things. I went for a flip in one once when Alan Cobham's air circus was up here. Wouldn't do it again, I wouldn't. No bloody fear.'

Sergeant Finch swung into his saddle. 'All right, you lot. On your feet. We'll take the Millwood Forest Trail back to camp. Come on! Fall in! Fall in!'

Kruger rose to his feet when dinner was over. The meal had been Thursday's customary offering of shepherd's pie: grey, watery mashed potato flecked with almost invisible specks of what could be ground meat which looked as if it had been added to the ingredients by means of a spray gun with an extremely fine nozzle.

He tapped his spoon on the table for silence and the buzz of conversation died away immediately.

'Our experts tell me that our vegetable harvest is exceptionally good this season,' Kruger announced without preamble. 'As you have seen, we are now enjoying generous portions of vegetables. Therefore I have decided that we will save at least twenty-five per cent of our produce as seed for next year. Potatoes and beans will be stored, and selected plots of other vegetables will be allowed to go to seed.'

There was a chorus of groans.

'What's the point, commander?' Ulbrick demanded. 'The war will be over before the year's out.'

'I pray that you're right,' Kruger replied. 'If the war is

over by the end of the year, then I promise you all the biggest feast of your life. But I always believe in planning for any eventuality, therefore my ruling stands.'

There was complete silence as Kruger sat down.

'He's crazy,' Harry whispered to Heinz. 'Everyone knows it'll all be over by the end of the year.'

'You know that,' Heinz retorted acidly. 'I know that. We all know that. The trouble is that the British don't know.'

'We've *got* to escape,' Harry whispered vehemently. 'I mean, well, it's not even a proper camp. We'll be a laughing stock when it's all over if we do nothing.'

'The guards have got proper rifles and proper bullets,' Heinz pointed out. 'And the fence is made of proper barbed wire.'

'You're scared?' There was an accusing note in Harry's voice.

'Of rifles and bullets, yes. And barbed wire is bad for my skin.'

'Your skin is all you think of,' Harry retorted.

'It's the only one I've got.'

'We'll have to think of something.'

'I'll tell you what, Harry,' Heinz suggested. 'You do the thinking. You're the one with brains.'

Harry wondered what he could say that would stir his friend out of his lethargy. He had an inspiration: 'That dentist will be back next week. And his drill will be even blunter.'

Autosuggestion at the mention of the German-hating driller-killer was enough to renew the throbbing in Heinz's abused jaw. He brooded for some seconds. 'We escape,' he decided.

On the next exercise walk, Harry nudged Heinz and pointed to a man in a blue uniform who was having a picnic with a girl. The couple were sitting on the grass where they could enjoy the view across Lake Windermere. It was an idyllic day. The girl was in a pretty summer dress, gathered modestly around her ankles; the man's tunic was unbuttoned; the lake was speckled with white triangles of sailing boats.

'What do you think of those two?' Harry asked.

'You can have the fellow, I'll have the girl.'

The man stood up for a closer look at the enemy as the ragged column approached. Some prisoners whistled appreciatively at the brief glimpse of underwear that the girl gave them when she scrambled to her feet. She clung to her escort's arm and stared at the Germans, her eyes wide and a little fearful.

'RAF,' Heinz murmured.

Harry was about to agree but they passed close enough to the couple for him to have a good look at the man's uniform. It was plain, unmarked. Harry switched his attention to the insignia embossed on the man's gilt buttons.

'No, he's not, Heinz. My God! He's Dutch! Royal Dutch Air Force. No wings. He's either ground crew or he's . . .' Harry's step faltered so that the prisoner behind nearly crashed into him. 'Heinz!' he whispered urgently. 'Memorize every detail of that uniform! I've got a brilliant idea!'

Not a flicker of emotion showed on Kruger's face as he regarded the two airmen. He tipped his chair back and exhaled slowly on his cheroot. 'So you propose stealing an aircraft,' he commented. 'Interesting. Tell me more.'

Harry did all the talking. 'Commander, those aircraft that keep appearing over here are trainers – two-seater RAF basic trainers. The biplanes are De Havilland Tiger Moths, and the monoplanes are Miles Magisters. The formations they fly and the sort of stunts they perform are typical of any service flying training school.'

'So?'

Undeterred by the scathing tone that had crept into Kruger's voice, Harry pressed enthusiastically on. 'They won't have a range of much more than five hundred kilometres – half that with the sort of aerobatics they do over the lakes. The formations come from the north and they always return north. That means that there's a flying training school no more than a hundred kilometres from here – about sixty miles.'

Kruger held up his hand for silence. He thought for a few moments, his eyes fixed unblinkingly on Harry, who returned the hard stare without flinching.

'So let us take one step at a time,' said Kruger at length, carefully tapping the ash off his cheroot. 'We assume that you escape from here. We assume that you find the flying school. We assume that you get into the flying school, that you find an aircraft that you've never flown before, and that it has full tanks, and that you manage to take off. Having assumed all that, oberleutnant, you will find yourself flying an aircraft with a range of no more than three hundred and fifty miles – which is not enough to reach France or Holland. So what, may I ask, is the point of your plan?'

'Simple, commander,' Harry replied. 'We never said anything about flying to France or Holland. We'll fly to southern Ireland where we'll be interned. And as for flying an unfamiliar aircraft – there's nothing to trainers: a control column, a rudder-bar, a few instruments – compass, rev counter, oil – and that's all.'

'That's all?'

'That's all,' Harry confirmed.

Kruger looked far from convinced. 'And how about the security at this . . . flying school?'

'If it's anything like the security at training schools, it'll be non-existent. We're not talking about an operational base, commander.'

'We're not talking about an escape yet,' said Kruger icily. 'How do you propose travelling north?'

Harry nodded to Heinz. The younger officer was hesitant at first but he warmed rapidly to his favourite subject. 'We were brought here on the London to Carlisle line, commander,' he said respectfully. 'We were taken off the train at Lancaster where we changed on to the branch line that took us to Windermere.'

Kruger nodded. It was how the majority of prisoners arrived at Grizedale Hall.

'North of Lancaster,' Heinz continued, 'the Carlisle line goes over Shap Fell. It's a very steep climb. In fact there was a lot of argument among railway engineers in the last century when the line was being planned because it was thought that the climb would be too steep for locomotives. The gradient is –'

'You mean the trains have to slow down when they're climbing Shap Fell?' Kruger interrupted impatiently.

'Yes, commander,' Heinz replied.

'All right,' said Kruger, stubbing out his cheroot. 'How do you propose getting out of here?'

'In two laundry hampers,' Harry answered promptly.

Amusement showed fleetingly on Kruger's face. He gave a theatrical sigh. 'Tell me, oberleutnant, have you read any escape stories of the Great War?'

'No, commander.'

'I think you should. In all of them, POWs on both sides were pouring out of their camps in laundry hampers. It's the oldest trick in the book. That's why the guards turn out all the hampers as they're loaded into the van. They've read all the stories even if you haven't.'

'But they don't *measure* the hampers,' said Harry evenly. 'They're nearly a metre high. A false bottom about a third of a metre up from the base will provide just enough space for us. We know, commander, because we've tried it. And they won't know about the extra weight because they always make us load them into the van.'

Kruger lit another cheroot to give himself time to think. He dropped the match in his tin lid that served as an ashtray. 'All right, gentlemen,' he said at length. 'You have my permission to make a start on serious planning.' He immediately killed the look of elation on Harry's and Heinz's faces by adding sternly, 'And that's *all* I'm giving you permission to do. If your plans aren't ready to my satisfaction by the end of October – before the onset of winter – I shall not permit your escape attempt until the following spring. Is that clearly understood?'

'Understood, sir,' said Harry crisply, saluting and breaking into a broad grin of triumph.

'Forty-one, sarge,' Chalky reported to Sergeant Finch.

Sergeant Finch scowled. 'You sure, White?'

'Positive, sarge. I counted every doorstop twice.'

Sergeant Finch's scowl deepened. Devilment was afoot. Jerry devilment. 'That's twenty less than last week. Did you check Hartmann's room?'

Chalky looked apprehensive. 'Well, no, sarge.'

'Why not?'

'Because . . .' Chalky floundered. 'Er – well – because –'

'Because Willi Hartmann bribes you with chocolate bars! Just like he bribes all of you!' Finch thundered. 'I know everything that goes on this camp. Everything! So don't you try pulling the wool over my eyes, corporal!'

Chalky decided that it might be unwise to point out that if Sergeant Finch knew everything that was going on, he would know what was happening to the disappearing doorstops.

Finch pulled on his forage cap and glowered at Chalky. 'This is a very serious matter, White. I shall take personal charge of an investigation. And if I don't get to the bottom of what's going on, it will be reported to Major Reynolds.'

Major Reynolds was not in the best of moods as he and Kruger confronted one another on the terrace. With the exception of Willi, who was eavesdropping behind the french windows, the prisoners had sensed trouble and had made themselves scarce.

'As far as I'm concerned,' Reynolds declared, 'we had an

114

agreement that you would ensure that the hall was not structurally damaged in any way.'

'It was an understanding, major,' said Kruger blandly. 'I don't recall entering into any agreements.'

'It amounts to the same thing, commander.'

Kruger lit one of his poisonous cheroots. For once Reynolds was too preoccupied to wonder where the German officer was obtaining them.

'Personally,' Kruger murmured, 'I would have thought that you had more important things to worry about than twenty missing doorstops.'

'Sergeant Finch takes it seriously,' said Reynolds, inwardly cursing his over-zealous adjutant. 'Therefore I have to back him up. Twenty, round wooden doorstops are missing. He has rightly pointed out to me that they're fixtures, that they're on the inventory of fixtures and fittings agreed between the War Office and the owners of Grizedale Hall, and that they will have to be replaced when the hall is de-requisitioned.'

'I will look into the matter,' Kruger promised.

'They will have to be replaced.'

Kruger nodded. With a deadpan expression, he said, 'I will set up a committee of inquiry.'

'You can't go holding court-martials,' said Reynolds, alarmed. 'That's contrary to the Geneva Convention.'

'It will be a *committee*,' Kruger stressed. 'It will report back to me with recommendations as to the best way to replace the missing doorstops.'

Reynolds looked relieved. The two men exchanged salutes.

'Willi!' Kruger called out when Reynolds had departed.

Willi sheepishly emerged from behind the french windows. 'Commander?'

'Have you got those forms for me?

Willi looked unhappy. 'I've been promised them tomorrow, commander.'

'How much?'

'Twenty half-pound bars of chocolate,' said Willi miserably.

'Twenty?' Kruger exclaimed. 'Well – I daresay you have at least a hundred bars in your room. How about the money?'

'Ten pounds in ten shilling notes, commander.'

'That's ample, and there'll be plenty left over for the escape fund. Incidentally, I am now a committee of inquiry. Who's been stealing the doorstops?'

Willi contrived to look suitably puzzled.

'Willi,' said Kruger mildly. 'Nothing goes on in this place that you don't know about. If you don't tell me who has been stealing the doorstops, Major Reynolds will receive information about a certain prisoner who bribes the guards to ensure that his room is never searched.'

Willi looked sorrowful. 'It's only a suspicion, commander. I'm not an informer but I think Oberleutnant Wappler and Leutnant Schnabel may know something about them.'

'What the hell do they want with twenty, round, wooden doorstops?'

'I don't know, commander,' Willi replied truthfully.

'Buttons,' said Harry proudly, reaching into his mattress and holding out a collection of domed, wooden buttons for Kruger's inspection. 'We discovered that the doorstops were made from a wood that was easy to carve. Each one took about four hours.'

Watched nervously by Harry and Heinz, Kruger carefully studied one of the home-made buttons. The embossed insignia of the Royal Dutch Air Force had been painstakingly carved on the domed surface, and the finished product had been carefully covered with chocolate foil wrapping paper. He handed the button back to Harry without comment.

'And this is Schnabel's finished tunic,' Harry continued, producing the garment. 'Our colour is the same as the Dutch uniform, so it was only the buttons and the shoulder marks that gave us trouble.'

If Kruger was impressed, he gave no sign.

Unnerved by the senior officer's silence, Harry pressed on. 'We've learned from Chalky that the Royal Dutch Air Force men who we sometimes see on the fells are what the British call "Free" Dutch. Most of them are pupil pilots at an elementary flying training school near Carlisle. There's also a lot of Poles there.'

'How near is Carlisle?' Kruger inquired.

'We didn't like to press him, commander. But at least we now know that the school is near Carlisle.'

Kruger nodded. 'Well, so long as you keep clear of the Dutch, your accents will pass unnoticed. When will you be ready?'

'In time for next week's visit by the laundry van,' said Harry hopefully, sensing that Kruger was about to give his consent for the escape to go ahead.

Kruger reached into his pocket and produced two type-written documents which bore the Royal Air Force crest. 'These are British Air Ministry form Twelve-fifties. They're temporary passes that will enable you to enter RAF establishments provided the smudged date stamps aren't looked at too closely.'

While Harry and Heinz were gazing speechlessly at the two documents, Kruger counted out some ten shilling notes on to one of the bunks. 'There's three pounds each in British currency, plus bus tickets, torn cinema tickets, and so on. All the bits and pieces that one would expect to find in a serviceman's pockets.'

'You . . . you mean that we can go?' said Heinz, speaking for the first time and omitting Kruger's rank in his excitement.

'Your plan is the best that has ever been submitted to

me,' said Kruger, turning to the door. He paused and nodded to the forms lying on the bunk. 'Make sure that you know your identities. I shall be testing you. One more thing – why did you have to use doorstops for the buttons? Why didn't you prise knots out of the floorboards? I'm certain Sergeant Finch hasn't counted them.'

Heinz gaped at his senior officer. 'Knots? You know, commander, we never thought of that.'

Kruger grunted. 'I shall inform Major Reynolds that you sliced up the doorstops to make a draughts set.'

Heinz was the first to speak after Kruger had left. 'The best plan ever submitted to me,' he said, reciting Kruger's words. 'Harry, I do believe he *actually* paid us a compliment!'

Harry grinned at his friend. 'There's only one problem from your point of view.'

'What's that?'

'The dentist comes on a Monday and the laundry van comes on Tuesday.'

The cramped space in the laundry hamper's false bottom made Heinz realize that the dull ache of his recently filled tooth was the least of his discomforts. Through the gaps in the wickerwork, he had a depressingly close-up view of khaki as the guards milled around the prisoners who were loading the hampers into the back of the van.

A jolt banged his jaw as the hamper was lifted. Another jolt banged it again when it was bundled roughly into the van. He heard the lid thrown open, a sound of rummaging in the soiled linen, shouted orders, and yet another jaw-jarring jolt as the hamper containing Harry crashed into his hamper. The prisoners were deliberately handling the hampers casually so as not to arouse the suspicions of the guards concerning the extra weight that had to be lifted.

'Okay, Mike!', yelled an English voice. 'Take her away.'

Darkness closed in as the van's rear doors were slammed

shut. The engine started up, gears were crashed, and the van started moving.

After ten minutes Harry decided that it was safe to make a move. He heaved upwards, dislodging the false bottom, and pushed himself upright amid a cascade of sheets and pillowcases. He helped Heinz disentangle himself from his hamper, then the two men busied themselves in the swaying van by fitting the false bottoms back into the hampers and replacing the linen.

Heinz cautiously released the internal locking bar on the vehicle's rear doors and peered out. The van was travelling over Hawkshead Moor, heading towards Windermere. As it slowed to negotiate a junction, Harry and Heinz pushed the door open wide and jumped out. They picked themselves up and leapt over a dry-stone wall where they spent a few minutes cleaning their disguised uniforms and taking stock of their surroundings.

Harry grinned at his friend. 'There's no doubt about it, Heinz, the old methods are the best.'

Heinz gingerly massaged his aching jaw. 'That's what that damned dentist said.'

The two escapees reached Windermere station without being challenged. Harry purchased two tickets for Carlisle. The prisoners' main worry was that most servicemen on leave in the Lake District would be using travel warrants instead of money. Their anxiety was alleviated when they saw a polish major ahead of them in the ticket office queue pay cash. Luckily there were no Dutch servicemen about. Two hours later, after an uneventful journey to Oxenholme, they changed trains and boarded a northbound train to Carlisle. To Heinz's delight, the locomotive turned out to be a class G2, normally used for hauling freight.

The two airmen found an empty third-class compartment and settled down. They decided that the best way to pass the journey was by pretending to be asleep. This would

119

minimize the chances of them being drawn into conversation with gregarious passengers.

After a short stop at Tebay, the train pulled away from the slate and granite station and began the long climb up Shap Fell. It was one stage of the journey during which Heinz found it impossible to feign sleep: he spent it with his nose to the glass, gazing out across the harsh terrain, and tried to picture in his mind the gangs of sweating navvies, working with pick and shovel, who had brought the plans of the brilliant nineteenth-century railway engineer, Joseph Locke, to fruition. Unlike his contemporaries, who included George Stevenson, Locke was an engineer who wasn't afraid of steep gradients. He said that a railway could be built over Shap Fell, and he proved that he was right. Heinz was disappointed that Harry wasn't in the slightest bit interested in Joseph Locke.

Despite his excitement, Heinz felt his eyelids becoming heavy. The soporific, rocking motion of the train gradually weaned his attention away from the passing scenery and his toothache, and he fell into a fitful sleep.

He was vaguely aware of the train stopping several times and doors slamming, but no one entered their compartment. The next thing he knew was Harry shaking him violently.

'Heinz! Look!'

Heinz blinked and was immediately wide awake. Sandwiched between the railway and a main road was a small grass airfield with Tiger Moths and Magisters lined up at dispersal points around the perimeter. A flight of five Magisters was actually taking off in formation.

'That's it!' cried Harry excitedly.

'My God,' Heinz breathed. 'What a stroke of luck.'

'We're going to have to jump,' Harry decided.

Heinz peered down in alarm at the blur of grass flashing by. 'But, Harry, the train's going much too fast.'

'You've been asleep for an hour,' Harry retorted. 'We're

only about two kilometres out from Carlisle, therefore we can't be far from the Scottish border. If we jump now, we won't have to deal with customs men and border guards.'

Heinz was about to protest his certainty that there was no such thing as Scottish border controls, but Harry had swung the door open.

'Harry,' Heinz moaned. 'We can't jump yet.'

'Listen,' said Harry in a reasoning tone. 'Look upon it as bailing out.'

'That's exactly what I am looking on it as,' Heinz complained. 'Did I ever tell you about my injuries from bailing out?'

Harry ignored Heinz's reply because the train had entered a cutting where there was no one to see them. 'Now!', he yelled over his shoulder, and promptly launched himself off the train.

Heinz gave a moan of despair and threw himself after his comrade. He managed to land on his feet, but his body, possessing the momentum of the train, performed a series of somersaults like a rag doll fired from a gun. He came to rest, lying on his back, fifteen yards from his original point of contact with the ground. He gazed up at the leaden sky and wondered which parts of his body, if any, were still usable. His jaw felt as if it had been dealt with by a team of horses who had first dragged it from his skull and then taken it in turn to kick it.

A shadow crossed his face. Harry was standing over him. The taller airman's face was streaked with mud and there were grass stains on his uniform.

'Get up and stop moaning,' said Harry.

Heinz stood unsteadily. 'I wasn't moaning.'

Harry supported his comrade by the elbow. 'Come on, Heinz. The first thing we've got to do is reconnoitre that airfield.'

Number 15 Elementary Flying Training School at Kingstown, near Carlisle, had started life as a private flying club in southern England before being taken over by the RAF. After a number of incidents during the Battle of Britain, one of which was a pupil on his first solo flight in an unarmed Tiger Moth biplane becoming involved in a dispute with an Me109, the school and all its predominately civilian staff were moved north.

As Harry and Heinz discovered from their vantage point in a section of unused sewer pipe near the unfenced perimeter, the majority of the pupils were Free French. Other nationalities included some Czechs, Dutch and Poles.

Heinz looked at his watch. There were three hours of daylight left and already apprentices were lining up two flights of refuelled Magisters and picketting them before pulling canvas covers over the wings. An hour later the airfield was deserted apart from some coming and going around the flight office, which was among a cluster of hangers and buildings near the main road.

The last movement was an hour before dusk when an apprentice hauled down the windsock.

'I never thought it would be so simple, Harry,' said Heinz gleefully. 'We've got a choice of thirty refuelled aircraft.' He made a move to scramble out of the pipe but Harry put a restraining hand on his arm.

'No. We wait until morning.'

Heinz stared at his friend in surprise. 'But there's an hour's daylight left, Harry. We'll be in southern Ireland before dark.'

'We're not going to southern Ireland,' said Harry firmly. 'There's not enough daylight left for where we're going.'

Heinz gave his comrade a puzzled look. 'What do you mean?'

'We're going to walk up to one of those Magisters in the morning as instructor and pupil. We're going to do it openly – just as everyone else does – and we're flying to France.'

Heinz forgot where he was. He sat bolt upright and clouted his head on the inside of the sewer pipe. The blow started his toothache off again but he ignored it. 'Harry – you're crazy! Those things haven't got the range. We'd have to land and refuel –'

'Listen, Heinz. Our luck has got us this far. I don't know about you but I don't fancy being interned in southern Ireland for the duration. Not when there's a chance that we might make it home.'

Heinz was silent for a moment. 'You mean that it never was your intention that we should try to reach Ireland?'

'That's right,' said Harry. 'We'll head south and refuel at an operational airbase. We'll say that we're on a training flight and that we lost our bearings.'

'Just like that?'

Harry nodded. 'Just the one refuelling stop and then we'll be home.' He punched Heinz playfully 'So let's get some sleep. This time tomorrow we'll be telling our story to Hermann himself.'

At 7.30 the following morning, Alan Graydon and a group of fellow apprentices untied the pickets that secured the eight Magisters of 'A' flight and removed the aircrafts' canvas covers. Unaware that two pairs of eyes were noting their every move, they swung the propellers in turn to warm up the engines and generally prepare the aircraft for another day's work.

'Reckon there'll be any flying today, Alan?' asked one of the younger apprentices.

Alan looked up at the low cloud-base. A light drizzle was falling and the wind was blowing at a moderate 15 knots from the south-west. 'Yes, I think so. It'll take more than this to keep the Poles grounded.'

By 8 am, several pupils and flying instructors of assorted

nationalities were taking their customary early morning stroll around the concrete perimeter track while the flight office decided the day's flying programme.

The windsock was hoisted – signifying that flying was to take place – and the flying school came to life. Aircraft were taxied to the marshalling area; instructors and pupils pored over charts spread out on wings; engines opened up; and formations took off at timed intervals.

Alan was covering the two remaining Magisters in his flight an hour later when an accented but pleasant-sounding voice bade him good morning.

Alan turned round. Two Dutch officers were regarding him – one short and one tall.

'Good morning,' Harry repeated. He nodded to the Magister. 'I am needing this aircraft please for my student.'

'Yes, sirs,' said Alan, pulling the covers off the Magister's twin cockpits and helping the two airmen on to the wing. 'But, sirs – you should be wearing your parachutes. It's against the rules to fly without them.'

Harry looked nonplussed for a moment as he and Heinz lowered themselves into their respective cockpits. Then his face cleared. 'Ah yes, we are not flying. The CO wants my student to have some more taxiing practice.' He gave Alan a conspiratorial wink. 'You know what the CO is like.'

Alan smiled. 'Yes, sir. I do know.'

Harry sat down. His joy at discovering that the Magister's controls were as basic as he had predicted and immediately understandable, gave way to alarm when he realized that he was sitting too low to see over the cockpit coaming. He turned round. There was no sign of Heinz in the rear cockpit. He realized in dismay that there was one thing he had overlooked: the Magisters' seats were designed so that the pilot's parachute pack served as a cushion.

Harry looked up at Alan, who was standing on the wing root, trying hard not to laugh. The apprentice held out two of the folded canvas covers.

'We always sit on these, sirs, when we taxi Maggies.'

Alan obligingly pushed the covers under the two airmen and saw them comfortably settled.

'Thank you,' said Harry. 'I am most grateful. You will now turn the prop please. Magneto switches are off. Brakes on.'

'She's warm, sir. She won't need priming.'

Harry operated the magneto switches correctly.

'Contact, sir?' queried Alan, his hands ready on the propeller.

'Yes, contact,' Harry confirmed.

Alan swung the Magister's propeller. The Gypsy engine fired immediately. He stood clear while Harry tested the engine. The engine settled down to a steady note. Harry gave Alan a thumbs up sign and the youngster dragged the chocks away from the wheels.

He watched the aircraft taxi away from the dispersal point and returned to his task of covering the remaining Magister. He heard the engine open up. He looked across at the aircraft as it turned west into the wind and wondered why the instructor wanted so much power for taxiing. To his amazement, the Magister gathered speed, bumping across the grass. The tail wheel lifted and the monoplane was airborne and gaining height as it flew over the railway track. After two minutes it had disappeared into the low cloud.

Alan groaned inwardly and cursed the two hot-headed Dutchmen who had made him an unwitting accomplice in a serious breach of the rules. He decided that the best thing would be to report the matter immediately to the officer in charge of 'A' flight.

Without flying suits or goggles, Harry and Heinz began to shiver with cold as they flew south. But they didn't care. They were free. They were flying again. For a while all thought of the hazards that lay ahead were set aside.

'Thank you, Graydon,' said Flight-Lieutenant Neads when Alan finished explaining what had happened. 'They'll find themselves on the receiving end of one hell of a rocket when they get back. Were they Poles or Dutch?'

'Dutch, I think, sir.'

Neads nodded and picked up his telephone. 'All right, Graydon. I'll notify the CO. And you had better report the matter to the chief engineer.'

Due to Kruger's careful rehearsals, the morning roll-call ruse to provide cover for two missing airmen succeeded admirably. Kruger had drilled the two prisoners to perfection: they were the shortest POWs in the camp so that the corporal counting the numbers of men in each row did not see them step smartly forward into the row in front as he made a note on his clipboard.

Harry and Heinz took it in turns to fly the Magister. While one held the controls, the other stamped his feet in order to maintain circulation.

After flying south-east for an hour, Harry gradually lost height, so they emerged from the cloud-base. Heinz correctly identified the city to their east as Leeds, and they climbed back into the cloud.

They had flown a hundred miles – just over a third of the Magister's range.

Flight-Lieutenant Neads looked at his watch. 'We'll give them another forty-five minutes,' he told Pat O'Hara, the flying school's chief engineer.

'Long enough for me to think of something particularly horrible to happen to Graydon,' muttered O'Hara.

Neads smiled. 'Don't be too hard on the lad, Pat. Those crazy Dutchmen can be intimidating when they want to be.'

'I'll intimidate them,' O'Hara growled. 'Do we know who they are, sir?'

'The CO's checking "B" and "C" flights now.'

It was inevitable that after two hours blind flying in cloud, with a compass as the Magister's sole navigation instrument, Harry's and Heinz's amazing streak of good luck should begin to run out.

'You take over for bit, Harry,' said Heinz. 'I can hardly feel my feet on the rudder bar.'

'Time we went down and looked for landmarks,' Harry yelled above the roar of the engine as he took control.

The Magister broke through the cloud-base. The two airmen stared aghast at the sea 1000 feet below. They had unknowingly crossed the coast at Skegness and were over the North Sea.

'Our easterly drift must have been —'

'Harry!' Heinz interrupted. 'I think the left-hand fuel gauge must have been stuck – it's just dropped to a quarter!'

Harry looked down at the simple fuel gauge that was set into the port wing root. It was showing a much lower reading than the starboard tank gauge.

'We'll have to fly west,' Harry decided. 'We can't be that far from the coast.'

'And be shot down as a raider?'

'Have you got a better idea?'

Heinz remained silent. The heady feeling of flying again had passed; he was too cold and miserable to care very much what happened, especially now that his tooth was aching again with renewed ferocity.

Flight-Lieutenant Neads replaced his telephone. He brooded for a moment. 'All the school's instructors and pupils have been accounted for,' he informed Pat O'Hara. 'Group are going to check Grizedale Hall and the Shap Fell Hotel camp to see if our two mystery pilots are escaped POWs.'

This time there was no fooling the guards during the snap roll-call. Under Sergeant Finch's hostile eye, each prisoner was required to fall out as his name was called. At the end of forty minutes, when the courtyard had been cleared, the names of two prisoners who had not been ticked off the list were left on his clipboard.

'Three prisoners missing, saar!' he said, crashing to attention in front of Reynolds' desk with such force that a trout rod tumbled from its wall hooks.

'Three?' Reynolds looked surprised. 'I thought it would be two.'

'Wappler – Harold; Schnabel – Heindrich; and Shultz – Herbert. Saar!'

Reynolds sighed. 'Sergeant, there's no need to call Leutnant Shultz's name at every roll-call.'

'Sorry, saar! But he is down on my list as a prisoner!'

Reynolds picked up his telephone and called the commanding officer of No. 15 EFTS. Once through, he gave the RAF officer the names of Harry Wappler and Heinz Schnabel.

The land that Harry and Heinz found and followed south was mile after mile of mist-shrouded Norfolk Broads. It was bleak and desolate, as uninspiring as the sea and the two fuel tank gauges that were showing empty.

'Some sort of marshland,' shouted Heinz.

'Well, at least it's flat,' Harry yelled back.

Heinz made no reply. He was too tired and miserable to care very much about anything, and his tooth was a white hot lance being thrust into his jaw.

At that moment the engine spluttered and picked up again. It fired again for a few seconds and then died for good.

'Don't give up hope yet,' advised Harry as he looked for a suitable field for a forced landing.

The duty engineer at the Horsham St Faith Bomber Command station near Yarmouth took the telephone call from the garage owner because the operations room staff thought that this particular problem ought to be his baby.

He listened incredulously and said, 'Yes, I've got all that, sir. Two Germans have landed in your paddock.' He caught the eye of his sergeant and gave him a despairing look before returning to the unreal telephone conversation. 'Tell me, sir. Are these Germans with you now? . . . I see. What sort of aircraft do they have? . . . Well ask them.'

There was a pause while the garage owner solicited the required information from his visitors.

'A Maggie?' queried the duty engineer in response to the garage owner's reply. 'Well, in that case, sir, they're not Germans. What about their uniforms? . . . Well, describe their buttons.'

The garage owner described the buttons on his visitors' tunics.

'Well, in that case, sir, they're telling the truth – they're definitely Dutch and not German. I'll be with you in fifteen minutes.'

'But you must refuel us,' said Harry with a contrived anger that Heinz could only admire. 'It is important that we are getting back today to our flying school.'

The duty engineer sighed and returned Harry's form Twelve-fifty. 'I'm sorry, gentlemen. But I don't have the authority to order a petrol bowser off the station.'

Harry gestured to the garage owner who was sitting on a workbench swinging his legs and watching the two airmen suspiciously.

'So – you must require this garage to refuel us. It is very simple.'

'Maybe,' said the duty engineer evenly. 'But the work that would have to be done on your engine after running it on MT fuel wouldn't be simple. Look, sirs, come back to Horsham St Faith with me. You can phone your flying

129

school, have a shower and a meal and a bed, and be away first light tomorrow.'

Harry glanced at Heinz and realized that they had no option but to go along with the duty engineer's suggestion. There was a slim, impossible chance that they could continue to brazen it out until the following day.

'What do you fly at Horsham St Faith?' Harry asked.

'We're a bomber station,' said the duty engineer cheerfully.

Harry grinned. With their luck maybe they could steal a bomber. That would give Hermann something to chuckle about.

'Tell you sommat, mate,' said the garage owner sourly, eyeing Harry and Heinz. 'Them's jerries. Came across enough of the bastards on the Somme, I did. I know a jerry when I see one.'

'But maybe not when you see two together, eh?' the duty engineer suggested pointedly.

An operations room officer wandered into the duty engineer's office. 'Where's our two flying Dutchmen, Bill?'

Something about his colleague's tone of voice made the duty engineer suspicious. 'Taking a shower. Why?'

The officer dropped a pink flimsy on the duty engineer's desk. 'Thought you might like to see this, old boy.' He grinned. 'It's an all stations alert from Group. This morning a couple of escaped *Luftwaffe* POWs stole a Maggie from Fifteen EFTS at Carlisle.'

There was a dead silence in the room. The duty engineer's face paled visibly. 'Carlisle?' he choked. 'Carlisle to here? In a Maggie? It's not possible.'

The officer shrugged. 'Could be if they ran their tanks dry, old boy.' He looked levelly at the engineer. 'Which they did.'

Harry turned his naked body blissfully under the shower, enjoying really hot water, an unheard of luxury at

Grizedale Hall. He broke off humming to bang on the partition between his shower stall and the next. 'Heinz. For God's sake cheer up.'

'I'm sorry, Harry,' Heinz's voice replied. 'But this tooth is really giving me hell.'

The duty engineer entered the shower rooms just as Harry resumed humming. He stared at the two stalls and the pair of naked feet visible below each door, before turning his attention to the two uniforms thrown casually over the back of a chair.

'Herr Wappler and Herr Schnabel, I presume?' the duty engineer called out. 'Is there anything else you need before dinner? How about new buttons for your uniforms? These might have woodworm.'

The humming stopped immediately. There was a pause and one of the doors slowly opened. The taller of the two escapees stood naked and dripping under the shower. He grinned amiably at the duty engineer.

'Ah. We are – what is the English expression – rumbled? Yes?' inquired Harry.

'I expect that expression will do,' agreed the duty engineer wearily, without rancour.

The other shower stall door opened. Heinz regarded the RAF officer sheepishly.

'So is there anything you need before dinner?' the duty engineer repeated.

Harry looked puzzled. 'We are to have dinner?'

'Oh yes. In the officers' mess. You're our guests of honour. The CO's refusing to hand you over until he's heard the full story from both of you as to how you did it.'

'There is something I need,' said Heinz, speaking in halting English. 'Could you please take me to a dentist?'

The repercussions of the remarkable escape bid by Harry Wappler and Heinz Schnabel resulted in Pat O'Hara, the chief engineer at Number 15 Elementary Flying Training

School, having to attend two inquiries and fill in endless forms before he got his Miles Magister trainer back.

Alan Graydon received only a 'ticking-off' for handing over a Magister to the POWs, but the RAF came in for harsh criticism about security at their flying schools. At the second inquiry they successfully shoved most of the blame on to the Navy with their assertion that Grizedale Hall's intelligence officer was a certain Commander Ian Lancaster Fleming, RNVR, who was not even present at Grizedale Hall when Wappler and Schnabel must have been planning their audacious escape. The buck, which the Air Ministry passed to the Admiralty, ended up on Admiral Godfrey's desk.

'There's one dickens of a rumpus over all this,' he grumbled to Fleming.

Fleming chuckled. 'So what's going to happen to our intrepid birdmen, sir?'

'They're serving twenty-eight days' solitary at Colchester and will probably stay there. Can't have them going back to Grizedale and gloating. What's more to the point, Fleming, is what are we going to do with you? Grizedale is still our biggest concentration of U-boat officers and I don't want us to lose our toehold there.'

Fleming steeled himself for what was coming. In the summer the Lake District was marvellous – fishing, riding – but he had no wish to spend the winter there.

'Anyway,' Admiral Godfrey continued, 'just to keep everyone happy, I've said that you'll be back there by the end of the week.'

Fleming groaned inwardly. Then he remembered Cathy Standish and his mood brightened.

Part Five

THE PRISONER
IN THE TOWER

Korvettenkapitan Hugo Forster made himself so inconspicuous during his first week at Grizedale Hall that the rumour circulating among the prisoners was that he had discovered a foolproof method of escaping and returning at will, and was therefore only present in the camp for roll-calls and meals.

His diminutive physical appearance made it easy for him to dissolve into the background to the point of invisibility. This unusual, chameleon-like talent was helped by his instantly forgettable face. On those rare occasions when he was spotted in the camp, he was invariably wearing the expression of a man who has just discovered that his mistress was the wife of a world heavyweight boxing champion.

To Willi's dismay, Kruger paused by the vegetable plot that had been allocated to Forster. The U-boat 'ace' lit a cheroot and snapped the match in two with his thumbnail – a sure indication that he was angry.

It was a fine morning in early September. The sun was shining from a clear blue sky and the first delicate, experimental tints of autumn were staining the valley. But the beauty of the surroundings failed to detract from Kruger's temper. He was recovering from a bout of influenza which had led to him finding more faults than usual during his fortnightly inspection tour of all the vegetable plots.

The plot that was the cause of Kruger's extreme irritation

was a wilderness of yard-high weeds that was dominated by a giant thistle and a clump of stinging nettles.

'Willi. You told me that all the plots had been allocated.'

'They have, commander.'

'This one obviously hasn't been allocated.'

Willi consulted his clipboard even though he knew the answer. 'Plot 114. I allocated it to Korvettenkapitan Hugo Forster on his arrival last Monday.'

'He's had six days to clear it. Why has nothing been done?'

'I don't know, commander. He's not been around much.'

Kruger looked sharply at Willi. 'What are you talking about? All the prisoners are around all the time except Leutnant Shultz.'

'He makes himself scarce, commander,' said Willi, wishing that Kruger wouldn't drag Shultz into the conversation.

'I haven't interviewed him, have I?'

'No, commander. Leutnant Shultz escaped before you arrived.'

'I'm talking about Forster!' Kruger snapped. 'Where is he?'

'In the room at the top of the east tower, commander. The one that no one wanted. He said that it suited him.'

'So why haven't I interviewed him?'

'He arrived while you were ill, commander. I thought it best –'

'Well, I'm not ill now. Tell Forster I want to see him in my office in fifteen minutes precisely.'

Kruger turned on his heel and strode towards the hall, leaving Willi cursing the number of steps he would have to climb to find the elusive Hugo Forster.

Alone in his tiny garret room at the top of the spiral staircase in the east tower, Forster read Eva's letter for the hundredth time before carefully folding it and returning it to its envelope. He turned on his side and stared longingly at the photograph on the wall by his bed. It was a picture of his month-old son, Ernst, whom he had never seen. Eva had enclosed the photograph with her last letter. She wrote every week without fail. The news about Ernst in her latest letter had been overshadowed by her excitement at being offered her old job back with the Foreign Ministry as a Spanish translator. Monday's post had also included a letter from his father. He had skimmed through it once. Its contents had made it impossible for him to read it again. His father had enthused about his son's continuation of the family's naval tradition; how his mother would have been proud of him had she been alive; that there was no dishonour in being a prisoner of war; and that there would be a hero's welcome for him in Dortmund when he returned home after the British surrender.

A hero's welcome! Dear God, if only they knew. . . . But soon they would know. They would all know: Eva, his father, all his friends in Dortmund, and one day – his son. It was only a matter of time before the whole sorry story emerged.

In his loneliness and misery, Forster would have wept but for the rap on his door. It was Willi Hartmann, his chest heaving from the climb up the spiral staircase.

'Commander Kruger wants to see you in his office now,' said Willi breathlessly while mopping the sweat from his brow.

Kruger finished reading the questionnaire and asked Willi to leave. As soon as the door closed behind the little Bavarian, Kruger inhaled on his cheroot and stared at Hugo Forster. He was unimpressed by what he saw. The young U-boat commander was clearly ill at ease. He fiddled nervously with his cap while waiting for Kruger to speak.

'This doesn't give much information,' Kruger remarked. 'You say your *U-501* was rammed but you don't say how.'

'We were forced to the surface by two destroyers that had depth-charged us.'

'The names of the warships?'

'One was HMCS *Moose Jaw* and I think the other was *Chambly*.'

Kruger raised his eyebrows. 'They were Canadian?'

'Yes, commander.'

'Were British ships involved in the action?'

'I don't think so, commander.'

'Congratulations,' said Kruger sarcastically. 'You're the first U-boat to be sunk by the Canadians. None of your officers are here, so presumably they all went down with *U-501*?'

Forster nodded unhappily. 'I think so, commander. I was –'

'You only *think* so? Surely you made it your business to find out what had happened to your own crew?'

Forster avoided Kruger's contemptuous gaze. 'No one would tell me what had happened to them.'

'In which case *I* shall find out what happened to them, Forster,' Kruger stated frostily.

'I think I'm the only survivor,' said Forster miserably. 'Why else would the British not tell me what had happened to them?'

'I can think of a thousand and one reasons,' said Kruger, angrily stubbing out his cigar. 'That being so, how is it that you survived and your crew have not?'

'I was first on the bridge after we'd blown our tanks. Both our periscopes and our hydrophone gear had been knocked out by the depth-charges, so I had no idea how close the destroyers were. The *Moose Jaw* rammed as soon as we surfaced.'

'How long did your boat take to sink?'

Forster hesitated. 'I don't know, commander. I was knocked unconscious.'

Kruger stared hard at Forster before returning his

attention to the questionnaire. 'Your boat was sunk on September 10th. Three weeks ago. Show me the injury that knocked you unconscious.'

Forster pointed to his temple. 'Something hit me here, commander.'

Kruger leaned forward and studied the side of Forster's head. 'It has healed remarkably well in three weeks, Forster. In fact, I can't see even a mark.'

'Nevertheless, that's where I was struck,' said Forster doggedly, showing a trace of irritation at the searching questions.

There was a silence while Kruger appeared to be trying to make up his mind about something. 'Very well, korvettenkapitan,' he said at length. 'You may go. I shall expect to see your vegetable plot cleared within the next two days.'

The two men stood, pulled on their caps and exchanged salutes.

Forster opened the door and hesitated. 'There is one thing, commander.'

'Yes?'

'Admiral Doenitz arranged a letter-code for use by captured U-boat captains.'

'What of it?'

'Do you use it, commander?'

'Perhaps,' said Kruger guardedly. 'Why?'

'Oh, it doesn't matter. I merely wondered.'

Willi was standing at the end of the corridor, idly gazing out of a window as Forster brushed passed. He returned to the office.

'What did you think of his story?' Kruger asked.

'I haven't heard it, commander,' Willi replied, his cherubic face a picture of innocence.

'Willi,' Kruger murmured. 'You're as big a liar as Korvettenkapitan Forster. The difference between you and him is that all you've got to hide are the contents of your room.'

*

139

'Major Reynolds!'

Reynolds jumped guiltily at the sound of the female voice. He didn't know why he felt guilty. It wasn't as if he was having an affair with Nurse Brenda Hobson, however desirable such an involvement would be, even though she was married; it was just that the sound of her voice had that effect on him. He turned and smiled at her as she clip-clopped across the courtyard. As usual, she was in a hurry.

'Good morning, nurse. A beautiful morning.'

'It's about one of the prisoners, sir,' said Brenda, coming straight to the point. 'Korvettenkapitan Hugo Forster. He was supposed to see me for a medical check-up this morning and he didn't show up. I don't have the time to go chasing –'

'I'll speak to Commander Kruger about him,' said Reynolds.

'Personally I don't give a damn if they all die of starvation provided I've got it recorded. You know how I like to keep my record cards up to date.'

'I'll speak to Commander Kruger about it,' Reynolds repeated.

'And while we're on the subject, sir, what do I do about my record card for Leutnant Shultz? Is he still officially a prisoner, or what?'

'I'll ask Sergeant Finch to check with the War Office,' said Reynolds hurriedly. 'Please excuse me. I have to go now.'

Like all Cathy Standish's parties, the one she threw at her spacious farmhouse to celebrate Ian Fleming's return was a great success. There was a plentiful supply of food and drink despite the wartime restrictions, and an even more plentiful supply of unattached young ladies: three commodities which, in reverse order of esteem, had a certain appeal to Fleming.

He disentangled himself from a conversation with Major

Reynolds and a lively little brunette – the daughter of a local landowner – and pushed through the crowd of farmers and their wives who were gathered around Cathy Standish.

'Cathy,' he said, taking her to one side. 'A quick word with you.' He nodded to Mrs Heelis, who was sitting on a sofa wearing an ill-fitting tweed suit, a dishevelled bonnet, and a faintly disapproving expression. 'Major Reynolds tells me that the elderly lady is Beatrix Potter.'

'That's right, Ian,' Cathy replied, smiling mischievously up at Fleming. 'Only you mustn't call her that. She's Mrs Heelis.'

'I thought she was dead. I'd love to be introduced to her. Do you think she'd dance with me?'

Cathy laughed. 'I doubt it, Ian. She never usually goes to parties. I think my invitation to a radio-warming party must've intrigued her.'

'What's happened to your boyfriend?'

Cathy's smile faded for an instant. 'Who?'

'The one togged up in tweeds you always have in tow. I've often seen you riding with him.'

'Oh, him,' said Cathy lightly, steering Fleming towards the sofa. 'He doesn't like parties either.'

'Where do you keep him when he's not at parties?'

'Mrs Heelis,' said Cathy brightly. 'This is Commander Ian Fleming.'

Fleming shook hands with Mrs Heelis. He was surprised by the coarseness of her skin. Obviously she was accustomed to hard, manual work.

'Good evening, commander,' said Mrs Heelis, returning Fleming's greeting. She studied him with sharp, perceptive eyes. 'Ah, navy I see. Well, I've no quarrel with the navy. At least the navy doesn't build prisoner of war camps all over the place and make off with all the vets in the area. The nearest vet lives miles away. It's a serious problem for large sheep breeders such as Cathy and myself. Isn't it, Cathy?'

'Very serious, Mrs Heelis,' agreed Cathy.

'Are you interested in sheep, Mr Fleming?'

'Only when they've taken their coats off and they're served with mint sauce,' Fleming replied.

Mrs Heelis laughed good-naturedly. 'I've nearly doubled the size of my flocks since the war started.'

'You're lucky in one respect, Mrs Heelis,' said Fleming. 'At least the war permits you to continue with your business.'

'Very true. Very true. And what is *your* business, Mr Fleming?'

'Oh, I've dabbled in stockbroking. And journalism.'

'Journalism?' sniffed Mrs Heelis. 'I've had more than my fair share of attention from journalists. They ask the most ridiculous questions about books I wrote over thirty years ago.'

'I'd like to be an author,' Fleming admitted.

'Oh? And what sort of books would you like to write?'

'I've not given it much thought, Mrs Heelis. Thrillers, I suppose.'

'Write for children,' said the old lady firmly. 'A discerning readership, Mr Fleming. And a most rewarding one.'

Cathy laughed. 'I can't see Ian writing for children.'

'I'll make you a promise, Mrs Heelis,' said Fleming, smiling. 'If I do become a thriller writer, I'll write at least one book for children.'

'May I interrupt a minute please, ladies?' said Reynolds. 'I'd like a quick word with Commander Fleming.'

'Oh, I suppose you want to talk about the war,' said Cathy. 'Well, don't be too long.'

Fleming made his excuses and moved to a corner with Reynolds.

'What's the problem, old boy?'

'Will you be visiting the hall tomorrow?'

'I expect so,' said Fleming. 'Why?'

'Kruger's asking a lot of goddamn questions about the whereabouts of a U-boat crew.'

142

'Hugo Forster's U-boat?'

Reynolds gave Fleming a suspicious look. 'That's right. How did you know?'

Fleming chuckled. 'I guessed.'

'Now look,' said Reynolds. 'Is there something going on that I should know about?'

'Why should you think that, old boy,' asked Fleming blandly.

'Because Kruger's getting tough. He said that no British newspaper has carried a report on the sinking of Forster's U-boat and he wants to know why. He's threatening to complain to the protecting power commission on their next visit if he doesn't get an answer.'

'Oh dear,' murmured Fleming. 'We don't want the Swiss poking their noses into our affairs, do we? I'll deal with it in the morning.'

A guard showed Forster into Reynolds' office. The U-boat commander gave a start of surprise at seeing Fleming sitting at Reynolds' desk.

'Good morning,' said Fleming pleasantly, speaking in German. He offered Forster a cigarette from his gold case and waved him to a seat.

'I thought you'd finished interrogating me in London,' said Forster suspiciously.

'Oh, I just wanted to see how you were settling in,' said Fleming lightly. 'I hear that your senior officer is Otto Kruger of *U-112* fame. You must have a lot to talk over.'

'I've told you everything that I have to,' said Forster nervously, glancing at the window in case any prisoners were in the courtyard. 'Name, rank and number, and names and addresses of my next of kin.'

Fleming chuckled. 'Funny thing, the Geneva Convention. It specifies the information that a prisoner of war may give his captors but it says nothing about what information captors can give their prisoners.'

'I don't understand.'

'So far we've not released any information about the loss of your U-boat.'

'So?'

'And what information we do release is up to us, of course.' Fleming gave a sly smile. 'And you to a certain extent.'

Forster swallowed. 'I still don't understand.'

'Really? Knowing Kruger's record, I rather fancy that he and the other prisoners will make life somewhat uncomfortable for you if the truth emerges.'

There was a silence. Forster raised his head and looked Fleming straight in the eye. 'Commander Fleming, I bitterly regret what happened. But I'm learning to live with the memory of those moments before my boat sank because at least I did what I did in the heat of battle. If I was to tell you the secrets of *U-501*'s equipment, it would be a calculated act on my part and therefore something I could never learn to live with.'

Fleming gave Forster a pleasant smile. 'Very well, old boy,' he said in English. 'It's your decision.'

Admiral Godfrey read through Fleming's proposed press release a second time and made a couple of minor alterations before initialling it as approved. He tossed the typewritten sheet of paper to Fleming.

'Is it true, Fleming?'

'Substantially – yes, sir.'

Admiral Godfrey grunted. 'Well, I only hope to God you know what you're doing.'

'I'm sure it will produce results, sir,' said Fleming, sliding the sheet of paper into his briefcase.

'It's about time, Fleming. As far as intelligence gathering on U-boats goes, one can hardly say that we're outshining MI6.'

'We will be soon, sir,' Fleming promised, patting his

briefcase. 'There will be developments as soon as this gets into print.'

'For Chrissake,' muttered Reynolds when he finished reading the front-page newspaper story. 'Is it too late to stop Kruger seeing this?'

'I'm sorry, sir,' said Sergeant Finch. 'Evans spotted Forster's photograph over the *Daily Mirror* story after he'd handed out yesterday's papers.'

Leutnant zur See Weiner Hertzog had sat his huge frame on a chair outside Kruger's office and was angrily reading the front page of the *Daily Telegraph*. His rudimentary grasp of English was sufficient for him to follow the gist of the story, and his anger mounted with each reading as the words became clearer. He heard footsteps on the stairway. Kruger appeared. Hertzog stood and gave the senior officer a smart salute. His bulk nearly filled the narrow passageway.

'Commander, if I could see you for a minute please.'

'Arrange an appointment with Leutnant Hartmann,' said Kruger curtly. He tried to pass Hertzog but the burly naval officer stood his ground despite Kruger's look of cold disdain. Hertzog was a hardened prisoner. His U-boat, *U-39*, had been sunk after an abortive attack on the *Ark Royal* during the first fortnight of the war against Britain. The long period in captivity had made him taciturn and short-tempered.

'Have you read about the loss of *U-501*, commander?' Hertzog's tone was respectful; it was his eyes that betrayed his anger.

'What about it?' inquired Kruger frostily.

'My brother was *U-501*'s radio officer.'

'I'm sorry to hear that, Hertzog.'

'So I think I've a right to know what's going to happen to that stinking little coward,' said Hertzog bluntly, still undeterred by Kruger's icy stare.

'There will an inquiry into the loss of *U-501* immediately after our liberation,' Kruger replied. 'For the time being, it would be best if we don't allow British propaganda to pre-judge the issue. Now if you will excuse –'

'You mean that you're going to do nothing?' This time Hertzog's tone was insolent but Kruger was a sound judge of men: he could see that Hertzog was simmering with rage and realized that no purpose would be served by getting angry in retaliation. Instead, he said calmly, 'If the newspaper reports about Korvettenkapitan Forster's actions are correct, then you have my word that he will pay the price.'

'And you have my word that Forster will pay the price, commander.'

'Meaning?'

'Meaning just that,' said Hertzog simply. Before Kruger could reply he turned on his heel and clattered his bulk down the stairs.

The *Altestenrat* – literally 'The Council of Elders' – had been convened by Kruger in the music room on the first floor of Grizedale Hall. It was an easy room to cover with sentries to warn of approaching guards, and the thick pile carpet in the elegant room tended to deaden the sound of heated exchanges.

Oberleutnant Karl Shriver of the *Luftwaffe*, a recent arrival at the hall, sat at the head table. He was flanked by Kruger and Hauptmann Paul Ulbrick. The three men had taken considerable pains with their uniforms to ensure that they were correctly turned out. They were all studying several British newspapers that were spread out on the table. Willi was sitting in a chair near the door where he could hear the warning signal from the lookouts. He had a pencil and paper at the ready to make notes of the proceedings. Facing the table were the rest of the council, which consisted of ten of the more senior-ranking officers from among the hall's inmates. To avoid accusations of showing

146

favouritism towards a fellow U-boat officer, Kruger had selected the members of the council so that its naval officers were in the minority, and he had appointed Shriver as the council's president.

Completing the scene – standing rigidly to attention in front of the table – was Korvettenkapitan Hugo Forster. His eyes were fixed on the wall behind Kruger and his two fellow officers of the council.

At 10 am precisely, Kruger looked up from the newspapers piled on the table and made no attempt to conceal his loathing as he regarded Forster. He nodded to Shriver.

Shriver turned to Ulbrick. 'Please proceed, hauptmann.'

'Korvettenkapitan Forster,' said Ulbrick, rising to his feet. 'This is not a court-martial, therefore you are not under oath. The purpose of this *Altestenrat* is to establish the truth concerning the loss of your *U-501* and its crew on September 10th, 1941. The facts will then be reported to your Admiral Doenitz together with any recommendations that the *Altestenrat* feels that it ought to make. Do you understand?'

'Yes, hauptmann,' said Forster woodenly, not taking his eyes off the wall. He was uncomfortably aware that Kruger was staring at him with an icy expression.

'Also, you are not obliged to answer any questions. However, if you do refuse, that will also be reported by Commander Kruger to the Flag Officer, U-boats.'

'I will answer what questions I can,' said Forster.

Shriver nodded to Willi, who started writing.

Ulbrick studied Forster for a few moments and said abruptly, 'Can you read English, korvettenkapitan?'

Forster licked his lips. 'A little, hauptmann.'

Ulbrick contemptuously tossed the *Daily Telegraph* across the table to Forster. 'Read that,' he commanded.

Forster stepped forward and stared down at the newspaper. His fingers shook slightly as he tried to turn the pages.

'It's below the headlines on the front page,' said Ulbrick scathingly. He picked up the other newspapers one by one. 'It's a major story in the entire British press. The *Times*: "U-boat captain abandons his command". The *Daily Mirror*: "U-boat skipper jumps ship".'

'It's not as bad as they make it sound,' Forster protested.

'Forty-three U-boatmen lost,' snapped Ulbrick. 'Tell me how you can make that sound less bad than it is unless the British are lying. Are they lying?'

'Well – no. But –'

'Did you or did you not abandon your boat?'

'Hauptmann,' said Forster desperately. '*U-501* had been cut virtually in two when –'

Ulbrick's scalp went back. 'Did you or did you not abandon your boat!'

'How can I be accused of abandoning my boat when it sank under me?' said Forster defensively.

Ulbrick's eyes opened wide. 'Did I say I was accusing you, korvettenkapitan? I'm sorry, I didn't mean it to sound like that. Obviously I touched a nerve.'

A laugh at the back of the room was silenced by a withering glare from Shriver.

'Let me rephrase the question,' Ulbrick continued. 'Did you leave your boat?'

'It left me when it sank,' said Forster.

Ulbrick picked up a handwritten sheet of paper. 'In your statement –'

'Account,' Kruger corrected.

Ulbrick smiled and bowed to Kruger. He returned to the attack. 'In your account of the action, you said that you were the first man on the bridge as soon as *U-501* surfaced. Why were you so anxious to be the first man out of your submarine?'

Forster looked appealingly at Kruger. 'That's not a fair question, commander. As you well know, it's normal for the commander to be the first through the hatch, especially when there's damage to be assessed.'

Kruger nodded. 'Yes, that's correct, hauptmann.'

'And what was the damage?' Ulbrick queried.

'I didn't get a chance to see the extent of the external damage because the *Moose Jaw* rammed the moment I climbed on to the bridge.'

'Surely you were aware of the warship's proximity?'

Forster shook his head. 'I had no idea the destroyer was so close. We'd been heavily depth-charged. The attack periscope and the sky periscope were useless, and so was our hydrophone equipment. The pressure hull was leaking badly and the boat was filling with chlorine gas. That's why I ordered the chief engineer to blow all tanks and surface.'

'So that you could escape,' Ulbrick remarked.

'Yes, of course.'

Ulbrick paused and glanced at the circle of listening officers. 'So that *you* could escape? What about your crew?'

'I was including my crew,' Forster answered. 'But first I wanted to see if there was a chance of retaliating with our 88-millimetre. There was a gun crew standing by in the control room.'

'Did you order them to action stations?'

'No. I never had the chance. As I said, the *Moose Jaw* rammed immediately – before our deck casings were above water.'

Ulbrick looked up from the note that Kruger had passed him. 'Presumably you realized that all was lost the moment the Canadian destroyer rammed you?'

Forster's unhappy gaze met his inquisitor's eyes for the first time. He nodded.

'Did you order your crew to abandon ship when you realized that all was lost?'

Forster hesitated. 'No,' he said. 'There wasn't time. I was thrown away from the speaking tubes and the klaxon button by the force of the impact. The bows of the destroyer sliced right into the bridge.'

'You were thrown into the water?'

Another hesitation. 'No.'

'So what happened, korvettenkapitan? Why is it that you are here and none of your crew is?'

'Look,' said Forster abruptly. 'The destroyer struck within a metre of where I was standing. The noise was deafening. I hardly knew what was happening. There was this terrible screaming noise – steel smashing into steel. Then the conning tower was keeling over. I remember hanging on to the periscope standard and then I must have climbed onto the conning tower's coaming – I don't know. I saw something in front of me and I jumped.'

'You jumped onto the *Moose Jaw*'s foredeck!' Ulbrick accused.

'I didn't know what it was at the time!'

'You saw a destroyer's deck in front of you? A few metres away? And you expect us to believe that you didn't know what it was?'

Forster began to get angry. 'Look. I couldn't see or hear properly. I knew my boat was going down fast. I saw something in front of me and I jumped.'

Ulbrick regarded his victim in contempt. 'You saw safety?'

'I jumped. It was an instinctive reaction.'

Ulbrick consulted his notes. 'I'm not a U-boatman, korvettenkapitan, but I know enough to know that the foredeck of a destroyer is much higher above water level than the conning tower of a U-boat, especially when the U-boat's conning tower has keeled over. Am I correct?'

'Yes,' said Forster tiredly, knowing what was to follow.

'Therefore your act of jumping from the conning tower on to the destroyer must have been carefully timed and judged. Hardly an instinctive reaction.'

'All I know is that it was an instinctive jump,' Forster asserted.

'You saw safety in front of you and you jumped?'

'I tell you I don't know what I was thinking at the time!' Forster almost shouted. He looked wildly around at the accusing faces. 'Surely you've all been in the same situation before? When you've had to bale out or whatever. Your actions are instinctive. You do things that you can't remember or explain afterwards.'

'I can remember exactly what happened when I was shot down,' said Ulbrick. 'In particular I can remember giving orders to my crew to bale out before doing so myself.'

'A U-boat's different,' said Forster feebly. 'Look, you must understand that I was grabbed by the crew of the destroyer who pulled me on to the foredeck. It wasn't a clean jump if that's what you mean.'

'You jumped off the conning tower's coaming?'

'Yes.'

Ulbrick looked scathing. 'Earlier on you said that your boat had sunk.'

'It did sink.'

'But it was still afloat when you jumped. It would have to have been otherwise how could you have jumped?'

'It was partially afloat.'

Ulbrick arched his eyebrows. 'Earlier you said that the U-boat had sunk when you were rescued, that it had abandoned you. Now we learn that it was afloat.'

'What I said earlier was –'

'What you said earlier was a lie!'

'I didn't lie!' snapped Forster, showing unexpected spirit. 'In the heat of battle –'

'There was no battle!' Ulbrick countered savagely. 'You were depth-charged. You surfaced. You were the first man out of the hatch and on to the bridge. Your boat was rammed and, like the coward you are, you abandoned it by jumping from the conning tower onto the *Moose Jaw*'s foredeck – exactly in accordance with the accounts in these newspapers!'

Forster stared straight back at Ulbrick. 'It is obvious that you are intent on attaching more importance to propaganda stories in the British newspapers than to my account. If I am guilty of anything, it is my inability to convey to you the horror of what it is like to be confronted by the bows of a charging destroyer bearing down on one at distance of a few metres.'

The silence that followed was broken by Kruger. He stood and contemplated Forster. The U-boat captain met the withering stare for a moment and allowed his gaze to drop to the floor.

'The most effective propaganda of all, Korvettenkapitan Forster,' said Kruger, speaking slowly, 'is that which is based on truth. The Canadian crew of the *Moose Jaw* will no doubt be encouraged to relate the story to newsmen so that the whole sorry account will be reported in the world's press – particularly the United States' press. Your cowardly act will serve the British admirably in their campaign to win support in the United States. It will help the American public to believe the lies that the British are circulating about U-boats opening fire on lifeboats crowded with survivors. Do you have anything to say in your defence?'

'I thought that this wasn't a court-martial?' said Forster, a hostile edge in his voice.

'It isn't,' Kruger replied. 'But I will be in touch with Admiral Doenitz and will notify him that we have established that these stories' – he gestured to the newspapers – 'are substantially correct. A court-martial is certain to follow after our liberation and I have no doubt whatsoever that you will be found guilty of abandoning your command and that you will be hanged.'

Forster's face paled noticeably. For a moment it looked as if he was about to collapse.

'Do you have anything to say?' asked Shriver.

Forster shook his head.

'Very well,' said Shriver evenly. 'All that remains now is for us to decide what to do with you until the liberation. Willi, escort Korvettenkapitan Forster outside for a few minutes.'

The discussion among the thirteen members of the *Altestenrat* concerning Forster's fate was opened by Shriver. He said bluntly, 'He'll have to hang, of course. There's no question about that.'

'I agree,' said Kruger. 'But we're here to decide what to do with him until the liberation.'

'Others here might decide for us.'

Kruger frowned. 'I don't understand.'

'He's certain to be punished by the other prisoners,' Ulbrick replied.

'In what way?' asked Kruger.

Ulbrick shrugged. 'I don't have to go into details, but there're a number of your U-boat colleagues who will come up with their own form of punishment for Forster.'

'In which case, those prisoners would face disciplinary proceedings under British military law,' Kruger replied impassively.

'Would you side with the British if such a thing happened?' asked Shriver curiously.

Kruger lit a cheroot. 'I'm not taking any sides but I will not condone officers taking the law into their own hands.'

'Then Forster will have to be transferred to another camp,' said an army major.

'And that means Canada,' remarked another officer.

There was a silence. All the prisoners went in fear at the threat of being transferred to Canada. There was the frightening thought that they would be thousands of kilometres from their homes and loved ones. Also, although most prisoners considered that a British capitulation was imminent, none of them had any doubts that

Canada would continue to fight on for years – perhaps even decades. Nothing provoked escape fever in the camp quite as much as rumours of an impending transfer to Canada.

'No,' said Kruger firmly. 'Over forty men died in *U-501*. I'm not having Forster escape justice by being sent to Canada.'

'That only leaves one option,' said Shriver.

'Which is?'

'Forster will have to withdraw from all camp activities.'

'He's never taken part in them anyway,' Kruger observed.

'I was thinking of a withdrawal of *all* privileges,' said Shriver. 'There are the instruction courses, and we control the distribution of mail and food parcels –'

'Stopping his mail and parcels would be illegal,' Kruger pointed out.

'We will be suspending them pending further investigations,' said Shriver smoothly. 'It would certainly hit him hard because he's always first in the mail queue on Mondays.' The *Luftwaffe* officer glanced at Willi. 'Leutnant Hartmann could look after Forster's mail and parcels until the liberation. I understand that the guards never search your room, Willi?'

Willi nodded.

The major laughed and said: 'No one has ever seen the inside of Willi's room.'

'Also, there's a guard who owes me a favour,' said Willi. 'I could ask him to let me have Forster's outgoing mail before it's passed to the censors. That way we'd be stopping all his mail.'

Shriver frowned. 'It's an effective short-term punishment but supposing Forster complains to Reynolds?'

'Reynolds won't listen,' said Kruger. 'Our arrangement is that all prisoners' complaints are channelled through me.'

'Very well,' said Shriver. 'We have a proposal. Is there a seconder?'

'I'll second it,' said the major promptly.

'I'm opposed to it,' Kruger stated. 'The proposed action is illegal.'

'That is not in dispute, Otto,' said Shriver mildly, using Kruger's first name with an easy familiarity that was unheard of among the prisoners.

'In which case, Shriver, you ought to be opposed to the proposal as well.'

'Otto, this isn't your escape committee in which you have the right of veto. You agreed that every member of this council should have a vote. All right, so you're opposed to the proposal. Are you also opposed to me putting it to the vote?'

Kruger tried to outstare Shriver and failed. He shook his head.

'Very well,' said Shriver, well aware that Kruger had failed to get his own way for the first time at Grizedale Hall. 'All those in favour of the total exclusion of Korvettenkapitan Forster from camp activities, including the suspension of his mail and parcels, please raise their right hand.'

The Monday morning mail and parcel distribution system devised by Kruger was an orderly affair – far removed from the noisy throng that used to gather in the courtyard outside Sergeant Finch's office window in the days when Ulbrick had been the camp's senior German officer. The bundles of letters and parcels were stacked in alphabetical order on one of the long, trestle tables in the common room in front of the huge marble fireplace. There were more parcels than usual on this particular Monday morning because the monthly consignment of American Red Cross parcels had arrived – each one about the size of two shoeboxes. They contained tobacco, chocolate, candy, condensed milk, powdered coffee, tea, sugar, and tins of food, in addition to shaving and toilet soap of a quality far superior to that available in the shops in wartime Britain.

Watched by silent, expectant prisoners who were crowding on to the gallery, Willi finished checking the mail against his trusty clipboard. At 10 am exactly, he settled into his chair behind the trestle table and called out: 'Prisoners A to H!'

The twenty or so officers who had been sitting on the stairs scrambled to their feet and swarmed eagerly across the hall to Willi. They formed an orderly line in front of the table with Forster first in the queue. Hertzog was immediately behind him.

'Forster, H. G.,' said Forster excitedly.

'Forster, H. G.,' Willi repeated without looking at his clipboard. 'Sorry. No mail or parcels. Next.'

Forster stared at Willi in astonishment. 'What do you mean? There's a letter from my wife.'

The buzz of conversation in the queue died away to an uneasy silence.

'You know the commander's orders,' said Willi uncomfortably. He pretended to be engrossed in his clipboard so that he didn't have to meet Forster's pleading eyes.

'But the ban doesn't include letters from my wife! It can't. I don't care about the parcels but –'

Willi looked embarrassed. 'I'm sorry, korvettenkapitan. But I'm only obeying orders. Next please.'

Forster's face went white. 'You can't stop my wife's letters!' he whispered. 'It's inhuman!'

'No more inhuman than what you did, Forster,' Hertzog growled. 'Now move.'

For a moment Forster seemed to be paralyzed with shock. Slowly he raised his eyes to the expressionless faces staring down at him from the gallery.

'Move, you stinking little coward!' barked Hertzog, giving Forster a sharp poke in the ribs with a forefinger the diameter of a broomstick.

It was as if the jab had unleashed a coiled spring. Forster spun round and swung his foot with savage force into Hertzog's groin. Hertzog gave a loud cry of pain and doubled up in agony. Willi half-rose to his feet and fell back as Forster lunged at him across the table. One of the trestles collapsed, sending Willi and Forster sprawling on to the floor amid a cascade of parcels. Before anyone had realized what was happening, Forster had snatched up the bundle of letters that had fallen from Willi's hand and was thrusting his way past the prisoners towards the french windows.

'Stop him!' Willi yelled.

An army officer lashed out wildly at Forster and caught him by the sleeve of his jacket. Forster retaliated by swinging a punch into the army officer's face, forcing him to break his grip. Forster recovered his balance. Still clutching the bundle of letters, he darted across the hall to the windows but was brought crashing down in a flying rugger tackle. He fought like a wildcat and managed to break loose from four prisoners who tried to pin him to the floor. Suddenly he was seized from behind by a pair of brawny arms.

The dishevelled prisoners who had attempted to restrain Forster fell back as Hertzog swung him aloft as though he was a sack of hay. The giant U-boatman gave a grunt and hurled Forster across the room. He crashed against a settee which fortunately cushioned his fall. He staggered to his feet. Blood was streaming from a deep cut over his left eye. His expression was one of unbridled fury. He was about to launch himself at Hertzog but was checked by a shrill blast on a whistle.

'Well, gentlemen,' said Sergeant Finch, moving from the french windows into the centre of the room. 'If this is a diversion, you should know by now that they don't work with me.'

'A quarrel,' said Willi, recovering the letters that were

scattered on the rucked carpet. 'An argument over a parcel. It is nothing.'

Finch grinned when he caught sight of Forster's battered face. 'Looks like you lost, mate. Still – your consolation prize is that you get to see Nurse Hobson.' He turned to the two guards who were standing in the doorway. 'Take this gentleman to the sickbay.'

As Forster was led away, he paused in front of Hertzog and wiped the blood from his eyes. The two men stared at each other, their expressions mirroring their mutual hatred.

'I remember your brother on *U-501*, Hertzog,' said Forster bitterly. 'It's a pity that you weren't serving with him. That way the loss of my boat would have meant the end of two pigs instead of one.'

Fleming returned to Grizedale Hall from London that day at 2 pm. He was parking his Bentley in the courtyard when he was accosted by Brenda Hobson with an offer of coffee in her sickbay.

A few minutes later he was appreciatively sipping the best cup of coffee he had tasted since ground coffee had become virtually unobtainable earlier that year.

'My God, nurse, real coffee. How do you do it?'

'It's an American blend. Chalky – er – one of the guards gave it to me,' Brenda replied, smiling. 'He gets a supply from the POWs who don't like coffee. It's funny the way the Americans send them so many food parcels.' She looked worried. 'You won't say anything will you?'

Fleming chuckled. 'It would be impossible to stamp out trading between the guards and the prisoners – and I don't suppose it does any harm.'

'How about Nazi bullying?' said Brenda suddenly. 'Does that do any harm?'

'Ah. Now we're coming to the reason why you've lured me into your sickbay. I had hoped that it was because you

158

either considered me in need of a soft hand on a fevered brow or because you found me irresistible. Tell me more.'

'There's a Korvettenkapitan Forster here – a U-boat captain. I'm sure he's being bullied by the prisoners.'

'Oh?' Fleming queried guardedly. 'Why do you think that?'

'This morning I put three stitches in a cut over his eye. He's a funny bloke. Doesn't say much even though he can speak a bit of English. Keeps himself to himself. He doesn't even work in the gardens and yet Kruger has a strict rule that all POWs have to do some gardening.'

'This is a "white" camp,' Fleming pointed out. 'Any bullying is not likely to be Nazi-inspired.'

'They're all Nazis as far as I'm concerned,' Brenda replied vehemently. 'I don't really care what they do to each other, but I object to them doing it on British soil and getting away with it.'

'Shouldn't you be telling this to Major Reynolds, my precious?'

Brenda gave a contemptuous toss of her head. 'He turns that blind eye of his to a lot of things that go on around here. If you don't believe me, ask him about Leutnant Herbert Shultz's escape or why Willi Hartmann's room is never searched.'

'Why do you think I ought to be interested?'

'You're responsible for camp intelligence, aren't you?'

'Well – sort of,' Fleming murmured guardedly. He glanced around the neat sickbay in a search of something to help change the subject. A framed photograph of a smiling young man in a sub-lieutenant's uniform caught his eye. He picked it up.

'Either you are or you're not,' said Brenda. 'If you're not interested, then I'm sorry to have wasted your time.'

'Is this your husband, Brenda?'

Brenda's expression softened. 'Yes. David.'

'You must introduce me sometime.'

'Oh, I hardly ever see him. But he might be home for Christmas. He said that the *Barham* is due for a refit.'

Fleming smiled. He put the photograph down and stood. 'Well, don't forget that I'd like to meet him. He's a lucky man to have you.'

Brenda was not susceptible to Fleming's charm. 'What are you going to do about Forster?' she persisted.

Fleming made a vague promise to look into the matter. He left Nurse Brenda Hobson a few minutes later feeling very pleased with himself. Things were moving on the Forster front.

Forster stretched out on his hard bed and started reading his prison library book for the fifth time. The ban even covered the loan of library books: he could neither return the book or withdraw a new one. He had avoided the evening meal but the pain from the cut over his eye and his misery made him forget his hunger.

He reached the foot of the first page and realized that not one word had registered because his mind kept returning to the letter from Eva that he knew was somewhere in Willi Hartmann's room. At first he toyed with the idea of creeping into the army officer's room and looking for the letter. After some thought, he abandoned the idea: it was a standing joke at the camp that it was easier to escape from Grizedale Hall than it was to get into Willi Hartmann's room.

By 9.30 that evening, Eva's letter was dominating Forster's thoughts. The more he thought about it, the more angry he became – not only with the attitude of Kruger and the members of the *Altestenrat* but with the whole system that had sent him to war and separated him from his wife and child. Maybe there was another photograph of the baby in Eva's letter? Maybe she had said which she preferred of the second names they had short-listed during his last leave? His last leave. . . . A heady weekend together. They had spent Saturday scouring the shops for baby things. Because of the shortages they had laughingly bought whatever clothes they could find, regardless of whether they were intended for a boy or a girl.

Forster could stand it no longer. He hurled the unread book across the tower room and swung his feet off the bed. He resolved to find Eva's letter whatever the consequences. If necessary, he would threaten Willi Hartmann with a knife. . . .

He emerged from his door and peered down the black, silent well of the spiral staircase. In the distance he could hear the camp choir rehearsing their last song of the evening. As he descended the stone steps, he thought he heard a sound. He turned round and listened. There was nothing. Or was there? He descended a few more steps. Suddenly a flashlight snapped on, its beam stabbing him in the eyes, dazzling him.

'Hallo, Forster,' said Hertzog's voice. 'Guess what I've come for.'

'Well, it won't be for a lesson in good manners,' Forster replied, surprising himself at how steady his voice sounded. 'Most pigs are too stupid to realize that they haven't got any to start with.'

There was a brief silence before Hertzog replied. 'That makes it two apologies I've come for,' he said softly. 'We'll start with the one for what you said about my brother this morning.'

'I meant every word of what I said and furthermore – I'll repeat it. I said that it was a pity that you weren't serving on my boat along with your brother because –' Forster got no further. He didn't see the clenched fist that burst through the light like an express train and slammed into his face. His head snapped back and a pyrotechnique display from a thousand Roman candles exploded in front of his retinas. As the fog closed in he was vaguely aware that he was falling backwards. Either that or it was space around him turning itself inside out.

Whatever it was, he didn't really care. . . .

There were voices. Faraway voices. Near voices. A vague, distant feeling of movement and a curious sense of total detachment from his body. He heard a question asked in a strange language to which someone mumbled an answer using his voice.

'Christ, what a mess,' said one of the voices.

'Sounded like him saying something about falling.'

'Bloody lot of stairs to fall down.'

'Lucky he didn't fall down the middle. Must be a hundred-foot drop down the inside of the tower.'

'You'd think those bloody Jerries would've noticed that he wasn't at breakfast. Okay, report to Major Reynolds and come back with a stretcher.'

The voices disappeared and the darkness returned, bringing with it the pungent smell of fuel oil, the whine of electric motors, and the familiar motion of a U-boat blowing its tanks and surfacing. He clutched the bridge ladder with one hand and released the hatch clips above his head. As he scrambled on to the bridge, he was immediately aware of a new noise, a noise that should not have been there. Barely had he straightened up when the destroyer's charging bows cleaved into the conning tower like a titanic axe. The force of the impact threw him violently against the periscope standard. The tortured, grating scream of steel grinding upon steel deafened and confused him. Through the maelstrom of whirling images, which included the sea reaching up to claw him away from his stricken U-boat, he glimpsed the safety rails that surrounded the U-boat's 'wintergarten' gun deck. He threw himself at the rails and clung to them with a strength fuelled by terror. His body was plunged up to his waist in the near freezing water and then his shoulders were nearly dislocated as the safety rail lifted to the swell. Suddenly there were shouts and the sound of running feet approaching, strong hands closing around his wrists and lifting him over the rails. In that despairing moment he realized to his abject horror that the safety rails belonged to the destroyer. He wanted to release his grip, to let the sea swallow him and his shame, but the brawny arms of the enemy seamen were lifting him on to the destroyer's foredeck. . . .

'Good morning, old boy,' said Fleming breezily, when Brenda showed him into the sickbay.

Forster looked up from the chair where he was sitting by the window and managed to scowl at his visitor despite the bandages that swathed his face.

'Ten minutes and no more, commander,' said Brenda sternly before closing the door behind her.

Fleming listened to Brenda's high heels tapping across the courtyard and sat down opposite Forster. He gave the German a broad grin. 'Well, well. And to think that I thought the war was over for you.'

'I fell down the stairs in the tower,' said Forster sourly.

Fleming chuckled. 'Four cracked ribs. Two teeth knocked out. Six stitches in your cheek. That was some fall.'

'It's a long flight of stairs.'

'Curious how you've become so accident-prone since the story of *U-501*'s loss was released. Now that you're a father, you've got to take care of yourself.' He reached in his pocket and produced an envelope. 'By the way, your wife's doing well for herself.'

'That's Eva's handwriting!' Forster cried. He half-rose from the chair to snatch the letter but Fleming held it out of reach.

'Steady on, old boy,' said Fleming, gently easing Forster back into his chair. 'It may be your wife's handwriting, but it's not addressed to you.'

Forster stared at Fleming in bewilderment. 'I don't understand. She would only write to me.'

'She wrote to the Red Cross in London wanting to know why she hadn't heard from you.'

'But I write to her twice a week!'

Fleming looked speculatively at Forster. 'If you have, your letters aren't reaching the censor's office. Any idea what could be happening to them?'

Forster opened his mouth to say something and changed his mind. He shook his head.

'Did you reply to her last letter?'

'Of course.'

'What do you think of her new address?'

Forster had no idea what Fleming was talking about and made the mistake of attempting to bluff. 'She thought she might find a smaller flat now that I'm stuck here.'

Fleming smiled. 'Nice try, Hugo. Obviously all your mail is being stopped somewhere along the line. Actually, your wife and son are in Lisbon. She's working at the German Embassy there. Is she the Eva Halderene who used to work there before the war?'

'Lisbon?' For a moment Forster looked startled. What was visible of his face relaxed into a smile. 'Oh, yes. Of course. She told me in her last letter that the Foreign Office had offered her her old job back. Lisbon is where we first met in 1936. I was crewing on the *Gorch Fock* – the navy's sail training schooner. We had called in at Lisbon and our embassy laid on a reception for us.'

Fleming regarded the German naval officer thoughtfully. 'How much longer do you expect to be here, Forster? How long before the invasion is supposed to take place?'

Forster gave a wry smile. 'It's no secret that it'll be before Christmas.'

'And when it comes, you'll be in worse trouble than the trouble you're in now.'

'Why should I be in trouble?'

'Let's put it the other way around. If you were a British submarine commander who had abandoned his command during a battle, we'd court-martial you and stand you up before a firing squad.'

Forster said nothing.

'You're a loser whatever happens,' Fleming continued. 'If there's an invasion, you'll be executed. And if the war drags on, the chances of the prisoners here letting you survive are nil. Either way, you'll never see your wife and son again.'

Forster continued to remain silent but the look of misery in his eyes was all the answer Fleming needed. Like the skilled interrogator he was, Fleming had manoeuvred his victim into a position whereby he was wholly dependent on him and listening carefully to every word. He pressed home his attack. 'There is a third course.'

'What's that?' asked Forster, making no attempt to conceal his eagerness.

'It would be easy enough for us to send you out to Lisbon to be reunited with your wife. From there we could send you both to Canada – British Columbia is a beautiful place. We'd give you new identities and money so that you could start a new life together, safe from the war and Adolf and his merry men.'

Forster stared at Fleming in astonishment. 'You could do that?'

'It wouldn't present any problems.'

'There's a catch.'

Fleming laughed. 'Of course there's a catch. We wouldn't do it out of the goodness of our hearts. We would require from you a full account of *U-501*'s radio ranging and location equipment and other gear including her cipher machine.'

Forster slumped back in his chair. 'I don't understand. I read in the papers that *U-570* surrendered to you in August.'

'We had to wait several hours after her surrender for the weather to moderate before we could get a prize crew aboard her,' said Fleming. 'Which meant that her crew had plenty of time to throw all her important equipment over the side.' He paused and studied Forster speculatively. 'Another part of the deal is that we will want you to spend several days with our experts going over *U-570* with them.'

'You're asking me to betray my country. I can't do that, commander.'

'We're asking you to betray a man who's going to destroy your country and the whole of Europe unless he's stopped.'

'In the meantime, the information I give you will be used to help kill thousands of my colleagues in the U-boat arm.'

'We want to bring the war to an end in order to save lives. Including the lives of millions of civilians such as your wife and son.' Fleming paused. 'Listen, Hugo. Our offer to you is the only way that you're ever going to see your wife again, unless, of course, she's allowed to visit you before your execution. A week's co-operation – that's all we ask. In return we'll do everything we can to see that you and Eva and your son start a new life in Canada. Go along with us, and you'll be reunited with her within two weeks.'

'And if I refuse?'

Fleming gave a faint smile. 'You'll be repatriated home to Germany in exchange for a sick Allied prisoner.'

Forster stared at the British officer. 'But I'm not sick!' he protested.

'According to the Red Cross, your OKM aren't quibbling. My guess is that they're keen to get their hands on you.'

There was a long silence before Forster replied. When he spoke, his voice was so quiet that Fleming had to lean forward to hear what he said. 'Nurse Hobson says that I can be returned to my room this evening. I like it there. It's quiet and I can think. Can I give you my answer in the morning?'

'Of course,' said Fleming cheerily, standing. He gave Forster Eva's letter. 'No reason why you shouldn't have this. See you in the morning.'

It was 3 am. Forster was back in his room at the top of the tower. He lay wide awake on his bed, agonizing over what to do while his heart ached for his wife and son. To accede to the British demands would be so easy and he would be united with Eva and Ernst. And yet he would have to live with the memory of his treachery for the rest of his life. On top of that, there would the constant, nagging fear that one day his son would discover the truth about his father. But if he refused, he faced disgracing his family and son, and certain death before a *Kriegsmarine* firing squad.

There seemed no way out – no third choice. . . . Or was there?

The pain in his ribs from the beating up Hertzog had given him was forgotten as he crossed to the tiny window and peered down to the courtyard. He estimated that it was twenty metres to the ground. It was a Saturday night when there were few guards on duty. If he made a noise, the chances were that no one would hear him. He came to a single, momentous decision. His mind cleared once he realized exactly what he had to do, but his movements became feverish. He dragged the blankets and sheets from his bed and knotted them together into one long rope. He tested its strength by passing it around the window bars and satisfied himself that it would support his weight.

Kruger's face was hard as he and Major Reynolds strode through the quarry-tiled passageway that led to Forster's tower. Sergeant Finch and two guards trailed along behind.

'I tell you, major, I have not sanctioned an escape by any prisoner,' Kruger was saying. 'There's probably a rational explanation. Maybe the drugs Nurse Hobson gave him have caused him to oversleep.'

'Was he at breakfast?' Reynolds demanded, pushing a door open.

'No,' said Kruger.

'Then goddamn it, why didn't you check then?'

The search party reached the door that opened into the tower. Reynolds was first to mount the spiral staircase, with Kruger close on his heels.

'I'll tell you something, commander,' said Reynolds over his shoulder. 'If he's been beaten up again –'

'He was *not* beaten up,' Kruger insisted. 'He fell. It was an accident.'

Reynolds suddenly stopped without warning, causing Kruger to nearly cannon into him. The Canadian officer was staring up the inside of the stairwell. 'Jesus Christ,' he whispered.

Kruger peered up over Reynolds' shoulder. The only indication of shock he gave was that he failed to draw on his cheroot for some seconds.

A pair of feet hanging down the inside of the stairwell were visible a few yards above Reynolds' head.

The two men silently climbed the stairs until they were level with Forster's hideously distorted face. The knotted sheet noose had cut so deeply into his neck that it was concealed by the discoloured, grossly swollen flesh.

'Jesus Christ,' Reynolds muttered again, unable to think of anything more original or appropriate to say as he stared at Forster's gently swaying body. 'Jesus bloody Christ. What in hell drove him to do a darn fool thing like that?'

Part Six

A GREAT
LITTLE ESCAPE

'I've had the visit from the Forestry Commission,' said Major Reynolds, waving Kruger to the chair in front of his desk. 'They've agreed that they're short of able-bodied men for the maintenance of Grizedale Forest and have no objection to clearing work being carried out by POW working parties.'

'Excellent, major,' said Kruger, lighting a cheroot.

'They've laid down a number of conditions.'

'Naturally.'

'Firstly, they insist that only fallen timber can be removed from the forest.'

'Understood,' said Kruger.

'Secondly, there must be no felling of standing timber unless for thinning purposes – and then the felling and coppicing must be under the supervision of the forestry warden.'

'That seems perfectly reasonable,' Kruger commented. 'We're not interested in the standing timber – only the tonnes of fallen timber that is being allowed to rot.'

Reynolds looked curiously at the senior German officer. 'You really think you can get the hall's central heating system working for the winter?'

'My engineering officers are confident of it,' Kruger replied. 'Only a few modifications are necessary to the main boiler to make it run on timber instead of coke.'

Reynolds thought for a moment. 'Well,' he admitted, glancing at the dormant radiator under his window. 'It sure is one helluva temptation after last winter.'

Central heating was rare in England but normal in Reynolds' native Canada. It was Reynolds' guess that Harold Brocklebank knew about central heating from his frequent trips to North America, which was why it had been installed in Grizedale Hall. Unfortunately, the War Office and the Ministry of Fuel and Power had decreed that Grizedale Hall should not receive an allocation of coke.

'The question is whether there's enough fallen timber in the forest to keep the furnace going through the winter,' said Reynolds.

'We have estimated that there's more than enough for us and that there will be plenty for the charcoal burners,' said Kruger. 'Six handcart loads per week will be sufficient provided we shut off the heating to the greenhouses and turn off the radiators in the bedrooms.'

'The administrative offices and the guards' quarters will have to be heated, of course,' said Reynolds craftily.

'Of course,' Kruger agreed levelly.

'Okay,' said Reynolds after a few moments' face-saving consideration. 'I'll authorize a switch from exercise walks to forest working parties.'

'Thank you, major,' Kruger stood, pulled on his cap and returned Reynolds' salute. 'There is one more thing, major. . . .'

'Yeah?'

'There's a rumour going around that we are to be transferred to Canada. Can you enlighten me please?'

'Where the hell did you hear that?'

Kruger gave a thin smile. He could hardly say that Doenitz's last letter had mentioned that a number of captured NCO U-boat crewmen were now writing home from Canada. Instead he said, 'It's just a rumour, major.'

'Well, that's all it is,' said Reynolds. 'As much as I'd like to be sent home, I've heard nothing about it, so I suggest that you forget it.'

The telephone rang. Reynolds picked up the receiver and

listened. 'Okay,' he said, 'I'll tell him.' He replaced the receiver and smiled at Kruger. 'We've got an old prisoner back.'

Kruger looked interested. 'You mean Leutnant Shultz?'

Reynolds' smile changed to a scowl. 'No, I don't mean Leutnant Shultz.'

Kruger was genuinely pleased to welcome Hauptmann Dietrich Berg back to Grizedale Hall. He shook the young officer's right hand, taking care not to jar his left arm because it was in a sling. Willi celebrated Berg's return by opening a prized bottle of whisky and pouring generous measures into three cups.

'And your eyes, Berg?' asked Kruger, concerned. 'They are healed?'

'Oh yes, commander. Perfectly. The British surgeons at St George's were magnificent.' He smiled happily at the two men. 'It is good to be back, commander. Er – the radio transmitter I built. Was any of the transmission heard by a U-boat?'

Kruger shook his head. 'I believe that a part of the transmission may have been heard. But the transmitter failure was before Brunel had a chance to send the important information.'

Berg looked disappointed. 'After all the trouble everyone went to to help me build the radio too.'

'It wasn't your fault, Berg,' assured Kruger. 'You did your best.'

'What have you done to your arm, Berg?' asked Willi, indicating the sling.

Berg glanced ruefully down at his left arm. 'Nurse Hobson said that she will be able to take the plaster off next week.'

'Yes. But how did it happen?' Kruger pressed. 'There was nothing wrong with your arm when you were taken off to hospital.'

'I broke it in hospital,' Berg confessed, tasting the whisky that Willi handed him.

Kruger sighed. Berg's tendency to be accident-prone was legendary but breaking an arm while in hospital was a considerable achievement. He glanced at Willi. The little Bavarian was having a hard time keeping a straight face.

'Tell me, Berg,' said Kruger. 'How does one set about breaking an arm while one's lying in a hospital bed?'

'It happened after I was able to move about. The British allowed me a lot of freedom around the hospital while my eyes were bandaged. I suppose they thought that a blind man didn't stand much chance of escaping.'

'It's a safe assumption,' Kruger agreed impassively.

'I worked out a theory that I could avoid objects by clapping my hands and listening to the echoes,' Berg enthused. 'After a few days I became quite good at moving about the corridors. I soon worked out where walls and obstructions were and how far away they were.'

'So you decided to escape?' Kruger queried.

'Yes.'

'By working out where obstructions were from the echoes when you clapped?'

'Yes, commander. In theory it ought to work. Bats can navigate by sound.'

'Yes, I know. Several million years' research and development has gone into their system. What went wrong with yours?'

'I reached the end of the corridor one night,' said Berg ruefully. 'I knew from my experiments that there was no obstruction and I was right – there wasn't an obstruction but there was a flight of stairs.'

Willi's cherubic face suddenly turned bright pink and he hastily blew his nose. Even Kruger appeared to be having trouble controlling his facial muscles.

'And that's how I broke my arm,' Berg admitted sadly. 'I didn't even know that I was on an upper floor of the hospital until I fell down the stairs.'

'Well, at least you're back in one piece,' said Kruger. 'All

174

your tools and your rock samples have been kept safe in your workshop. You can even have your old bedroom back, but I've re-allocated your vegetable plot.'

Berg pulled on his cap and saluted with his good arm. 'Thank you, commander. You are most kind.' He turned to leave and paused while searching for the right words.

'Commander. . . .'

Kruger raised his eyebrows questioningly. 'Yes?'

'I would like to plan another escape. With proper planning this time.'

Willi made a strange noise into his cup of whisky and even Kruger's voice sounded unnaturally calm when he replied. 'Why, Berg?'

'I heard a rumour that we're all to be transferred to Canada. A British army surgeon told me. He said that it would be a good thing when we're all sent there.'

The smile disappeared from Willi's face.

'Yes, we're always hearing these rumours,' said Kruger with studied casualness. 'But sending prisoners of war to another country is contrary to the Geneva Convention. Somehow I don't think the British would do that.'

'That's exactly what I said. The surgeon pointed out that there's also an article in the convention that requires POWs to be moved out of a war zone. He said that the entire country is a war zone now.'

Willi blinked in alarm. It was perfectly true that the whole of the United Kingdom was now a war zone. On a number of nights *Luftwaffe* raiders had raised the already high morale of the POWs by being heard over the Lake District.

'Well,' said Kruger sceptically, 'I daresay the word of an army surgeon is as reliable a source as any. You have an escape plan of course?'

'Not yet, commander. But I would like your permission to plan a breakout.'

Kruger avoided Willi's eye. 'Really? For how many?'

'Three, commander, Myself, Oberleutnant Max Kluge and Leutnant zur See Brunel. We used to talk about it before I was taken off to hospital.'

Kruger nodded. 'Very well, Berg. Personally, I think that you should stick to your geology and cuckoo clocks, but you have my permission provided that you go no further than making plans and on condition that you say nothing about this ridiculous Canada rumour. Is that understood?'

'Yes, commander,' said Berg gratefully. 'Thank you very much.'

'Canada,' breathed Willi unhappily after Berg had left the room. If we're sent to Canada, we could still be POWs long after the invasion.'

'I shouldn't take any notice of half-baked rumours,' Kruger replied. 'And I'd be grateful if you talked to no one about this.'

'Good afternoon, Ian,' said Reynolds when the operator put him through to Fleming's London number. 'We're all wondering when we're going to see you back here. My phone doesn't stop ringing – inquiries from the local ladies.'

The two men exchanged pleasantries for a few minutes before Reynolds got down to the real reason for the call. 'Ian, I was wondering if you could do me a big favour. You've got some pretty good contacts in Western Command. Do you think you could find out from them if there's anything in these rumours about Number One Camp being transferred to Canada?'

Reynolds listened for a moment before replying to Fleming's query. 'Well, sure, I'd like to know. It's my home, remember. . . . Okay, Ian – if you can find out something, I'd be very grateful. See you next week.'

'*Please*, Fritz,' Berg begged. 'Just one small hole to test my theory.'

'What theory?' Brunel demanded, busily raking over his vegetable plot to remove Berg's footprints.

'That the topsoil is deeper in some places than others.'

'There's no more than about thirty centimetres of soil anywhere,' Brunel declared. 'Go down two spade depths and you hit granite.'

'Max didn't hit granite on the corner of his plot when he dug a hole for me.'

'Well, you get Kluge to dig another hole in his plot. I'm not messing up mine. Not now that it's nice and clear for the winter.'

'Only a small hole,' Berg pleaded. 'I could easily fill it in again with my good arm.'

Brunel proudly surveyed the expanse of neatly raked bare earth that was his plot. Not a trace of weed or vegetable was to be seen. It was the way he liked it. It was easy to keep tidy. Rows of vegetables made life difficult, and luckily the topsoil wasn't deep enough for those winter vegetables such as leeks and parsnips which stayed in the ground for months and always looked a mess. He sighed. 'Where do you want me to dig this hole?'

'Just here,' Berg replied, measuring out ten paces into the middle of the plot and leaving deep footprints where Brunel had just raked. He scratched an 'X' in the soil with a stick.

'Well,' said Brunel grudgingly. 'So long as it's the only hole you want.'

'Oh, it is,' said Berg eagerly.

Brunel looked suspiciously at Berg. 'Is this anything to do with an escape plan?'

'Well, yes. Sort of.'

'I hope it doesn't involve me.'

'But of course it does. Remember how we used to talk about escaping together? Max, you, and me?'

'That was before I discovered just how much of a liability you can be,' Brunel retorted.

'Dig the hole please, Fritz, and we'll talk about it later.'

Brunel grimaced and started digging while Berg cast an

177

anxious glance at Sergeant Finch who was sitting in his watchtower.

'I won't get much further than this,' Brunel commented when he had reached a depth of about eighteen inches.

Berg urged Brunel to keep digging.

The hole Brunel dug was small – no wider than his spade – but, to his surprise, he succeeded in reaching a depth of two feet without encountering rock. Berg looked eagerly on.

'Give me your rake,' said Berg excitedly.

Brunel handed the gardening tool to Berg, who stood the handle upright in the bottom of the hole. He held it awkwardly with his good hand and pushed down. To Brunel's astonishment, two feet of the rake's wooden handle disappeared into the ground before it encountered rock.

'You see?' said Berg, looking very pleased with himself as he withdrew the rake and started kicking soil into the hole. 'There's more than a metre of topsoil on this part of your plot.'

'I don't want to attempt an escape with you,' Brunel warned.

Berg chuckled. 'All right then. But there's no reason why you shouldn't grow root vegetables here next year.'

Brunel looked pained. 'There're two very good reasons why I shouldn't grow root vegetables anywhere next year. Firstly, we'll be liberated before next year. Secondly, I can't stand root vegetables – either to eat or look at.'

Kruger's expression was inscrutable as he studied the neatly drawn map of the camp and grounds that Berg had proudly spread out on his desk. 'Very pretty,' he remarked. 'Do I hang it on my wall or what?'

'I shouldn't do that, commander,' said Berg worriedly. 'The fault line might give the game away if the British saw it.'

'What game? What fault line?'

Berg traced his finger along a finely shaded pencil line

that started at the eastern end of the hall and ran south-wards across the vegetable plots and under the perimeter fence. 'I'm certain that there's a fault in the granite stratum, commander. By that I mean a step in the layer of rock. It's now filled in with soil. My guess is that the step runs beneath the hall and out across the grounds.'

'A step?'

'It's where the entire stratum has fractured and lifted about two metres on one side. It probably happened during an earthquake shortly after the last ice age when the land recovered from the weight of the ice. It's quite a common phenomenon where land has been covered by ice. Norway is still lifting a few centimetres each century.'

'All very interesting for one of your geology instruction courses,' Kruger murmured politely. 'Let me know when you'll be bringing the subject up and I shall make a point of attending.'

Berg stared at Kruger in surprise. 'Oh, I wasn't thinking of that, commander.'

'Then what is the purpose of this drawing?'

'I'm sorry, commander, but I thought that was obvious. If the fault is continuous, it means that we can dig a tunnel along it.'

Kruger looked sharply at Berg and saw that the young officer was serious. 'I think, Berg,' he said slowly, 'that you had better show me what you're talking about.'

Kruger and Berg reached the eastern end of the terrace and leaned on the stone-balled parapet. They watched the activity on the vegetable plots as the prisoners took advantage of the mild November afternoon to finish preparing the ground for the winter. To the left of the two men, a party of prisoners were busily sawing and chopping broken branches into three-foot lengths for burning in the boiler. Each piece was added to the growing mountain of timber stacked against the wall of the servants' quarters. Two guards were patrolling the southern perimeter fence, and Sergeant Finch was sitting in his favourite position on the rickety firewatching tower where he could see everything that was going on and translate every innocent activity into an element of the mass breakout which he knew was imminent.

'We're standing right over the fault now,' said Berg, speaking in a conspiratorial whisper even though there was no one nearby.

'*If* it extends under the hall,' Kruger pointed out.

'I'm positive that it does, commander. It stretches for a long way. I don't want to point, but you see that outcrop of rock on the skyline in the field just beyond the watchtower? I think that's part of the fault where the wind has eroded away the topsoil.'

'All right,' said Kruger. 'Assuming that you're right, why isn't the fault visible across the grounds of the hall?'

'That's simple,' Berg replied. 'Over the centuries, rain has washed soil down from the hills which has silted up against the side of the fault. Also, it's a safe bet that Harold Brocklebank had any visible outcrops earthed over when the grounds were landscaped.'

Kruger lit a cheroot and inhaled slowly while staring thoughtfully across the grounds. 'How deep could the tunnel be?' he asked at length.

'No deeper than the lower stratum of rock, of course,' said Berg. 'Which is about two metres below the surface. That won't be a problem because ninety per cent of the tunnel's length will be underneath the vegetable plots, which the British never inspect, of course. Ventilation ducts can be easily arranged at intervals, disguised as compost heaps with straw over them – that sort of thing.' He glanced sideways at Kruger's face in the hope of seeing a flicker of enthusiasm for the project, but the U-boat commander maintained his usual disinterested expression as he studied the line the tunnel would follow.

'It wouldn't be enough to end the tunnel on the other side of the wire,' Kruger pointed out. 'You would have to continue under the road and come up on the other side of that dry-stone wall.'

Sensing approval of his scheme, Berg nodded enthusiastically. 'Also, the wall would hide the opening from the camp, commander.'

'Which means that the tunnel will have to be at least two hundred metres long. Correct?'

'About that,' Berg agreed.

'How much soil would have to be removed?'

'About one hundred cubic metres, commander. Spread over all the vegetable plots, it would add no more than five centimetres to their overall level – which will never show because winter digging raises the level of the soil by aeration anyway.'

Kruger dropped his cheroot and ground the butt with his heel. 'All right, Berg. I'll convene a meeting of the escape committee for tomorrow. I shall want you, Brunel and Kluge to attend as well.'

Berg watched apprehensively as Brenda nibbled away at his plaster cast with a pair of sharp scissors. She managed to slice away two inches of plaster, exposing pallid and puckered skin.

'Did you see Grizedale Hall being built?' asked Berg. It was a question he had been carefully rehearsing since he had learned that Brenda was a local girl. He winced as she thrust cold steel between his tender forearm skin and the unyielding plaster cast.

'Certainly not,' said Brenda sharply. 'It was built around the turn of the century. Do I look that old?'

'I'm sorry,' said Berg apologetically.

'God, this is tough. What did they mix into it? Cement?'

'I don't know. I was unconscious when it was put on.'

'Usually it goes soft in water.'

A large piece of plaster fell away and landed painfully on Berg's toe. He made no complaint.

'Of course,' said Brenda, working the scissors vigorously back and forth under the plaster and against Berg's newly healed bone, 'I used to come here a lot when I was going out with old Brocklebank's chauffeur.'

'That must seem like a long time ago,' said Berg. He suddenly realized that he had said the wrong thing again and added hastily, 'I mean – there have been many changes. The war and such things.'

'Oh gosh, yes,' said Brenda, wrenching away some more plaster and returning to the attack with her scissors. 'The parties that old Brocklebank used to throw!' She giggled. 'Harry and me used to get quite tiddly on the wine that was left over.'

'Tiddly?'

'Drunk. You know.'

'Ah yes.'

Brenda gave an extra hard push with the scissors. The remains of the plaster cast suddenly split without warning. The scissors slipped and she stabbed Berg so hard that one blade sank an inch into his delicate skin. He gave a loud yell of pain and yanked his arm away with the scissors still embedded in his flesh. He clamped his hand over the wound and the action slashed the scissors' free blade across his knuckles. What was left of the plaster around his arm began staining red with blood.

'Oh hell!' Brenda exclaimed, snatching the scissors out of the wound. 'I'm terribly sorry, hauptmann, really I am. You must think I'm an awful clot.'

'It is nothing,' said Berg calmly, as though being stabbed was an everyday occurrence. 'You must not worry please.'

Brenda continued to apologize profusely while she bathed the stab wound in a dish of saline solution. Berg watched woodenly as tendrils of blood gradually stopped oozing out of his arm.

'I'm afraid it'll need at least four stitches,' said Brenda, still red with embarrassment as she examined her handiwork.

Berg left the sickbay ten minutes later. His arm felt curiously light without the plastercast, but the pleasure of being free of its weight was offset by the dull ache from the stab wound and the stitches.

As he crossed the courtyard, something started nagging at the back of his mind. Perhaps it was something that Nurse Hobson had said? But he wasn't sure.

The three members of the escape committee, Kruger, Hauptmann Paul Ulbrick, and Hauptmann Karl Shriver, watched intently as Brunel and Kluge helped Berg stand a table on its side on the floor of the music room. Brunel's expression suggested that he disapproved of the demonstration.

'What happened to your arm, Berg?' inquired Kruger, noticing Berg's bandage.

'Nurse Hobson stabbed me when she —'

'Well, I'm pleased to see that you managed to ward off the blow with your arm. Continue with your demonstration.'

Berg cleared his throat and pointed to the table's now vertical top. 'This is the side of the fault in the granite stratum, gentlemen, and the floor is the base of the fault. That will give us a stable floor and side to the tunnel.'

'The fault is filled in with topsoil, I presume?' Shriver queried, glancing at the sketch plan in front of him.

'Yes, hauptmann.'

'How do you propose shoring-up the tunnel?'

'That's simple,' Berg replied. He nodded to Brunel.

The diminutive naval officer sighed. He leaned a four-feet-long piece of floorboarding against the table and crawled through the triangular-shaped arch formed by the table and the floorboard. He scrambled to his feet and pointedly brushed the dust off his trousers.

'I estimate that we will need two boards or lengths of straight branch for every metre of the tunnel,' said Berg. 'We'll be just below the surface so there won't be much weight of soil to support.'

Ulbrick broke the brief silence that followed. 'It all seems too simple,' he observed.

Brunel's nod of agreement earned him a scowl from Berg.

'I hardly think two hundred metres of tunnel could be described as simple,' said Kruger drily. 'What we have to decide is whether or not Hauptmann Berg's proposal is worth pursuing.'

'It's an interesting idea,' said Shriver, studying the plan again. 'But I see many problems. The plan doesn't show the entrance to the tunnel. Presumably, you intend cutting down through the floor of a room in the servants' quarters? Sergeant Finch's snap searches are extremely thorough. Concealing an opening from him over a long period is going to be impossible. Also, how does one transfer one hundred cubic metres of soil from the tunnel to the vegetable plots?'

'Not all the minor details have been worked out,' said Berg.

Shriver looked frosty. 'The location of the tunnel's entrance is hardly a minor detail, Berg.'

Brunel suppressed a snigger.

'Berg has proved that a tunnel is possible,' Kruger intervened. 'For the moment I propose instructing all prisoners to provide him with whatever co-operation he needs to complete his planning. Are we all in agreement with that?'

The escape committee remained silent. Kruger turned to Berg, Brunel and Kluge. 'So it's up to you and your two comrades now, Hauptmann Berg. We agree in principle with the tunnel, but that's all for the time being. Dismissed.'

Kruger waited until the door had closed behind the three men before speaking again.

'As you know, gentlemen, the old rumour about our transfer to Canada has started circulating again. But this time I have evidence that a number of our men have been sent there.'

The other members of the escape committee remained silent but Kruger saw the momentary flicker of apprehension in their eyes.

'This may be wishful thinking on my part,' Kruger continued. 'But I have a suspicion that the British may not be too keen to transfer this camp if we establish a reputation for habitual escaping – not when there's a neutral, unguarded border for us to cross into the United States. We will let Berg continue with his planning. If he comes up with a practical scheme, we will take it over and organize a mass breakout.'

For the next three days Berg wrestled with the question of where to start the tunnel. But no matter how many rough sketches he made of the hall's ground-floor plan, or how many times he and Kluge strolled around the grounds making mental notes of their paces, a solution to the problem eluded him. Also, his concentration was spoilt because, for some unaccountable reason, his thoughts kept returning to his conversation with Nurse Hobson when she had stabbed him.

'I've decided that I want nothing to do with your damned tunnel,' said Brunel the following Monday morning as he, Kluge, and Berg joined the dozen or so prisoners in the common room who were excitedly opening their letters and parcels. 'It sounds too dangerous for me.'

'Nothing much has been decided yet,' Kluge pointed out.

'That's what is worrying me.'

'Surely you want to escape?' said Berg.

'Not by digging a tunnel, I don't,' Brunel replied, ripping the wrapping paper off his parcel. 'And certainly not with an accident-prone liability like you.'

A prisoner clapped Berg on the back. 'Hey, Berg. We hear you're planning a mass escape. Any chance of Dormitory Six joining in?'

'My God!' Brunel yelped. 'Look what my sister's sent me!' He produced a bottle of Reisling from his food parcel and held it proudly aloft.

'You're lucky it didn't break,' a prisoner commented. 'Do we have a party tonight?'

'How about now?' another prisoner suggested.

'At 11 am?'

Berg stared at the bottle of wine. His eyes seemed to glaze over with shock. He suddenly grabbed Brunel by the arm. 'Fritz! I need your help!'

'You're not having my wine.'

'I don't want it. But I need your help downstairs.'

'In a minute.'

'No, now . . . ,' Berg insisted. '*Please*, Fritz.'

Brunel sighed. 'Very well then. Just so long as you don't expect me to start digging a tunnel.'

Berg excitedly clattered down the stairs with Brunel in tow.

'We'll need some tools from my workshop first,' said Berg breathlessly. 'It was crazy of me not to have noticed it before. Crazy.'

'What was?' Brunel demanded, having to break into a trot to keep up with Berg.

'What's the one thing that's missing from this place, Fritz?'

'Women?'

'No. No. Much more important than women.'

'What could be more important than women?'

The two men entered Berg's workshop.

'Nothing is more important than women,' Brunel declared, as Berg rummaged among his tools and produced a home-made cold chisel. 'Except wine maybe.'

Berg beamed delightedly. 'That's right, Fritz – wine.'

'What?'

'Grizedale Hall hasn't got any wine cellars! And yet a mansion like this *must* have been built with them!'

Berg kept watch while Brunel knelt down and worked the cold chisel into a joint in the quarry-tiled floor. The room they were in had been part of the butler's parlour in the days when Grizedale Hall had been a stately home.

'Try lifting now,' Berg urged.

'I haven't got the chisel right in yet!' Brunel hissed in reply. 'Just you keep your eyes and ears open! God knows why I get myself involved in your lunatic schemes.'

Brunel prised upwards, slipped his fingertips under the edge of the tile and eased it up. Underneath was the hall's original subfloor consisting of a layer of sand over a bed of rammed hardcore.

'Try one of the tiles in the centre,' Berg suggested, hiding his disappointment.

'I tell you, it's a waste of time.'

'*Please*, Fritz. Only, I can't do much with this arm since Nurse Hobson stabbed me.'

Brunel replaced the tile and went to work on one that Brunel pointed out. It lifted easily to reveal fresh, white concrete beneath. He stared at it in amazement.

'You see!' said Berg triumphantly.

Brunel made no answer but set to work to lift a neighbouring quarry tile. It took him less than five minutes to expose a rectangle of concrete set into the hardcore subfloor. The concrete was a metre square and it emitted a hollow ring when Brunel rapped it with the cold chisel.

'Will it lift in one piece?' asked Berg.

'I don't know,' Brunel replied, tapping the concrete again. 'It sounds thin enough. We ought to report this to the commander.'

'Try lifting it,' Berg begged.

By now Brunel was curious to see what was under the

concrete. He levered upwards very carefully and was able to lift the thin slab of concrete in one piece to reveal a wooden trapdoor complete with brass lifting ring. He grinned up at Berg. 'Sorry, Dietrich. Looks like you were right. This has to lead to the wine cellar. The British made a lousy job of concreting it over.'

Berg forgot about his lookout duties. He knelt down beside Brunel and helped him lift the trapdoor. It opened easily on oiled hinges, releasing a musty smell of dry rot. Berg nearly dropped his matches in his excitement but he eventually managed to strike one. The light flickered on a steep flight of timber steps that disappeared into the darkness.

Before Brunel could counsel caution, Berg lowered himself feet first through the opening and started to descend the stairs. As his head reached floor level, there was the sound of collapsing, rotten timber. Berg looked at Brunel in panic. The sudden grab he made at the edge of the hatchway was a fraction of a second too late. Brunel was also too late trying to seize Berg's wrist. The army officer gave a cry of terror and dropped with a sickening thud on to the stone floor of the cellar ten feet below.

'Amazing,' said Ulbrick, holding his candle high and peering the length of the cellar between the rows of wine bottle racks that were stacked high with empty bottles. 'To think that this has been here all the time.'

'It's lined with lead but I don't believe it will be difficult to cut through,' said Kruger. 'Most important, its volume is double the volume of the soil from the tunnel. And those racks will make excellent shoring boards.'

Ulbrick nodded. 'Will there be enough air to seal a digging party in here for an entire shift?'

Kruger nodded. 'Possibly. While Berg was waiting for the plaster cast on his ankle to set, he told me that it ought to be possible to dig four metres per day. I hope that can be bettered.'

The two men climbed the ladder out of the cellar and watched while Brunel and two prisoners concealed the trap-door. Brunel had bonded the original quarry tiles to a square piece of plywood which dropped neatly into place. He checked that the quarry tiles over the trap were flush with the floor and quickly rubbed some wood ash into the joints. The operation took less than thirty seconds. There was no sign that the floor had been disturbed when he stood up.

'Excellent, Brunel,' said Kruger approvingly. 'Incidentally, you did a good job lifting Berg out of the cellar. The British accepted his story that he fell over the step outside his workshop.'

'Thank you, commander.'

Kruger nodded. 'This evening we shall draw up the lookout rotas and the digging party shifts. We start cutting the tunnel tomorrow.'

Brunel was surprised. 'Surely we'll be waiting for Hauptmann Berg to come out of hospital before starting work, commander?'

Kruger shook his head. 'Major Reynolds told me that with a septic arm and a broken ankle, Berg isn't expected out of Barrow General for at least four days. That's providing he doesn't come to any more harm in hospital. I want forty metres of tunnel excavated for him by then. You'll be in charge of the digging parties.'

Brunel looked nervously from Kruger to Ulbrick and tried to read some meaning into their impassive expressions. 'It's very kind of you, commander, but I'm sure Berg would prefer to make the first cut himself. He worked hard on planning —'

'What Berg would or would not prefer is of little consequence,' said Kruger crisply. 'Work on the tunnel starts tomorrow.'

Berg hopped slowly and painfully down the ladder into the cellar by taking most of his weight on his good arm. His left

189

foot was completely swathed in a bulbous plaster cast that was about as big as a bucket and roughly the same shape. It meant that it was too large to fit between the rungs of the ladder. Fortunately, Nurse Hobson's stab wound was healing satisfactorily. Brunel handed him down his crutch and Kruger steadied his elbow as he tucked it under his armpit and pivotted around to survey his surroundings.

Two naked light bulbs illuminated the cellar. The wine bottle racks had been dismantled and their component timber planks stacked neatly against one wall. At the far end two prisoners were treading down a heap of soil. But it was the triangular hole cut in the wall three feet above the floor that held Berg's attention. It was over three feet wide at its base and of about the same height on one side. A prisoner was hauling on a cord that led into the opening.

Without saying a word, Berg hobbled forward and stooped to peer along the tunnel. It had only the one vertical wall which, as he had predicted, consisted of a cross-section through a fractured granite stratum. The tunnel ran straight for fifteen metres before curving to the left. It was lit at five-metre intervals by low wattage light bulbs that were recessed into the roof. The shoring boards were cut to the right length and precisely positioned. Two parallel timber planks with raised sides served as rails to guide the truckle-mounted box that the prisoner working at the tunnel entrance was hauling towards the cellar.

'You're to be congratulated, Berg,' said Kruger. 'We found the fault exactly where your measurements said it was. We've dug twenty-five metres. I had hoped to have dug more by now. The first ten metres was no problem, but now we're running into shale and small rocks.'

'Thank you, commander,' said Berg, straightening up. Above the opening was a noticeboard bearing the names of the prisoners working the four-hour shifts. Everything was well organized and functioning efficiently.

'Well?' Kruger inquired. 'What do you think?'

Berg did his best to hide his disappointment. The tunnel project had been his pet scheme and one that he had looked forward to starting.

'Well?' Kruger repeated.

'Twenty-five meters is a remarkable achievement,' said Berg. 'I'm very grateful to you.'

The box laden with soil trundled to a standstill in the tunnel opening. The prisoner unhooked its cords and connected them up to an empty box. He rapped twice on the rails and the box disappeared down the tunnel.

'The railway is the only modification we've made to your original design,' said Kruger. 'It makes removing the debris that much easier.'

'Yes, of course,' Berg replied, hoping that he didn't sound disappointed. 'How many men are working at the face?'

'Two – just as you suggested. There is one cutting the soil away and another loading it into the box.'

The two men watched the prisoner add the contents of the box to the heap of soil and debris that was being trodden down.

'My name isn't on the rota, commander,' said Berg respectfully.

'That's correct,' Kruger replied.

Berg peered at the noticeboard again. 'It says that Brunel is the engineer in charge of the tunnel, commander. Yet Brunel was against an escape.'

'He's not now that I've discussed the matter with him,' said Kruger cryptically.

'But the tunnel was my idea, commander, therefore I thought that –'

'I can understand your disappointment, Berg,' said Kruger. 'But you are in no state to go crawling along tunnels just yet, whereas Brunel is very fit and very small. Besides, I have some much more important work for you. I will visit you in your workshop after lunch.'

'This is an odd request from Kruger, sir,' Sergeant Finch commented, dropping a letter in Reynolds' in-tray. 'He wants to redesign the layout of the allotments.'

'*Commander* Kruger,' Reynolds stressed, picking up the letter and reading it. 'He may be the enemy, but I guess we should stick to the formalities. It's warm in here, huh?'

'Very pleasant, sir. I wish there was a radiator in my office.'

'Have a word with Commander Kruger. I guess it wouldn't be any trouble for his engineering officers to fix you up with one of the unused radiators from the dormitories.' Reynolds finished reading the letter. 'What's so odd about this?'

Finch shrugged. 'It just struck me as odd, sir.'

'It would be odd if he wanted to do it during the growing season. November is about the best time.' Reynolds wrote 'OK' at the foot of letter, signed it, and tossed it into his out-tray. He looked up and saw Finch's disapproving expression. 'What's the matter, sergeant?'

'Nothing, sir.'

'Aw, come on. I know that look. You have my permission to speak freely.'

'I think you give in far too easily to that Jerr- to Commander Kruger, sir.'

'I don't give in to anyone,' Reynolds corrected. 'Either I agree with a request or I don't agree.'

'You always agree to his requests.'

'He's never made an unreasonable one. Okay, so maybe I shouldn't've let him take over the distribution of mail and food parcels, and maybe there is too much prisoner control in the kitchens – but it's taken a load off our shoulders. And yours in particular.'

'I wasn't thinking of that, sir. I think he's planning something.'

'Sure he's planning something,' Reynolds retorted irritably. 'He's always planning something. And it's your job to find out what it is – which you won't find out in here talking to me.'

Kruger picked up the unfinished miniature pendulum clock. It was barely the size of a matchbox. The tiny Gothic numerals on the varnished clock face were a work of art in themselves. 'Very clever, Berg,' he admired. 'Some of these parts must have been virtually impossible to carve, especially with your arm and two missing fingers.'

'Oh, I manage, commander,' Berg replied self-effacingly. Kruger's presence in his workshop made him ill at ease. He talked to conceal his nervousness. 'I learned to manage without those two fingers years ago, and I did most of the work on that clock before Nurse Hobson stabbed me. I used floorboard knots for the parts that have to take wear because they're hard. It took me three weeks to make –'

'I'm sorry that you won't be able to work on the tunnel,' Kruger interrupted.

Berg smiled apologetically. 'Oh, please don't worry, commander. I could never have made that sort of progress by myself.'

Kruger hesitated. 'Tell me, Berg. Just how keen are you on escaping?'

Berg looked surprised. 'Very keen, commander. Kluge, Brunel and I used to talk about nothing else. And now with these Canada rumours. Why do you ask?'

Kruger shrugged. 'I'm sorry, Berg. I misjudged you. I had formed the opinion that you really prefer solving problems, that escaping was just another problem to be solved and that you wouldn't be so interested in escaping once you had solved the problem.'

Berg shook his head. 'All three of us want to escape more than anything else in the world, commander.'

'In that case, you will need three of these,' said Kruger, placing a civilian identity card on Berg's workbench.

'That's our last one. You'll have to make replicas because I don't want that one to leave the camp.'

Berg opened the card and was relieved to see that it did not have to bear a photograph of the owner. He opened a drawer and took out a magnifying glass, which he used to examine the identity card. 'It's poor quality paper. I don't think that will be too much trouble. But the printing. . . .' He peered closely at the card. 'Well . . . I suppose it will be possible to make three copies.'

'How?'

'Well, there's only one method and that's hand-lettering with Indian ink. Kluge is brilliant at lettering. He does all my clock faces.'

'I want you to carve printing blocks, Berg. All three cards must be identical.'

Berg blinked in surprise. 'Blocks, commander? But that would take weeks!'

'You won't be escaping until the spring.'

'But I thought –'

'That I would permit a winter escape? An individual escape with the officer provided with the necessary travel warrants, perhaps – but not three of you. You would attract too much attention and be forced to sleep rough. I can't allow that in the winter. Besides, your arm and ankle won't be strong enough for at least another three months.'

Berg was so shocked that he momentarily forgot who he was arguing with. 'But my arm and ankle are healing nicely. They'll be perfectly –'

'I don't like having my orders questioned,' Kruger observed mildly. 'Now, about your identity cards. You're a genius at wood-carving, Berg, therefore I do not think that making blocks will present you with problems that you can't overcome.'

Berg examined the identity card and made a conscious effort to focus his mind on the problem. 'I suppose it might be possible to carve founts of different print styles,' he said.

Quite suddenly he became absorbed as his fertile brain raced ahead, anticipating problems and seeking solutions. 'Yes, that's it, commander. I could make a wooden *forme* to hold the individual founts and set one line at a time. It might even be possible to make a proper platen and ink the *forme* with a hand-roller. In fact, making a wooden printing press wouldn't be that difficult. We could print all sorts of documents. A camp newspaper?'

Kruger smiled. 'Let's not get too far ahead of our immediate objectives, Berg.'

'And with a printing press, commander, we'd be able to print dozens of identity cards – not just three.'

Kruger nodded and picked up the identity card. 'Yes, I had thought of that, Berg.' He moved to the door. 'I'll get Willi to check the questionnaires. I believe there are two ex-printers among the prisoners.'

'Yes, commander. Also it would be a great help if Konig and Endelmann could help make the founts. They're fantastic wood-carvers.'

'I'll have a word with them,' Kruger promised as he left the workshop.

Berg made no reply: he was already deeply absorbed, preparing a preliminary sketch of a home-made printing press.

Finch sat in his rickety firewatching tower with Corporal White and glowered suspiciously down on the whirl of activity taking place on the reorganized vegetable plots. Over fifty prisoners, working to string lines, were busily treading new paths between the plots and moving wheelbarrow loads of rotting compost around. Even the toolshed that the prisoners had built for their gardening implements was being dismantled and moved to a new position.

'Bloody odd, the whole thing,' Finch muttered to Chalky.

'What's that, sarge?'

'All that work.'

'What about it?'

'It's all so bloody pointless.'

Corporal White glanced down at the vegetable plots. 'Looks a lot tidier than the old layout. All them compost heaps in a straight line. Funny how the Jerries like everything all neat and tidy.' He lowered his voice. 'I expect you've heard the little whisper that I've heard, sarge?'

Finch wasn't particularly interested; Corporal White was always hearing little whispers. 'Oh?' he said boredly, watching a prisoner position a compost heap so that it was perfectly aligned with all the other compost heaps. 'What sort of whisper?'

'It's only a rumour of course, sarge.'

Finch began to get angry. 'Okay, so let's have it.'

'That they're planning a mass escape.'

There was a pause before Finch replied. 'Are you certain?'

Corporal White nodded sagely and glanced over the side of the watchtower. 'It seems that they're going to grow giant runner beans and use them to pole-vault over the wire, sarge.'

While Sergeant Finch was threatening Corporal White with extreme physical violence, Kruger – grim-faced and silent – was striding along the corridors towards the servants' quarters. There was no indication which of the loafing prisoners were lookouts – none gave any obvious signal – but Kluge was already waiting expectantly for him by the wine cellar's open trapdoor when he appeared in the butler's parlour.

'More shale?' queried Kruger.

'Worse,' said Kluge tiredly, wiping the grime from his sweat-streaked face. 'Brunel thinks it's solid rock.'

Kruger went quickly down the ladder into the cellar. The evidence of the problems that the digging shifts had encountered was the large heap of rocks – some were small boulders – that had been removed from the tunnel.

A prisoner helped Kruger change out of his uniform into a pair of working trousers and a muddy sweater. He also slipped out of his shoes and socks because he wouldn't be needing them – there was nowhere to stand up in the tunnel.

'Brunel's waiting for you at the face, commander,' said Kluge as his commanding officer carefully laid himself chest down on the wooden passenger trolley. 'Don't forget to keep your feet tucked in.'

'Ready,' said Kruger cryptically.

Kluge jabbed an electric bell-push button three times. The cord attached to Kruger's trolley tightened. Helped by a push from Kluge, the trolley began rumbling jerkily along the tunnel, bumping over the joints in the wood track.

Kruger instinctively lowered his head and pulled his shoulders in. He was by no means a broadly built man yet there was barely enough room for his body to clear the shoring timbers. Despite the ventilator pipes whose openings were concealed by the compost heaps, the air in the fifty-metre length of tunnel was dank and humid: it stank of sweat from the men who had laboured in it for the past two weeks and reminded Kruger of the smell of a U-boat's interior after several weeks on patrol. He chanced a brief glance ahead and saw Brunel's face illuminated in the pool of electric light at the tunnel's face. The tiny naval officer was sweating as he hauled on the cord, pulling Kruger towards him. He stopped work when the trolley drew level with his feet.

Kruger lifted himself off the trolley and discovered that there was enough headroom for him to kneel. 'What's the trouble, Brunel?'

'This is the trouble,' said Brunel savagely. He gave the face an angry blow with his palm and made room for Kruger to squeeze alongside him. 'A boulder. God knows how far down it goes.'

Kruger ran his fingertips over the rock's surface. It was a slab of delicately shaded pink Coniston granite. Massive and immovable. 'How about going round it?' he suggested.

'It'll be impossible,' Brunel replied. 'We're only half a metre beneath the surface here anyway and the ground above is Werner Leyden's plot – the steepest part of the slope. If we dig to one side, we're certain to break through above ground level. And trying to go round it will mean putting a junction in the track and excavating enough room for someone to transfer the trollies from one track to the other. It'll double the time taken to empty just one box, which is taking long enough as the tunnel gets longer.'

Kruger rarely resorted to cursing, but he felt that an expletive was justified on this occasion. After that both men were silent for some moments.

'So that's it,' Kruger murmured phlegmatically. 'Well . . . at least it's kept our minds occupied.'

Brunel swore and ineffectually punched the rock face. 'So what do we do now? Fill it all in to keep our minds occupied?'

Kruger thought for a moment. 'How about getting Berg to take a look?'

'You think he's capable of shifting half a dozen tons of granite boulder?'

'I think he's capable of coming up with a suggestion,' Kruger replied equitably.

'Explosives would shift it,' said Berg brightly, steadying himself on his crutch while a prisoner brushed the dirt from the tunnel off his clothes.

Kruger groaned. 'I had hoped for a practical suggestion from you.'

Berg looked hurt. 'But that is a practical suggestion, commander.'

'Even if we could get hold of explosives,' said Kruger icily, 'has it occurred to you that even Sergeant Finch could hardly fail to notice an explosion right in the middle of Werner Leyden's cabbage patch?'

Berg thought for a moment. 'There are a number of difficulties with using explosives,' he admitted. 'But it still remains the quickest and easiest way of breaking up that boulder.' He smiled at the circle of faces that were staring at him in the cellar. 'I made the study of explosives my hobby when I was at school and college.'

'Is that how you lost your fingers?' Kruger inquired.

'Yes, commander. Would you like to hear about some of the various explosions I have been responsible for?'

Not only had Leutnant Walter Hilgard served on the *Bismarck*, but he was built like it as well. Unlike the *Bismarck*, he was a survivor – helped to a considerable extent by his 220 pounds of bone and muscle. Before the war he had been a chef at the Kaiserhof Hotel in Berlin and often boasted about the times when he had cooked for Hitler. The Fuehrer's diet and that of the prisoners had much in common in that it was largely vegetarian. For that reason, Kruger had appointed Hilgard as Grizedale Hall's officer-in-charge of catering. Complaints about Hilgard's cooking were rare but that was due more to his fiery temper and dexterity with a meat cleaver than to his culinary talents.

It was his meat cleaver that he rested a massive arm on when he saw Berg hobble into his domain. 'If you're another complaint about my *crêpe suzettes*, I'll cut your bloody head off and boil it for brawn,' he threatened.

'No, I haven't come about that, Hilgard.'

'You try making *crêpe suzettes* with dried eggs. It's not easy.'

'They were delicious,' Berg enthused, saying the first thing that came into his head. 'Nice and crunchy.'

'So what do you want?'

'You've got a bag of potassium nitrate in here which I –'

'I've got what!' Hilgard boomed in astonishment, his

voice rattling the saucepans hanging on the wall of the kitchen.

'Shh!' said Berg, glancing nervously at the open door where two guards were talking. He swung his weight forward on his crutch so that he could whisper in Hilgard's ear. 'You've got a large bag of potassium nitrate. I need it please.'

'I've got no such thing in my kitchen! I never use chemicals in my cooking.'

'Listen,' said Berg patiently. 'When I did my stint in here, I remember that there was a ten-pound bag of saltpetre in –'

'You can't have that!' said Hilgard indignantly. 'I need that for curing the rabbits.'

'But you don't need it. We hardly ever snare rabbits any more – we've wiped them all out.'

Neither Berg or Hilgard saw Kruger approaching.

'I'm not parting with my saltpetre,' the naval officer declared. 'If you've snared any rabbits, then you should bring them to me for curing and not try to do it yourself.'

'What's the trouble, leutnant?' Kruger inquired.

'This idiot wants my saltpetre, commander.'

'That's correct, leutnant,' said Kruger. 'I would be grateful if you would kindly let him have it sometime today when it's quiet.'

Hilgard gaped at Kruger. He was about to argue but changed his mind. 'All right,' he said sulkily. 'I'll bring it over. But there's no one in the camp as good as me at curing rabbits.'

Kruger nodded his thanks and left.

'By the way, Hilgard,' said Berg. 'Do you ever use sodium chloride in your cooking?'

Hilgard scowled angrily. 'Of course not. No chemicals – that's my rule – even if I could get them.'

'Just as I thought,' Berg murmured. 'Sodium chloride is common salt.'

Sergeant Finch stopped wheeling his bicycle. He was standing directly over the spot where the troublesome granite boulder lay. He sniffed deeply and looked suspiciously at Leyden and Willi. 'I can't smell a thing,' he declared. 'It's all your bloody imagination.'

'I'm sorry, sergeant,' said Leyden. 'I've been working this vegetable plot for two weeks now. Every time I come out here, I can smell gas.'

'I can smell it too,' Willi chipped in.

Finch sniffed again. 'There's nothing. Just clean Lake District air. Which you lot don't deserve, I might add.'

'I know gas when I smell it,' said Leyden.

Finch looked exasperated. 'How can there be a smell of gas out here? We're a hundred yards from the kitchens.'

'Maybe the gas pipe goes under the garden?' Willi suggested.

'But the road is up there!' said Finch, gesturing in the direction of the hall. 'Why would the gas company route their main this way, for God's sake?'

'Maybe Harold Brocklebank insisted that the pipe was laid this way?' Willi observed. 'After all, he didn't allow the kitchens to be built in the main hall, did he? Perhaps he was scared of the fire risk.'

'All right. All right,' said Finch impatiently, wheeling his bicycle back to the drive. 'I'll report it, but I still say that it's your imagination.'

Berg peered through the boiler's mica inspection port. 'All right,' he said, straightening up and hobbling out of the way. 'It's ready.'

The prisoner in charge of the boiler swung the furnace door open and used a pair of long-handled stoker's tongs to drag several blazing baulks of timber on to the boiler room floor. 'How much do you need?' he asked Berg.

'About two kilos.'

The prisoner grunted and busied himself with a shovel,

scraping lumps of smouldering charcoal off the burning timbers.

'That's fine,' said Berg when there was enough charcoal scattered on the floor to fill a bucket.

The two men broke some of the larger lumps to make sure that they were blackened right through and spent five minutes pounding the charcoal to a fine dust with coal hammers.

Berg had a bag of good-quality charcoal powder tied under the armrest of his crutch when he hobbled out of the boiler room. He was also looking very pleased with himself. All he needed now was sulphur. He knew where to find that: there were several sticks of it in the greenhouses where it was used for fumigation purposes.

The chill, cutting edge of the November wind sweeping across the fells from the north-east brought with it the first flurries of snow.

Reynolds stood with Kruger and Willi in the middle of the vegetable plots. He turned up the collar of his greatcoat and sniffed while Kruger looked questioningly at him.

'Nothing,' said Reynolds. He sniffed again. 'No. Nothing at all.'

'I can't smell it so strongly today,' Willi admitted.

'Yeah,' said Reynolds, anxious to get back to his office. 'I guess the wind is too strong, huh, commander?'

'I expect so,' Kruger replied. 'The smell was certainly more noticeable yesterday.'

Reynolds thrust his hands in his pockets and thought for a moment. 'Okay. I'll report it to the gas company. Let's see what they say.'

Kruger, Ulbrick and Brunel watched intently as Berg sprinkled two tablespoonfuls of saltpetre on to a brick. He made a hollow in the centre of the heap of white powder and mixed in smaller quantities of the sulphur and the charcoal dust. The concoction turned black as he stirred the ingredients together.

'There we are,' said Berg proudly. 'Twenty grammes of black powder – or gunpowder as it's better known. Stand back please, gentlemen. Oh, please don't worry – it only explodes when it's ignited in a confined space such as the breech of a musket or cannon.' He grinned and added, 'Or underground.'

The three officers took a step backwards. Berg remained seated but leaned back in his chair. His plaster-encased ankle stuck out awkwardly from under his workbench. He struck a match and plunged the burning head into the powder. There was a loud whoosh and a burst of brilliant white light that lasted for less than a second. Sparks and lumps of burning gunpowder splattered across Berg's workbench. He extinguished them by deftly flicking them with a handkerchief. The draught from an open window quickly cleared the acrid fumes from the workshop.

Berg proudly examined the blackened patch on the brick. 'You see, gentlemen? Not a trace of the powder left. I've got enough ingredients for five kilos of gunpowder which I've calculated is just the right amount to shatter the rock. Of course, we'll have to remove the railway track and shoring boards from at least ten metres of the tunnel – and fill it in. We don't want any traces around for the British to find when they inspect the crater.'

Brunel thought he could smell something burning.

'How will you ignite the charge?' Kruger asked.

'That's simple, commander. I'll imbed an exposed torch bulb filament in a priming charge. Apply a battery to the wires, the filament glows, sets off the priming charge – and bang – no more rock.'

Brunel became convinced that he could smell something burning.

'Yes,' Kruger persisted. 'But where will you operate the charge from?'

'The tool shed.'

'Is that safe?'

'Fifty metres?' said Berg confidently. 'Oh yes. It won't be that big an explosion.'

'Just enough to shatter a twenty-tonne chunk of granite,' Ulbrick observed scathingly.

'That's right,' said Berg animatedly. 'Granite is brittle. The shock will probably shatter it into a dozen pieces, possibly more. When we fill in the crater, all we have to do is make sure that the fragments are buried where they won't be in the way.'

Ulbrick shook his head doubtfully. 'I still think it's the most lunatic idea –'

'I agree wholeheartedly,' Kruger interrupted. 'But right now it's the only one we've got. Either we try Berg's scheme or we abandon the tunnel.'

'Something's burning,' said Brunel, but no one took any notice of him.

'That's what's worrying me: that it *is* Berg's scheme,' said Ulbrick. 'They have a habit of going wrong.'

'Nothing can go wrong with this plan,' Berg declared. He twitched his nose and wondered if the burning smell was his imagination. 'I'm always extremely careful with explosives and take all the necessary precautions.'

'Berg,' said Brunel quietly.

'Yes?'

'I think some of that black powder went astray just now.'

'Really? Where?'

'Your plaster cast is on fire.'

The gas company engineer frowned over his maps, which he had unrolled on Major Reynolds' desk. 'I'll be honest with you, major, we just don't understand it. Maybe there's an old main down there that Harold Brocklebank had installed by the old Furness Gas Company. If so, we don't know anything about it. Their records were destroyed before the Great War, and there's nothing on our maps.'

'The pressure test showed that there's a leakage,' Reynolds pointed out.

'The loss was very slight,' said the engineer patiently. 'Well within tolerance. Personally, I think your POWs are playing a practical joke on you.'

'Not very practical if we can't see the point of it,' Reynolds observed. 'Okay, Mr Williams. Thank you for coming. We're sorry to have wasted your time.'

Willi's timing was perfect: he opened Kruger's door just as Corporal White was passing.

'Ah, Chalky. Do you have time for a drop of whisky?'

It was an offer Corporal White could not refuse, not even at eleven o'clock in the morning.

'This gas leak is annoying us,' Willi remarked as his guest tasted his drink.

'Why's that, Willi?'

'It's making us prisoners look such fools. The commander is very angry with us. We can smell gas and yet you British cannot. I have tried telling him that it's only to be expected, but he won't listen.'

The NCO was puzzled. 'Why should you be able to smell it and not us?'

'But it is only natural,' said Willi. 'We eat plenty of chocolate and you eat none.' He opened a drawer and produced a monster one-kilogramme bar of Swiss Toblerone. 'Surely you know that chocolate sharpens the sense of smell?'

Chalky shook his head numbly while goggling at the huge bar.

'It is true,' said Willi. 'My brother is a doctor. He told me. Chocolate improves your sense of smell, he said. You have heard that the Swiss keep their country very clean?'

Chalky nodded.

'They have to because they have a heightened sense of smell from eating so much chocolate,' said Willi, holding the bar out to Chalky. 'Try it if you don't believe me. You eat that chocolate and I am sure that you will be able to smell that gas leak.'

The bar disappeared inside Chalky's battledress blouse before Willi could blink. 'Perhaps I should try two bars?' Chalky suggested. 'Just in case one doesn't work.'

Willi opened his drawer again and produced a second bar which vanished as quickly as the first one.

'How long do you think it'll take to work?' Chalky queried.

'Oh, by about noon tomorrow.'

'And if I do smell gas, should I report it?'

'Oh definitely,' Willi murmured. 'It will be your duty to do so.'

Chalky fidgetted.

'Problem?'

'Well,' said Chalky reasonably. 'I'm going to feel a bit of a chump if I'm the only guard that smells this gas leak. Maybe if you let me have another couple of bars for me mates. . . .'

Willi sighed and opened his drawer for the third time.

Berg's bomb weighed nearly ten pounds and completely filled a wooden case the size of a shoebox.

To install it, Berg had to work at the tunnel face while lying flat on his stomach on the trolley. Ignoring the ache in his arm and ankle, he cut the string that secured the bomb to the trolley and slid it into the hole that Brunel had excavated beneath the slab of granite. He took special care not to damage the two lengths of fine enamelled copper wire that were connected to the bomb's firing charge. A final push with a board and the bomb was in position. He backed the trolley a few metres along the track while playing out the wires until one of the ventilation openings was above his head.

'Leyden!' he called softly.

'Ready,' Leyden's voice answered from the ventilation hole.

'I'm pushing the wires up now.'

Berg threaded the ends of the wires into the tube.

'Okay,' said Leyden. 'I've got them.'

There was a gentle tug on the wires. It took a minute for Berg to uncoil the sixty-metre lengths of wire and feed them through the ventilation tube. He rapped three times on one of the rails when he had finished, which was the signal for Brunel to haul him back into the cellar.

'All ready, commander,' he reported to Kruger as Brunel and one of his assistants helped him off the trolley.

'Excellent, Berg,' said Kruger. He turned to Brunel. 'All right. You had better start filling in. Ten metres back from the face should be more than enough. Correct, Berg?'

'Correct, commander.'

Kruger nodded. He looked regretfully at the glowing butt of his cheroot before dropping it and grinding it underfoot. 'All right, Berg,' he said. 'Get the wires connected up to the shed ready for tomorrow. After that I want to see what progress you've made with the printing press.'

'I think it's working, Willi,' said Chalky as he mounted the terrace steps. 'I ate half a bar this morning and I'm certain I could smell gas just now.'

'Yes,' said Willi drily. 'Your sense of smell will be at its best at noon tomorrow.'

'Will it fade when the chocolate's finished.'

'I suppose it will,' said Willi cautiously.

'A pity. I shall miss it.'

As Willi returned Chalky's bland smile, he had an uncomfortable feeling that he had met a fellow expert in the useful arts of bribery and blackmail.

At eleven the next morning, an hour and ten minutes before Berg's bomb was due to be detonated, Brunel reported to Kruger that the filling in of ten-metres of tunnel had been completed. Also, Berg had wired up the bomb and was sitting in the shed awaiting the signal. Kruger thanked him and glanced at his watch. The timing of his visit to Reynolds was critical.

Berg crouched in the toolshed and peered through the grimy window. From his vantage point he could see the terrace steps. Nearer to the shed, about fifty metres away, was Leyden's vegetable plot. A light drizzle was falling and the only activity was a few prisoners tending their reorganized plots. Berg checked the two wires that disappeared through a crack in the shed floor and carried out a final test on the toggle switch and battery. Everything was in working order.

A movement outside caught Berg's eye. Exactly on time, two prisoners appeared. One was carrying a bundle of short wooden stakes and a length of ribbon made from bits of rag. The other was armed with a hammer. They worked steadily for ten minutes, knocking a circle of stakes into the ground around Leyden's vegetable plot. They strung the ribbon from the stakes and returned to the main hall.

Berg slid his plaster-encased ankle under the tiny workbench and sat down on a box to wait.

Reynolds had just finished speaking on the telephone to Fleming in London when Kruger was shown into his office.

'This gas leak is getting serious, major,' said Kruger, coming straight to the point. 'I demand that something is done about it before any of my officers are injured. I've closed off an area of the vegetable plots and I must say that I'm disappointed to note that you are not treating the matter as seriously as I am.'

Reynolds tried not to look too exasperated. 'For God's

sake, commander, the gas company experts are convinced that there's nothing there and, if there is, that there's no danger.'

'That smell is now so strong that it *must* be dangerous,' Kruger stated firmly. 'Come out and see for yourself if you don't believe me.'

At a minute to noon, Berg saw Corporal White and Private Jones appear. The two guards strolled along one of the paths between the vegetable plots. They reached the circle of wooden stakes, which they proceeded to investigate with great interest. Something appeared to distract Chalky. He looked around in surprise and sniffed the air. He said something to Private Jones. Both men sniffed hard and seemed to agree on something. They abandoned their inspection of the staked-off area and hurried off in the direction of the hall.

Berg started worrying about the bomb. Had he got the ratios of the three ingredients right? Would it be big enough? Would the detonating charge work? A minute passed. He told himself that it was too late to change anything now, and to stop worrying.

Reynolds forgot Kruger's presence and looked sharply at Chalky. 'Are you certain of this?'

'Positive, sir. So's Private Jones, sir. We could both smell it. Plain as anything it was.'

'Perhaps we should both investigate?' Kruger suggested.

Reynolds nodded. He stood and pulled on his cap. 'All right, Corporal White – you and Jones go on ahead.'

Chalky saluted and left the office.

As Reynolds was putting his greatcoat on, he said to Kruger, 'I have something to tell you outside which I want you to treat as confidential, commander.'

Kruger made no reply. He followed Reynolds out into the courtyard and fell in step beside him.

'It's about these goddamn Canada rumours,' said Reynolds. 'I've heard from a reliable source that there are no plans to move the Number One camp for the time being.'

'How sure are you of this, major?' asked Kruger expressionlessly.

'Like I said, it came from a reliable source. I can't go further than that.'

At five minutes past noon, Berg saw a prisoner up-end his spade and start cleaning it. It was the warning signal that told him to get ready. He moved the toggle switch into the centre of the toolshed's workbench and connected its two wires to the battery's terminals.

Willi stepped through the french windows on to the terrace at seven minutes past noon, just as Kruger and Reynolds rounded the corner of the building and headed towards the vegetable plots. A hundred yards away in the toolshed, Berg reached for the toggle switch while keeping his eyes fixed on Willi.

Kruger and Reynolds reached the first vegetable plot. They were approximately seventy yards from Leyden's plot with its fluttering ribbons tied to a circle of stakes.

Berg's fingers were posed expectantly on the toggle switch. He didn't take his eyes off Willi for a second.

Willi whipped out a large, spotted handkerchief and blew his nose.

'When is Commander Fleming returning, major?' Kruger asked Reynolds.

'In his own good time. Why?'

'Oh, nothing.'

Reynolds glanced sideways at Kruger and realized that there was something different about the U-boat ace. He was about to speak when Berg's bomb went off with a tremendous WHUUMPH!

A shock wave punched through the ground and hammered into Reynolds' body with what seemed like enough force to ram his feet into his groin. The blast followed through an instant later, hitting him like an express train and making him stagger backwards. He recovered his balance and stared in dumbfounded horror as a column of rocks, soil and flame erupted out of the ground and roared high into the air like the by-products of Mount Vesuvius on a bad day.

One particular small boulder climbed higher than its neighbours. Reynolds watched in stunned disbelief as it soared like a brick albatross into the grey sky It reached the top of its trajectory and curved gracefully over. The rest of its journey consisted of a rapid downwards acceleration that ended with it plummeting with unerring accuracy straight into the toolshed, which it successfully reduced in an instant to a heap of splinters and firewood.

The spectacle's finale was a mighty howl of anguish from Berg.

That evening Kruger called an emergency meeting of the escape committee. His opening remarks dealt with the amazing success of Berg's gas leak and bomb ruse. The gas board engineers had been baffled by the explosion but had decided that it must have been due to a freak seepage of natural gas through the rocks. Whatever the cause, they had decided that it was most unlikely to happen again. Best of all, the troublesome boulder had been shattered into over forty fragments, all of which had been recovered by the prisoners with Reynolds' consent because Kruger had told him he was keen to rebuild one of Grizedale Hall's rockeries.

'It means,' Kruger finished, 'that we should have no more major problems when work is resumed on the tunnel.'

Shriver was puzzled. 'I don't follow you, commander. Surely the work is to continue.'

'I propose resting the tunnel project until the spring,' Kruger replied.

There was a chorus of groans. 'We might be in Canada by then!' Ulbrick protested.

'I doubt it very much.'

Shriver smiled. 'Or we might be liberated by then.'

'I doubt that very much too,' said Kruger coldly.

Shriver was about to dispute Kruger's views but was interrupted by a rap on the door. Willi entered and handed Kruger an envelope. It was still slightly limp from when he had steamed it open.

'With Major Reynolds' compliments,' said Willi.

'You've read it, of course, Willi?'

Willi knew better than to lie to Kruger. He nodded guiltily.

'Then perhaps you would be good enough to tell us what it contains.'

Willi swallowed. 'Some good news, commander. Major Reynolds says that he has heard from Barrow General Hospital. The compound fracture of Hauptmann Berg's leg isn't as bad as was first thought. And if he gets over his concussion, he should be back with us in time for Christmas.'

The brief silence that followed was broken by Ulbrick. 'You said "good news", Willi,' he said accusingly.

The next day Reynolds had a sudden thought. 'You know something, sergeant?' he said to Finch, who was filling in some requisition forms. 'I do believe that Kruger has run out of those poisonous goddamn cigars. I didn't see him smoking one yesterday.'

Part Seven

BOMBERS' MOON

For the third night in succession the eerie wail of Ambleside's solitary air raid siren, echoing across the fells, was heard at the camp. The floodlighting and perimeter fence wire lighting were extinguished almost immediately so that the hall did not provide the marauding bombers with a landmark.

Kruger signalled to Willi to turn off the light in the office before he cautiously drew the blackout curtain aside and peered out. The ghostly light of a full moon shining from a clear sky bathed the frost-covered grounds. The spidery silhouette of the firewatching tower was visible above the conifers of Grizedale Forest. He heard whistles blowing from the direction of the guards' quarters.

'Molde! Braun!' he snapped. 'Get a move on! They're turning out the blackout guard!'

There was enough moonlight in the room for Leutnant Victor Molde and Oberleutnant Klaus Braun to finish blacking-up their faces with shoe polish. They knew from timings made during the previous raids that they had less than three minutes before the number of soldiers patrolling the grounds was doubled.

The two bomber pilots were each wearing seamen's black trousers and jumpers. Willi helped them into their kitbag harnesses and ensured that the bags were settled comfortably on their shoulders. Berg's home-made wire cutters were pushed securely into a sling around Molde's waist. Kruger checked that the terrace thirty feet below was clear before hurling the knotted blanket rope out of the window. One end of the rope was tied to the radiator.

The two would-be escapers exchanged hurried handshakes with Willi. Kruger shook hands with Braun as the *Luftwaffe* officer swung his leg over the windowsill and grasped the rope.

'Good luck, oberleutnant.'

Braun gave Kruger a broad grin. 'Thank you, commander. I'll write.' He realized his mistake before he had finished the sentence. 'Commander, it was a slip of the tongue.'

'A slip that could get you shot!' Kruger snapped. 'From the moment you put those clothes on you were Dutch seaman Hans Menckin on your way to Londonderry via Liverpool. I'm sorry, Braun, but your escape is out of the question.'

'Oh, for God's sake!' Braun protested, almost shouting. 'You can't stop –'

'Molde!' Kruger interrupted. 'Don't stand there gawping. Get down that rope!'

After an uncertain glance at Kruger and Braun, Molde climbed over the windowsill and went hand over hand down the rope. He dropped the last ten feet, landing lightly on his feet, and vaulted over the terrace's parapet before Kruger started hauling the rope up. Luckily the two guards who appeared on the terrace at that moment did not see the last few feet of rope disappearing into Kruger's office.

'This is absurd!' Braun protested. 'We've worked hard planning this escape.'

'Not hard enough.'

'But you're crazy! You can't let Molde go alone.'

'Molde will manage perfectly well without you,' said Kruger curtly. 'Take off that kitbag please, and return to your dormitory.'

Braun returned Kruger's icy stare. 'After this, commander, you will find that you have lost the respect of the *Luftwaffe* officers here.'

'Oh, I don't know, Braun. I rather imagine that the *Luftwaffe* football team will be pleased to discover that they haven't lost their centre forward.'

Braun slipped the kitbag off his back and nearly threw it at Willi before storming out of the office.

Willi said nothing. He was about to turn the light on when the anti-aircraft battery to the east near Windermere suddenly started pouring a steady stream of shells into the sky. Kruger was tempted to peer out of the window but he knew from his experience of the previous two nights that he would be unable to see anything out of the south-facing window.

'Odd,' he commented to Willi. 'That's the third night in succession that that battery has opened up. If the target is Barrow-in-Furness, it doesn't say much for the *Luftwaffe*'s navigation.'

After a hundred-yard dash from the hall across the grounds, taking advantage of the shadows thrown by shrubs, Molde threw himself down between two wheelbarrows that were standing side by side on the open expanse of the vegetable plots. They had been strategically positioned earlier that day to provide the necessary cover for an escape bid should there be yet another bombing raid. Once he had allowed three minutes after the first two-man patrol had passed the point where he intended to cut through the wire, he had five minutes before the next patrol were within fifty metres. He kept very still and waited.

Molde was relieved that Braun was not accompanying him. During the twenty-four hours planning that had gone into the impromptu escape, Braun had adopted a carefree attitude. He had preferred to spend the day telling his circle of prisoners about how he would be fooling the British rather than getting down to serious study of maps and routes.

The reason why Kruger had sanctioned the winter escape was because Braun spoke perfect English without an accent and because Molde had often camped in the Lake District before the war. Both men were athletic, which would stand them in good stead when it came to stowing-away on a neutral ship in Liverpool. Also, the finds of litter clearing parties and Willi's bribery of the guards meant that both men were well-equipped with identification and travel documents.

The anti-aircraft guns started firing just as he decided to make the final sprint to the fence. He twisted his head round and watched the probing beams of the searchlights and the points of tracer fire climbing with deceptive laziness into the sky.

Molde knew all about British flak. There was the curious, unreal feeling of watching the tracer reaching up with what seemed unbelieveable slowness and then appearing to accelerate madly as it neared its target; the dull shocks of shells passing right through an aircraft without exploding and then the nightmare kaleidoscope of flying instrument glass as had happened when one exploded in the nose and another a second later in the tail, killing his gunners and toppling his Junkers into a spin.

The young pilot offered a prayer of deliverance for the aircrews of the unseen aircraft and wondered if they were from his *gruppe*.

The first patrol were more interested in the battle raging in the east than the barbed wire fence they were supposed to be guarding. Molde watched them until they were out of sight. As he began the final dash for the wire, he heard the unmistakable sound of an over-revving engine of an aircraft in an uncontrolled dive.

*

'Bloody hell,' breathed Private Jones. 'It sounds like they got one!'

He and Chalky paused near the firewatching tower and stared eastwards towards the sound of the diving aircraft. The searchlight beams swung southwards about their axis like the spokes of a celestial wheel as they hunted for their lost quarry. One beam momentarily illuminated a cluster of white specks and immediately swept back to pinpoint five parachute canopies hanging in the sky.

Chalky gave an exclamation of annoyance and dropped his cigarette. 'Come on, Jonesy, they'll be wanting us to go and hunt for the bastards. On a bloody freezing night like this too. Bleedin' Jerries.'

'Parachutes!' Kruger exclaimed angrily, drawing his head back into the office. To Willi's amazement, he grabbed the bundle of knotted blankets and dropped it out of the window. 'Willi! Go after Molde and bring him back!'

Willi's portly frame stood rooted to the floor in terror. 'I'm to what, commander?' he queried faintly.

'Go down the rope and bring Molde back. There'll be search parties combing the fells for that aircrew – he doesn't stand a chance of getting away. Go on, man! Move!'

'But, commander –'

'Don't argue with me, Willi. I ordered you to attend Ulbrick's keep fit sessions for an occasion such as this – now get down that rope!'

Willi knew better than to argue, especially as Kruger's temper had not been good of late since he had either run out of the toxic little cheroots or had given up smoking. He moved trance-like to the window and lifted a plump leg over the windowsill.

'You'll need this,' said Kruger, putting the rope in Willi's virtually lifeless hands. 'Good luck.'

*

Molde was working the wire-cutters through the last strand of barbed wire when he heard someone running towards him. He looked over his shoulder and gazed in amazement at the apparition charging across the wide strip of grass that was used for sports practice. Willi paused uncertainly at the trip wire, uncomfortably aware that the guards wouldn't hesitate to take pot shots at him if he was seen. He stepped over the low wire and flopped down beside Molde like a wounded sea elephant.

'What the hell do you want?'

Willi's heaving chest continued hoovering air in and out of his lungs for some moments before he could gasp out Kruger's order.

'Don't be bloody crazy!' Molde hissed in reply, returning to the attack on the wire.

'*Please*, Molde,' Willi begged. 'You must come back. He'll kill me if you don't.'

'Tell him I was gone by the time you'd reached the fence!'

The last strand parted. Molde bent it out of the way and started wriggling through the hole. Willi grabbed hold of his ankle.

'You stupid bastard!' Molde hissed angrily. 'Leggo!' He tried kicking himself free but Willi hung on to his leg with a grim determination born of fear.

'Molde, I beg of you. You must come back. Please!'

Molde replied by planting his free foot on Willi's face and shoving with all his strength. He broke free, wormed the rest of his body through the wire, and scrambled to his feet.

'Oh God,' Willi wailed to himself as he watched Molde running towards the trees. 'He'll kill me. He'll kill me.'

'Tut tut,' said Fleming sympathetically, wandering up behind Reynolds and Finch, who were ruefully examining the hole in the wire. 'Never mind, gentlemen. You've got me back. Who have we lost?'

'Victor Molde, *Luftwaffe*,' said Reynolds bitterly.

'Ah,' said Fleming knowingly. 'In that case there's no chance that the hole was made by Leutnant Shultz trying to get back in?'

Reynolds was clearly not amused by Fleming's joke. 'Good morning, Ian,' he said stiffly. 'Good to have you back.'

Fleming nodded. 'I knew there'd been an escape. I was stopped at two road blocks.'

'It's this stupid single fence,' said Finch angrily. 'We need two fences with the outer one electrified.'

'Not a bad idea,' Fleming observed.

'Try telling the War Office,' said Reynolds. 'They say that every yard of barbed wire is needed for beach defences.' He nodded to the firewatching tower. 'I only managed to get that thing by scrounging it from the Forestry Commission.'

'How's Kruger been keeping?'

Reynolds scowled. 'That guy's been impossible just lately.'

'I think I can guess why,' said Fleming, chuckling.

Fleming tapped on Kruger's door and entered. 'Good morning, Otto. Long time no see.'

Kruger's expression as he looked up from his desk was the nearest that Fleming had ever seen to hope on the U-boat commander's face.

'Good morning, commander.'

'I expect your lookout system told you that I was coming?'

Kruger smiled wryly. 'I knew someone was coming who was not German. That is all.'

'Your security system is better than ours,' Fleming observed, unbuckling his briefcase. 'Prisoners breaking out by the score; people smuggling stuff into the camp. Look what I managed to get past the guards yet again.'

Kruger took the huge box of German cheroots that

Fleming held out. 'I am very grateful to you, commander,' he said, unwrapping one of the cigars and lighting it.

Fleming grinned. 'An early Christmas present, old boy. I've found you another supplier. He said that he's only too glad to get rid of them. No one else can stand them. I think his stocks will last you until the end of the war.'

Kruger exhaled slowly, releasing a cloud of acrid fumes. 'And how long will that be, commander?'

With ten minutes to go before the Wehrmacht referee blew the final whistle, the noisy, aggressive football match between the *Luftwaffe* and the *Kreigsmarine* was still a goal-less draw. If results were according to number of supporters, the *Kriegsmarine* would have been well ahead because their representatives at Grizedale Hall outnumbered both the other services – a reflection on the intensity of the Battle of the Atlantic that was now being fought.

After a foul that was blatant, even by the standards of Grizedale Hall, the referee awarded a penalty kick to the *Luftwaffe*. The supporters crowding along the touchline fell silent as Braun squared up to the ball. He was about to begin his run-up when his attention was distracted by the sight of Sergeant Finch climbing the ladder to his favourite perch on the firewatching tower.

The combination of a target, still air and his frustration at being denied the chance to escape decided Sergeant Finch's fate. As Braun's foot slammed into the ball, he knew instinctively that the kick was a good one.

Sergeant Finch settled down on his seat. He bent down and started unscrewing the searchlight's rusting switchbox that was screwed to the watchtower's boarded surround. Of all the problems in his life, the searchlight and its ancient wiring was the most persistent; it was for ever blowing fuses. Requisitions for new equipment were just a waste of time and paper – they disappeared into the War Office machine and were never heard of again. He was about to pull the front off the switchbox when a splintering crash right by his ear caused his heart to catapult into his throat and try to crawl out of his ears.

'My God,' Ulbrick whispered to Braun as Sergeant Finch's infuriated face appeared at the hole that the football had punched in the rotten boards. 'I think there's going to be trouble.'

Ulbrick was right. Finch almost slid down the ladder with the football clutched under his arm and stormed across to the prisoners.

'Who kicked this?'

'I did, sergeant,' Braun answered 'Did it scare you?'

Finch calmed down and his manner became calculating. 'I find it very strange, Oberleutnant Braun.'

'You find what strange, sergeant?'

No one noticed Kruger appear. He regarded the crowd of prisoners for a moment before stepping over the trip wire and picking up a piece of timber that Braun's football had dislodged from the tower.

'I find it strange how your talent with a football has suddenly deserted you,' Finch replied.

Braun smiled. 'It comes and goes like your sense of humour, sergeant.'

'Really, oberleutnant? Well let's see how *your* sense of humour survives a ten-year sentence for sabotaging a War Office installation.'

A silence fell as the prisoners sensed that Finch was not joking.

Braun forced a laugh. 'You are not serious?'

'Aren't I? You're under arrest, oberleutnant. How much more serious would you like me to be?'

'What's the trouble?' inquired Kruger from the back of the crowd. The prisoners made a path for him through their midst. In his hand was the piece of timber from the tower. 'Good afternoon, Sergeant Finch. Do you have a problem?'

'Oberleutnant Braun is the one with the problem, commander. He's under arrest for sabotaging a War Office installation. That kick was deliberate.'

Kruger crumbled a piece of the tower's timber in his fingers. 'But the tower is still standing, sergeant. Just. As you can see – it is rotten.'

'That's not the point –'

'But it is the point,' Kruger insisted. 'I saw what happened. It was an accident.'

'I can fight my own battles, commander,' said Braun in German.

'It was a deliberate act of sabotage,' Finch declared.

Kruger shook his head. 'It would only be sabotage if Oberleutnant Braun knew that the timber was in this condition, sergeant. Timber this thick would normally withstand a football hitting it. Oberleutnant Braun has never been up the tower. Therefore, if he's charged, the question is certain to arise: how did he know of the tower's condition? Did a guard tell him? Passing information to the enemy? There may have to be a separate inquiry.'

Finch glowered at Kruger. 'What the hell are you talking about, commander?'

'I expect I am making as much sense as you with your talk of sabotage,' said Kruger evenly. 'It was an unfortunate accident which I am certain Oberleutnant Braun is anxious to apologize for.' He turned to Braun. 'Is that not so, oberleutnant?'

For a moment it looked as if Braun was prepared to continue the argument, but he thought better of it and muttered a grudging apology to Sergeant Finch, which the British NCO accepted in the same spirit in which it was offered.

'Let it happen again, oberleutnant,' Finch warned, tossing the football to the referee, 'and you'll find yourself in serious trouble.'

Kruger nodded his approval. 'Thank you, Braun.'

Braun acknowledged and rejoined his team mates as play resumed. Kruger pointedly ignored Finch and turned to watch the match for a few minutes, inhaling on the last inch of his cheroot. He dropped the butt, ground it into the grass and walked away. Finch pounced on the butt immediately and examined it with an expression that was a mixture of bewilderment and frustrated rage.

Kruger was sitting writing at his desk when he heard the warning whistle. He looked up expectantly just as there was a rap on the door.

'Come!'

The door was opened by Braun.

'You wanted to see me, commander?'

'Come in, Braun. Close the door. Take a seat.'

Braun did as he was told. He lounged languidly in his chair while regarding Kruger with undisguised hostility. 'Thank you for dealing with Sergeant Finch, commander.'

'That was a remarkably stupid thing to do, Braun. But that's not what I wanted to see you about. It would seem that Molde is still free.'

Braun remained silent.

'When the bomber was shot down during the raid, I tried to cancel his escape as well, in case there would be search parties out on the fells hunting for parachutists. Willi claimed that he was too late and that Molde had already got through the wire.'

Braun shrugged. 'So Willi told me. What has it got to do with me? Or are you going to admit that you were wrong in stopping me from escaping?'

Kruger gave a thin smile. 'I doubt if you'd be interested if I said that my reasons arose out of concern for your safety.'

'For once, commander, your judgment is not at fault. Thank you for telling me about Molde.' Braun stood. 'Now if you would excuse me, I have a coaching session with my reserve team.'

'I've not finished, Braun. Please sit down.'

Braun sat and contrived to look suitably bored.

'As a U-boatman,' said Kruger, ignoring Braun's insolent expression, 'I know very little about flying problems. I wish to pick your brains. I hope you have no objection?'

'Go ahead,' said the pilot disinterestedly.

'For the past two nights there have been abortive *Luftwaffe* raids on Barrow-in-Furness. At least I'm assuming that the target has been Barrow. Why have the bombers been going off course?'

Braun flushed angrily. 'Commander, am I here to listen to your criticism of the *Luftwaffe*?'

'No, Braun. You're here for me to listen to you. I recall that you were shot down on a Barrow raid. Am I correct?'

Braun nodded. 'Yes. Despite the difficulties, Barrow was a priority target for my group. It probably still is in view of the raid two nights ago.'

Kruger looked interested. 'Was the target the Vickers submarine construction yard?'

'Yes.'

'Well there's hope for us yet, even if the *Luftwaffe* are unloading their bombs all over the Lake District.'

'I'm sorry, commander, but I don't follow you.'

'Co-operation between the *Luftwaffe* and the *Kriegsmarine*,' Kruger commented. 'It used to be non-existent. U-boats returning across the Bay of Biscay to our bases at Lorient and St Narzaire were never provided with air cover. The result was that the RAF threw anything that could fly at us. Sunderlands, biplanes – even lumbering old Walrus amphibians. These raids on Barrow would suggest that some co-operation lessons have been learned. Why else would the *Luftwaffe* bomb submarine yards?'

'I was opposed to the raids.'

Kruger raised an eyebrow. 'Oh? May I ask why?'

'I couldn't see the point in risking aircraft on such a difficult target when there are juicier targets nearer to home. The war will be over soon. What difference will the production of a few submarines a month at Barrow make to the British war effort?'

Kruger gazed thoughtfully at Braun for a moment before opening a desk drawer and removing its contents. He pulled the emptied drawer right out from the desk and turned it over. He placed it in front of Braun. Drawn on the underside of the drawer's plywood bottom was a detailed Indian ink map of the Lake District and nearby coast, showing roads, railways, towns and villages. Also included was Barrow-in-Furness.

'Neat, commander,' Braun observed.

'All escapees' maps are copied from this master.'

'Including the one I wasn't given a chance to use?'

'Why is Barrow a difficult target?' asked Kruger.

'Is this some sort of trial that the *Luftwaffe* is on, commander?'

'Not unless you know of something that the *Luftwaffe* should be on trial for, Braun,' said Kruger acidly. He gestured to the map. 'I would like to know what the problems are with Barrow.'

Braun studied the map. 'Well, firstly, there's the distance. It's over a thousand kilometres from our base. It's even further than Liverpool. Which means that we have to sacrifice some of our bomb payload for extra fuel – which also means, when we find Barrow, our bombing has to be that much more accurate.'

'That's understood,' said Kruger. 'But why do your bombers always seem to end up here over the Lake District, several kilometres north of Barrow?'

Braun smiled ruefully. 'That's what happened to me when I was shot down. Barrow's at the extreme effective range of our radio navigation beams. The tendency to drift north could be due to distortion of the beam caused by the high ground around here, or – as we believe – that the British have found a way of interfering with the beam. No one was ever one hundred per cent certain. What we were certain of was that Barrow was a swine to find.'

'But the lakes are such obvious landmarks. Surely it would be not be difficult to correct one's course for Barrow from them?'

'It's not that simple, commander,' said Braun, his hostility towards Kruger forgotten for the time being. He pointed to Barrow and to nearby Walney Island. 'A glimpse of a lake through a break in the cloud can easily be mistaken for the channel between Barrow and Walney Island. You see the similarities? Also the lakes are roughly the same width as the channel.'

Kruger studied the map in silence for a moment. What Braun said was true: there were remarkable similarities between Barrow's topography and that of the lakes. He sat back in his chair and steepled his fingers. 'So what would you say is the solution, oberleutnant?'

Braun shook his head. He added jokingly, 'What's needed in this area is a distinctive landmark.'

Kruger's expression remained serious. 'What would you call a distinctive landmark?'

'I'm sorry, commander, I'm not sure I understand you.'

'What detail is visible from the air during a full moon?'

Braun thought for a moment. 'Well . . . virtually everything that's visible during the day. Houses, gardens – even the white rings the British have painted round tree trunks.'

'The white rings around trees? You surprise me, oberleutnant.'

'The difficulty isn't so much spotting landmarks,' said Braun. 'It's identifying them correctly to obtain an accurate bearing.'

'The white rings round trees. . . .' Kruger mused. 'Fascinating. I had no idea.'

Braun looked puzzled. 'Why are you asking these questions, commander?'

Kruger was lost in thought before he replied. 'What are

the chances of your group taking another crack at Barrow during next month's bombers' moon?'

Braun smiled. 'Well . . . our *Geschwader* doesn't give up that easily. And as I said, Barrow is a priority target for my group. Yes, they'll be back.'

'Good,' said Kruger. 'In that case, we'd better make sure that we are ready for them. I shall need your help, oberleutnant. I hope you are in agreement?'

'That depends on what you want,' said Braun cautiously.

Molde thought he heard a seal bark. After three attempts to engage his sleep-drugged mental gears, he succeeded in co-ordinating the various facial muscles that were required to open an eye. He thought he saw something that looked vaguely like a grey, uninviting sky viewed through the neglected roof of a broken-down barn. Upon opening both eyes, he discovered that what he was looking at was in fact a grey, uninviting sky viewed through the neglected roof of a broken-down barn.

As reason returned like an unwelcome black tide, he realized that he was cold, bitterly cold despite the layer of straw covering his body. But there was an exception: the small of his back was surprisingly warm. After a minute's contemplation, the reason for his warm back became apparent: someone was breathing down it. It wasn't ordinary breathing. As the gusts of warm humid air blasted down his spine like clouds of steam, he reasoned that it just wasn't possible for anyone to breathe like that unless they were on the verge of a catastrophic failure of their bodily systems. He reached out a cautious hand and his fingertips encountered a bristly chin. Above the chin were soft, sensual lips and a pair of flaring nostrils.

Molde twisted his body around and found himself staring a horse in the eye. The horse took grave exception to the liberties that his hand was taking and promptly bit it.

*

Sergeant Finch was sitting morosely in his firewatching tower like a khaki vulture. All was not well within his well-ordered little world. He treated the absence of Leutnant Molde as a personal insult. If he hadn't been so intent on his brooding, there was a faint chance that he might have spotted certain surreptitious activities going on under his nose. On the other hand the prisoners were masters at disguising their nefarious deeds, so burying a long length of rope under a few inches of top soil hardly tested their undoubted talents. The rope led across the vegetable plots and disappeared in the general direction of the drive. Some prisoners were covering the rope with soil that they were excavating from bean trenches and others were raking soil over the rope. Where it ran across open grass, it was being covered with heaps of dead leaves.

The working party filling in potholes in the drive were so preoccupied that they appeared not to notice the laundry van until the driver hooted at them. He rested his arms impatiently across the steering wheel while the prisoners unhurriedly gathered up their tools.

One prisoner distracted the driver's attention for a crucial moment with an obscene gesture to ensure that he did not glance in his mirror. While the driver was leaning out of his window, trading insults with the prisoner, Brunel darted out of the rhododendrons beside the van, rolled underneath the vehicle, and lashed the end of the rope to its rear axle.

As soon as the road was clear, the driver angrily slammed the van into gear and accelerated towards the hall. The prisoners watched, fascinated, as the rope snaked after the speeding vehicle. All the prisoners who had been working in the grounds to cover the rope moved clear as soon as they saw the van move off. Their movements were unhurried but purposeful. Suddenly the rope leapt three feet into the air, showering soil and leaves in all directions, and snapped taut with a loud twang. The firewatching tower's timber leg that had the other end of the rope looped around it snapped like a matchstick and was yanked out of place as though it had been struck by a giant, invisible sledgehammer.

The driver of the van leapt from his seat to find out what it was that had jerked his vehicle to a standstill, nearly hurling him through the windscreen in the process. His attention was immediately rivetted by the sight of the tottering firewatching tower and therefore he didn't see Brunel quickly untie the offending rope and drag it out of sight.

Unable to withstand the increased load, the tower's three remaining legs bowed inwards. A six-inch diameter cross-brace – about the only sound timber in the tower – hung on grimly for as long as it could. When it finally gave up the unequal struggle, it emitted a tremendous crack like a pistol shot and fell away in two pieces. For some seconds nothing but habit kept the tower upright as it swayed drunkenly in the breeze, defying gravity for several moments before the entire structure crashed down on itself like a pole-axed giraffe.

It wasn't only the welter of collapsing, splintering boards and struts that every prisoner who witnessed the scene would remember for the rest of his life, or the pyrotechnique display of blue sparks when the searchlight power cable shorted out; what would be indelibly etched on every man's memory was the expression of abject terror on Sergeant Finch's face in those few seconds before he was unceremoniously buried under a huge pile of rotten timber that had once been his beloved firewatching tower.

As soon as he heard the sound of a car start, Molde climbed down from the bales of straw and, taking care to avoid Caligula – as he had named the horse – because its hobby was collecting bits of his anatomy, he tiptoed to the door and peered through a crack.

He was just in time to see Fleming's Bentley swing into

the farmyard and swerve sharply to avoid ramming a Morris as it backed out of a garage.

'Ian,' said Cathy delightedly, winding down the window of her car. 'I didn't know you were back from London. This is a lovely surprise.'

'Surprise being the operative word,' said Fleming, stepping down from the Bentley's running board and leaning on the Morris's driver's door. 'Actually, I only got back yesterday. I thought I'd pop over to see if you were all right. You heard about last night's escape?'

'Oh yes,' said Cathy, giving Fleming a dazzling smile. 'Ambleside police rang me up this morning. I got John to check all the outhouses.'

'John?'

'The son of one of my tenants. You've seen him. He often goes riding with me.'

Fleming remembered the young man in the smart tweed suit. 'Oh, yes.'

'It's sweet of you to come over, Ian, it really is. I've left all my livestock in the care of a tenant because I'm just off to spend a few days with my sister at Kendal to help her with her early lambs.'

'I wish I could join you.'

Cathy laughed. 'I can just see you chasing ewes all over the fells.'

'I'll have you know that I'm an expert at chasing women.'

Cathy laughed again. 'Don't I know it. Anyway, if you're around after three o'clock next Friday afternoon, do drop in for a cup of tea, won't you? Must fly now. Byee!'

Fleming said goodbye and watched the Morris drive off. He returned to his own car and followed Cathy out of the farmyard. Had he glanced back at the farmhouse, he would have seen a young man wearing an immaculate, expertly cut tweed suit watching his departure from an upstairs window.

Molde straightened up and turned round in time to avoid

Caligula who was stretching a long neck and bared teeth in his direction. Luckily the beast was tethered. He climbed up to his bed on top of the bales of straw and considered his next move while eating quarter of a bar of chocolate from his kitbag. He was ravenously hungry and he needed all his self-control to prevent himself from wolfing down the entire bar. He decided that it would be best to stay in the barn until nightfall. By then the British were certain to have rounded up the aircrew of the crashed bomber, and the soldiers and police looking for him would probably think that he was a long way from the camp by then. In the meantime there was nothing to do except sleep and try to keep warm.

Before curling up in the straw, Molde helped himself to a drink from Caligula's water trough when he thought the belligerent beast wasn't looking. It was looking and it did its best to take a lump out of his rear as he dived for safety.

Reynolds was particularly annoyed by the disruption of the camp's routine caused by the collapse of the tower. His fishing tackle was in need of attention; he had been looking forward to revarnishing his favourite pike rod.

'It was sabotage,' he declared angrily to Kruger, having summoned the German officer to his office. 'There is no other word to describe it!'

'I would dispute that,' Kruger replied. 'There are other words such as accident, and –'

'That was no accident, commander, and you know it wasn't.'

'I might've been killed,' Sergeant Finch chimed in, much aggrieved.

'Sergeant Finch might've been killed,' said Reynolds, picking up a fly and examining its bedraggled feathers.

'I suggest you ask the forestry warden about the condition of that tower,' said Kruger evenly. 'It is common knowledge that it was rotten before it was moved here, and that was over a year ago. He once told prisoners on a working party that he was surprised that it had stood for so long.'

'The state of the tower is immaterial,' said Reynolds testily. 'What matters is that it was deliberately destroyed by your officers.'

'Can you prove that?' Kruger countered.

'That's for a court-martial to decide.'

Kruger looked exasperated. 'Who are you going to charge? The entire camp or just me? If it does go that far, then I shall insist on calling the forestry warden to testify as to the tower's condition.'

'The matter's out of my hands once I submit a report.'

Kruger decided that it was time to bring the conversation around to the subject that was uppermost in his mind. 'Major Reynolds,' he said, being deliberately hesitant. 'I have a suggestion to make which may offer a way out of this dilemma.'

'Oh yes?'

'Without prejudging the question as to why or how the tower collapsed, I suggest that we build you a new watch-tower.'

Reynolds blinked and dropped the fly he had been playing with. He stared incredulously at Kruger. 'You mean the prisoners to build a new tower?'

'Precisely.'

'You're crazy. I could never permit that.'

'Why not? There's plenty of timber available in the forest which the working parties are clearing. Hauptmann Shriver was a civil engineer before he joined the army. I'm sure he could design an excellent tower, complete with a proper ladder and a decent observation platform with sides and a roof to protect the guards from the wind and rain. Also I need a project to keep my men occupied, if only for a few weeks. There's not much gardening to be done at this time of year.'

Reynolds glanced at Sergeant Finch for support but his NCO was staring at Kruger with an expression that was a curious mixture of hostility and suspicion.

'There's a very good reason why I can't permit it,' said Reynolds. 'The Geneva Convention prohibits the employment of POWs on construction work of a military nature. Clearing the forest and gardening – that's fine, but I can't allow you to go building prison camp watchtowers. Thank you for the offer, commander, but it's out of the question.'

'But a firewatching tower is *not* a military structure,' Kruger pointed out. 'It is no more military than the drive that we are for ever rebuilding.' He saw the uncertainty on Reynolds' face and pressed home his argument. 'What you use a firewatching tower for is entirely up to you. And because we will most likely be salvaging timbers from the wreckage of the old tower, our rebuilding work can be classed as maintenance.'

'Well . . .' said Reynolds doubtfully. 'I guess there's no harm in –'

'I have a suggestion,' said Kruger resolutely. 'You defer submitting a report until we have rebuilt the tower. Is it a deal?'

Molde opened an eye and promptly closed it. His brain was messing him about again. He kept his eyes tightly closed and decided that his brain could work a smart hallucination when it felt like it. This particular one was brilliant. For one thing it had got rid of Caligula. For another it was in colour – the lights glinting on the silver tureen cover were in glorious, living Technicolor. But the crowning achievement was the inclusion of smells – real smells – smells you could set to music: coffee, fried eggs, bacon and toast, and home-made blackcurrant jam like his mother used to make.

Molde sat up, picked the straw out of his hair, and avoided looking in the direction on the door where the hallucination was lurking. And yet the mouth-watering odours were as persistent as a Hamburg prostitute. Slowly, he looked up. He was now wide-awake but the hallucination refused to go away: the folding table was still there and so were the pieces of bone china, together with the silver tureen cover over a dinner plate, and a coffeepot. He lowered himself to the floor and approached the table. He lifted the tureen cover and solemnly regarded the fried eggs, ham, and sausages that were gently sizzling on the over-heated plate. He picked up the coffeepot. It was hot to the touch and felt full.

Molde's first inclination was to grab his kitbag and run but he realized that whoever had provided the meal was probably covering the barn with a shotgun until the police or army arrived. There was only one sensible thing to do: he dumped a bale of straw in front of the table and sat down to eat the best meal he had had since his capture.

Hauptmann Karl Shriver was already making some preliminary sketches as he listened to Kruger outlining his plans for a new watchtower.

'It needs to be the same height as the old tower,' Kruger was saying. 'About fifteen metres high, I imagine. I'm particularly anxious that we show the British just how good our civil engineering can be, and it must be finished before the next full moon.'

Shriver gave Kruger a questioning look. 'That gives us about twenty-five days. Not very long.'

'It's imperative that it's finished by then.'

'Why, commander?'

'That's when the camp is due to be inspected by a high-ranking British army officer,' said Kruger smoothly. 'If there's no tower, questions are likely to be asked.'

Shriver continued with his drawing. 'Have you spoken to Braun about the tower?'

'Why should I?'

'He was the one that organized the tower's demise.'

Kruger gave a rare smile. 'I'm very grateful to Ober-leutnant Braun. He has given us a problem to test our resourcefulness.'

'It'll be tested all right,' said Shriver dolefully, shading the watchtower's pitched roof on his drawing. 'The biggest problem is going to be getting hold of long enough lengths of timber for the legs.'

'Can it be built using short lengths?'

Shriver considered and made some amendments to the drawing. 'I suppose it would be possible to build the tower up as a series of arches, with the arches getting progressively smaller – yes – that would be the best approach.' He showed the drawing to Kruger.

'Very neat, hauptmann. It looks right.'

Shriver nodded. 'There's an old adage about something being right if it looks right. This would make quite a sturdy structure. I haven't worked out the exact dimensions, but there need not be any timbers in it over three metres long.'

'Will we be able to salvage any of the timbers from the old tower?'

'I doubt it,' said Shriver, smiling. 'Most of them are fit only for burning in the boiler. Maybe some of the nails and spikes could be reused.'

'There's only one thing wrong. The observation platform must have a flat roof.'

'But that's absurd,' the army officer protested. 'A pitched roof made from split pine will not only look attractive, but it will be easier to make weatherproof.'

'It must have a flat roof,' Kruger insisted.

'And where do we get roofing felt from?'

'How about some of the linolcum from one of the unused dormitories?'

'Well I suppose it will do,' said Shriver doubtfully. 'But it won't be as effective as a pitched roof.'

'A flat roof please, hauptmann. As large as possible to

provide plenty of overhang protection for the tower's occupants. I would be grateful if you have the final drawing ready by this evening so that I can show it to Major Reynolds in case he disappears on a fishing trip tomorrow.'

As soon as Molde heard footsteps approaching the barn, he jumped down from the bales of straw. In case his would-be captor was nervous with a shotgun, he held his hands high above his head and mentally rehearsed the English phrase 'don't shoot' several times.

The latch was lifted and the door pulled open. Light streamed into the barn, making it difficult for Molde to see the man standing against the light. But there was no mistaking the silhouette of a shotgun draped over the man's forearm. The barrels were pointing at the ground.

The door swung closed. Molde saw that the man was about his own age. He was very English-looking and wearing an immaculate, expertly cut tweed suit.

'Don't shoot. I am unarmed,' Molde blurted out.

'I'm very pleased to hear it,' the young man answered. 'Please don't worry – there's no ammunition in this thing.'

Molde gaped in amazement at the young man. There was nothing very extraordinary about what he had said. What was extraordinary was that he had said it in German; not German as an Englishman would speak it, but with a distinct Saxony accent.

'You must be Leutnant Molde,' said the young man pleasantly, 'Correct?'

Molde nodded dumbly, his mind racing.

'I hope you enjoyed your meal?'

'Oh, yes, fine,' said Molde.

'I'm glad,' the young man smiled beguilingly. 'They mentioned your name on the radio this morning. I knew you were in here because you left a foot sticking out of the straw when you tried to hide. I moved the horse to another outhouse. He can be a bit touchy about sharing his accommodation.'

'Who the hell are you?' Molde eventually managed to stammer out.

The young man smiled disarmingly and gave a little bow. 'Leutnant Herbert Shultz of the *Kriegsmarine*. I used to be a prisoner of war at Grizedale Hall.'

Willi was armed with his trusty clipboard when he finally tracked Ulbrick down in the common room.

'No,' Ulbrick declared empathically when he had heard what Willi had to say. 'I refuse to have anything to do with Kruger's latest hare-brained scheme. It's bad enough having to do gardening, but I draw the line at collaborating with the enemy.'

'It's not collaborating,' said Willi.

'Building the British a new watchtower? If that's not collaborating, then I would like to know what is.'

'A number of officers will be in serious trouble with the British if a new tower isn't built,' Willi pointed out.

Ulbrick grunted. 'That's their problem. I had nothing to do with pulling the bloody thing down.'

'Everyone's got to help,' said Willi. 'And besides, it'll be something to do.'

'There's plenty to do. There's newspapers to be read. Chess games to be played. Radiators to be sat on. I lead a full life.'

'I'll put you down for tomorrow's forest working party,' said Willi, writing on his clipboard. 'Everyone has a job. Any officer refusing to co-operate will lose their privileges. Commander Kruger's orders.'

'And what will our commanding officer be doing? Nothing as usual. After the liberation there's going to be lot of embarrassing questions asked about Commander Kruger, and a lot of prisoners here are going to supply a lot of embarrassing answers.'

'That's where you're wrong,' said Willi, consulting his clipboard. 'He's got himself down for the last job of all on the tower.'

Ulbrick looked surprised. 'What's that?'

'He hasn't said on the work schedule,' said Willi. 'But according to the list he's drawn up, he will be driving in the final nails. Do I tell him that you're refusing to co-operate?'

Ulbrick muttered a curse under his breath. 'What do I have to do?'

'Report in the courtyard tomorrow morning immediately after roll-call.'

Work on the watchtower started the following day as soon as the forest working party returned with a handcart laden with lengths of pine. Shriver personally examined each timber. Those suitable for use in the tower were handed over to a working party to have the bark stripped off, and the rejected timbers were loaded on to the woodpile outside the hall's central heating boilerhouse.

The first stage of the operation – the digging of four deep trenches for the leg stays – was completed on the first day. During the rest of the week, the leg stays were set upright into the ground like piles. They provided a firm base for the legs to be positioned with temporary supports until the cross-bracing members were spiked permanently into place.

Shriver's design approach was to opt for cross-halfing joints wherever possible because they were simple to cut and stake. Only where strength was paramount did he insist on the more complex tusk tenon joints. Tools such as tree saws, sledgehammers, augers and chisels were loaned by the forestry warden.

By the end of the week, the tower was fifteen feet high. Progress slowed down for two days after that because a derrick – used for lifting heavy timbers – had to be designed and built, and positioned securely on top of the tower.

*

Cathy folded her table napkin and poured coffee for herself and her guests. She smiled warmly across the dinner table at Molde and Shultz in turn. 'Well,' she said. 'This is a lovely surprise. Two men to look after me. I'm going to be thoroughly spoilt, I know it.'

Shultz took her hand in his. 'Cathy,' he said gently. 'I have had a wonderful time with you. I do not think I will ever be able to repay you for your hospitality.'

Cathy's smile faded. 'But . . .' she prompted.

'It is time I moved on.'

'But, Bertie, you can't leave me. Where would you go? Back to the hall?'

Shultz looked faintly embarrassed. 'I do not know. Perhaps I will be able to find a ship at Liverpool to take me to southern Ireland – or even Sweden.'

Cathy stared down at the table and toyed absentmindedly with her napkin ring. 'When do you want to leave?'

'Tomorrow. Cathy, I am sorry, really I am –'

Suddenly Cathy brightened up as though she had made a determined effort to push the inevitable out of her mind. 'Let's worry about that tomorrow. Tonight we'll have a party. Just the three of us.'

'You're seeing Nurse Hobson tomorrow for your check-up, aren't you, commander?' Willi queried apprehensively, looking up from his newspaper.

Kruger glanced at his home-made wall calendar. 'That's correct, Willi. What of it?'

'Can you remember the name of the ship her husband was transferred to?'

The anxious note in Willi's voice alerted Kruger. 'The *Barham*. Why?'

'That's what I thought.' The little Bavarian continued reading, his face drawn and pale.

Kruger began to get annoyed. 'Willi, do you mind telling me what's the matter?'

Willi passed Kruger the newspaper he was reading. 'It's on the front page, commander. HMS *Barham* was torpedoed in the Mediterranean three days ago.'

Kruger read the news item in silence. It was terse, and to the point: on 25 November 1941, the battleship *Barham*, a veteran of the Battle of Jutland during the Great War, had been torn apart by a cataclysmic explosion following a torpedo attack by a U-boat. The mighty ship had sunk almost immediately, taking over eight hundred men to the bottom.

'Hell,' breathed Kruger softly.

'Maybe she won't come in to work tomorrow?'

'She will,' said Kruger emphatically.

The following day Cathy crammed Leutnant Herbert Shultz's kitbag with food. She tried hard not to cry but when Shultz appeared in the kitchen, wearing his original dark trousers and rollneck pullover instead of one of her late husband's tweed suits, she finally broke down and wept.

'Please, Bertie,' she pleaded between her tears. 'Stay just a few more days.'

'I have to go now, Cathy. I have been free for a year and I have only got five miles from the camp. Someone at home might start asking questions.'

'But there'll be police and the army still out looking for Victor.'

'But I am not Victor.' Shultz kissed the inside of her palms. 'We have had some lovely times together, Cathy. I do not know how I will ever be able to repay you.'

'You will write, won't you, Bertie? You promise?'

'Of course I will. And I will be back as soon as this stupid war is over.'

'That could be years,' Cathy sobbed. 'What am I going to do in the meantime?'

'Victor will look after you.'

Cathy struggled to bring her tears under control. She clung to Shultz. 'I don't want Victor, I want you.'

'I will be back, Cathy,' said Shultz, gently disengaging Cathy's fingers. 'I promise.' He picked up a wallet that was lying on the kitchen table. 'Is this the money?'

Cathy nodded. 'Thirty pounds. I hope it's enough. And the identity card is in the kitbag.'

Shultz kissed her. He pulled on a greatcoat and buttoned it up. 'It is more than enough. God bless you, Cathy. Thank you for everything.' He swung the kitbag on to his shoulder, opened the kitchen door and left the farmhouse. Cathy watched him walking across the farmyard. He reached the gate, turned around and waved, and then was gone.

She stood at the window for several minutes, gazing with unseeing eyes at the farmyard gate where Shultz had vanished. She felt in her apron pocket and took out the identity card that she had stolen during a visit to a tenant's house. Perhaps leaving it out of the kitbag had been selfish but she had been unable to think of anything else that would bring Bertie back to her.

A polite cough behind prompted her to hurriedly stuff the incriminating identity card back in her pocket and turn around.

Molde was standing in the doorway, looking uncomfortable in an expertly cut tweed suit, despite the fact that the suit was a perfect fit. Cathy stared at him.

'Er . . . Does it look all right?' asked Molde, embarrassed by Cathy's silence.

'All right?' Cathy echoed hollowly, taking a trance-like step towards Molde. 'All right?' There was a dazed look in her eyes.

'I thought that perhaps the waistcoat needs altering. Not too much. Perhaps it is a little loose at the front, do you think?'

'You're perfect!' said Cathy abruptly. 'You're stunningly, marvellously perfect!'

Suddenly, to Molde's surprise and alarm, she launched herself across the kitchen, threw her arms around his neck, and held him in a powerful grip. 'Victor!' she cried. 'You're perfect! Absolutely perfect! You won't ever leave me, will you? Promise me. *Please, please* promise me.'

As Molde steadied himself by circling his arms involuntarily around Cathy's waist, he couldn't help wondering what he had let himself in for.

'Get undressed and get on the scales,' Brenda told Kruger. There were dark shadows under her eyes and her voice lacked its usual briskness. She checked Kruger's weight and entered the information on her record card.

'You can get dressed now.'

Even Kruger was deterred by the ice in her voice. He tightened his tie and said. 'Nurse, we were all very upset to hear about what happened to your husband.'

'Thank you, commander,' Brenda replied calmly, without looking up from her desk.

Kruger's eyes went to the photograph of the smiling young man and the child. 'Is that your son?'

Brenda slipped the card back into the index drawer and slammed it shut. 'Yes.'

'He looks like his father. You must be very proud.'

'Yes, I am.' She looked at Kruger for the first time and he was immediately aware of the hatred in her eyes. 'What's it to you?'

'What is his name?'

'Stephen.'

'How old is he?'

'He's seven on New Year's Eve . . . Commander, I would appreciate it if you would leave now before I say something that both of us might regret.'

Kruger pulled his cap on and turned to the door. 'It will be Christmas soon, nurse. If there's anything that I can do, or any of the prisoners can do –'

Brenda suddenly flared up. 'Haven't you done enough? You and all the other bastards like you in your cowardly U-boats? Or have you come in here to gloat?'

'I want you to know –'

'I don't care what you want me to know. All I want from you right now is for you to get out!'

Fleming finished his monthly report to Admiral Godfrey and read it through. Something in his nature revolted against using padding, with the result that the report – his eighth – only covered a single side of a foolscap sheet. In general, his appearances at Grizedale Hall had not produced a flood of intelligence, and his effc.ts to learn about German radio ranging and location development from Kruger and other prisoners had got nowhere. There had been exceptions in other fields of technical development, such as the time in September when he had helped a captured U-boat officer with his divorce papers. From that officer, Fleming had learned about an anti-Asdic device called *Pillenwertha* that was being fitted to all U-boats. Apart from that, his posting had been a disappointment, although Admiral Godfrey had generously commented after one particularly meagre report that what intelligence had been obtained was providing valuable corroborative evidence.

Fleming sighed and decided that it was time for him to return to London for a spell. He was sealing the report in an envelope when Kruger tapped on his door and entered.

'Otto,' said Fleming, genuinely pleased. 'This is a pleasure. Please take a seat.'

'I would prefer to stand,' said Kruger stiffly. 'This won't take a minute.'

'Fire away, old boy.'

'I'm sure you are aware that some prisoners have been in the habit of selling unwanted items in their parcels to the guards – shaving soap, that sort of thing.'

Fleming chuckled. 'I know it goes on,' he replied, wondering where the conversation was leading. 'Why?'

Kruger seemed lost for words for a moment. He reached into his pocket and laid an envelope on Fleming's desk. 'I know that this is unorthodox, commander, but the prisoners have organized a collection to buy some Christmas toys for Nurse Hobson's son. There's fifteen pounds in this envelope. Perhaps on your next trip to London, you would be kind enough to spend it for us?'

Fleming was too taken back to reply immediately. When he did, it was to shake his head and push the envelope back across his desk. 'I'm sorry, commander. Tell the prisoners concerned that it is a generous thought, but I can't do it.'

'Then perhaps Major Reynolds will be willing to help?'

'It's not because I'm not willing, Otto,' said Fleming hastily. 'It's simply because there are hardly any toys to be had in the shops right now. What toys there are disappear on to the black market right away. I'm sorry.'

Kruger nodded and pocketed the envelope. 'I would be grateful if you said nothing about this to Nurse Hobson.'

'Understood,' Fleming replied.

By the end of the first week in December, the watchtower was nearly up to its full height, and lacked only the covered observation platform.

It held the promise of being a magnificent structure. All the timbers were carefully varnished before they were fixed in position, and Shriver's attention to detail was such that he had a special team of five men at work whose sole responsibility was to build the spiral staircase that wound its way up through the centre of the gracefully tiered timber arches.

Even Sergeant Finch, who still mistrusted Kruger's motives in wanting to build the tower, found himself grudgingly looking forward to when it would be finished.

'It's going to be a fine Christmas present, sergeant,'

Major Reynolds had observed when they had inspected the unfinished structure.

Sergeant Finch had cautiously agreed with him.

The prisoners organized a rapturous welcome for Berg when he arrived back at the camp. He eased himself down from the back of the truck and looked around in surprise as the cheering prisoners swarmed around him. He barely had time to exchange handshakes with Kruger and Willi when two prisoners scooped him on to their shoulders and carried him around the grounds at the head of a cheering mob.

Those prisoners who had arrived at the hall after Berg had been carted off to hospital stared in amazement at the curious spectacle. One even plucked up the courage to ask Kruger who the new arrival was, and why wasn't he being put in solitary confinement?

After the months of soft living with Cathy, Shultz was having a miserable time on the run. A day's walk had taken him to Windermere railway station but he had turned away into a side street because the station forecourt was swarming with civilian and military police who were meticulously checking every passenger's identity card. The next day he discovered that it was exactly the same at the smaller stations of Staveley and Burneside.

He spent two shivering, thoroughly miserable nights in a shepherd's stone shelter high up on Wansfell Pike overlooking Lake Windermere. On the third night he lit a small fire in the fireplace. He decided that he didn't care if someone came to investigate the smoke. As luck would have it, the wood stacked up in the shelter was tinder dry and burned without smoke. As he sat staring into the flames, the same questions kept running through his mind. Why had Cathy left the identity card out of his kitbag? Had she left it out accidently? Or had she done so deliberately? And if so, why?

'It certainly is good to have you back with us, Berg,' said Kruger during the evening meal.

Berg beamed around the crowded common room. 'It's great to be back, commander. In three months my leg should be back to its former strength.'

'And your concussion? Its after-effects can be most unpleasant,' Kruger observed.

'Sometimes I get a ringing in my ears,' said Berg dismissively. 'But I've got used to it now.'

'Well, let's hope you haven't brought back any more rumours from hospital about our transfer to Canada.'

Berg chuckled and sliced up the extra sausages he had been given. 'I heard nothing this time, commander. Only the ringing noise in my ears.'

Kruger watched Berg's knife expertly slitting the sausages open. 'I see that your skill with your hands hasn't deserted you, Berg.'

'Oh, not at all, commander. I kept my hand in at the hospital by making all sorts of things.'

'Good. Because I've got some work for you.'

Berg looked interested. 'On the tower? I'd enjoy that – it's a fascinating project.'

'No,' said Kruger, shaking his head. 'Not on the tower, but on something almost as important.' He went on to briefly outline what he wanted Berg to do.

'I'll be delighted to help,' said Berg, smiling warmly. 'I can't think of anything else I'd rather do.'

Molde surprised himself at how easy he found it to slip into a routine at Cathy's farmhouse. When the weather was fine, he went riding with her on the high fells. At other times she found innumerable small jobs for him to do in and around the farmhouse and its outhouses. Caligula soon learned to accept him as part of the household and an uneasy truce was agreed between them which the cantankerous horse was inclined to forget. The only irksome aspect of living with Cathy was having to make himself scarce whenever she had visitors. But, on the whole, the life was agreeable and the occasional moments of daytime boredom were more than offset by the tempestuous night-time events that Cathy loved to stage in her bedroom.

Berg was kept frantically busy from the day after his return and was rarely seen outside his workshop. Brunel was press-ganged into helping him and, after some initial objections, soon become absorbed in acquiring the skills necessary to operate Berg's home-made woodturning lathe with a reasonable degree of proficiency. After two days he surprised himself by making a matching set of four wheels out of a fruit packing case. That they had to be made again because Berg's first experiment with home-made axles went badly wrong was hardly his fault.

It took Shultz five minutes to smash a hole in the layer of ice that covered the tarn. He dipped his fingers in the freezing water and hurriedly withdrew them. He decided to remain dirty. Anyway, there was always a wind blowing so he could never really smell himself. The water in the ice pool became still. Shultz looked at his reflection and was shocked by the appearance of the fearful, unshaven apparition that stared back at him. It was hard to believe that five days living rough could do that to a man. He was cold, miserable and hungry, and had had enough. He stood up and was dismayed to discover that he now had diarrhoea to add to his problems. He decided to give himself up at the nearest police station.

At 10 am on 8 December, Shriver reported to Kruger's office. He gave his senior officer a smart salute and said, 'The tower is finished except for the work you said that you wanted to do on it, commander.'

'Excellent, hauptmann,' said Kruger, lighting a cheroot.

'You've done an excellent job. My congratulations. I will need a hammer and some clout nails.'

'They're ready on the platform for you, commander. Everyone is waiting,' Shriver replied, eyeing the ten-feet high roll of black linoleum that was standing in the corner of the office.

'Thank you, hauptmann. Give Major Reynolds my compliments and tell him I'll be along in five minutes.'

Shriver saluted and left.

The hall sounded curiously empty and quiet as Kruger went down the main staircase with the roll of linoleum tucked under his arm. He paused at the french windows to gaze across the grounds at the watchtower, rising solid and dependable above the trees. Shriver had gone to considerable pains shaping the timbers to ensure that the tower was symmetrical. The result was that from a distance it looked as though it was of steel girder construction.

All the prisoners were standing at ease in parade formation near the foot of the tower. Shriver, Braun and a few other senior German officers were standing in the front row. They were flanked by all the guards on duty. Major Reynolds and Sergeant Finch were standing side by side facing the parade. Even Fleming was watching from a distance.

Kruger made his way around the vegetable plots and walked to the head of the parade. He stood the roll of linoleum on end and shook hands with Reynolds and Sergeant Finch.

'I guess this is a great day, commander,' Reynolds observed. 'I've just delivered a little speech congratulating everyone who has worked on the tower.'

'We have all worked on it, major,' Kruger replied. He gestured at the roll of linoleum. 'Even I have a job to do. I have to waterproof the observation platform's canopy. The final task of all.' He caught Braun's eye and correctly guessed that the young pilot was having to work hard at preventing himself from bursting out laughing. He picked up the roll of linoleum. 'Am I correct in assuming that the question of a report concerning the collapse of the old tower is forgotten?'

Reynolds grinned. 'What report, commander?'

Kruger nodded. 'Thank you, major. If you will forgive me, the tower will be ready for handing over in about fifteen minutes.'

With that, Kruger walked beneath the structure and tied the roll of black linoleum to a rope that was hanging down from the observation platform. As he climbed the spiral staircase, he noticed minor constructional details such as the fact that the balustrade had been sanded smooth so that there were no splinters waiting for an unwary hand. He reached the spacious observation platform and glanced down at the sea of faces looking up at him. It took him a few seconds to haul the linoleum up to the platform and push it through the trapdoor on to the flat roof. He pocketed the hammer and a box of nails and climbed through the trapdoor.

Unrolling the linoleum in the strong breeze posed an expected problem, which he solved by placing the linoleum in its approximate position and temporarily tacking it down at the corners. The orientation of the roof covering was vital. He used a pocket compass to confirm that it was correctly aligned before he started nailing it down in its final position. It took him ten minutes to make sure that the linoleum was securely fastened to the canopy. He trimmed off the surplus linoleum with his pocket knife and stood up to study his handiwork with a dispassionate eye.

Painted across the linoleum in three-feet high white letters was the single word: **BARROW**. Beneath the solitary word was a broad arrow, over six-feet long, that was pointing south-west towards Barrow-in-Furness.

Kruger had used poster paint for the giant sign, which

meant that it would not survive many Lake District down-pours. He prayed that it would last until the bombers came that night or the night after.

The one thing Berg enjoyed doing most in his workshop was painting. There was a particular satisfaction to be derived from sanding a carefully worked piece of timber to a mirror finish before applying successive coats of lacquer and rubbing down each coat when it had hardened. Provided it was done carefully, what was originally a rough lump of wood could be made into something that looked like polished steel.

He and Brunel made a good team, and the results of their labours – lined up on the shelves – were a testament to their painstaking craftmanship.

Shultz dithered outside the tiny police house at Hawks-head, uncertain what to do. A woman passed by and wrinkled her nose in disgust. She made up Shultz's mind for him. He pushed the door open and shuffled into the house. A uniformed police constable was reading a newspaper while resting his feet on a pot-bellied boiler. He lowered the paper and gazed suspiciously at the thing confronting him. His nose gave an experimental twitch.

'Good evening,' said Shultz politely. 'I am an escaped German prisoner of war and I wish to give myself up.'

Police Constable Harry Tinker was Hawkshead's acting village policeman while Sergeant Webb was on leave. The last advice Sergeant Webb had given Harry before leaving was to tell him to watch out for a tramp named Soapy Sam who would do anything during the winter months to get himself in a police cell for the night. Under no circumstances was Soapy to be allowed into the police house because it had to be fumigated afterwards.

'Clear off,' said Harry curtly.

'But I'm an escaped –'

'I said – clear off!'

'But –'

'OUT!' Harry lent emphasis to his request by threatening Shultz with a truncheon which he clutched in his right hand while he used his left hand to hold his nose.

Shultz wandered forlornly out into the cold and wondered what to do next.

Brunel and Berg waited until 11 pm before they decided it was safe to make a move. They had remained in the workshop after lights out, crouching in the dark behind the workbench, hardly daring to breathe as the guards checked that the place was empty.

They carefully wrapped the smaller items in rags and placed them in a sack which Berg tied across Brunel's shoulders. Brunel checked that he had some suitable lengths of wire in his pocket and pulled on a pair of thick woollen socks while Berg opened the door and peered cautiously across the courtyard. He waited until two guards strolled by and then signalled to Brunel.

The diminutive officer raced cat-like across the courtyard and crouched under the window of Brenda's sickbay. He carefully slipped a length of bent piano wire under the sash catch and teased it into position. After a while he managed to slide the catch back and open the window. He disappeared into the sickbay and emerged a minute later clutching the now empty sack in his hand. He raced back to the workshop, grinning triumphantly.

'Nothing to it,' he whispered to Berg.

'Fine,' said Berg. 'Now for the rest. Can you manage the car as it is or shall we wrap it up?'

'I'll take it as it is,' Brunel answered.

'Well, mind you don't scratch it.'

By midnight all the results of Berg's and Brunel's labours had been safely transferred to the sickbay.

Unknown to the two men, another prisoner was also out

and about that night when he should have been locked up in the main hall.

'Schumann, John, Leutnant!' Sergeant Finch yelled, calling out the names from his roll-call list that he knew virtually by heart.

'Present!'

'Shulke, Jacob, Oberleutnant!'

'Present!'

'Shultz, Herbert, Leutnant!'

'Present!'

'Siemens, Wolfgang, Hauptmann!'

'Present!'

Sergeant Finch suddenly froze. His eyes narrowed. Someone was playing silly buggers. 'Who answered to Herbert Shultz's name?' he bawled indignantly.

'I did, sergeant!' answered a voice from the back of the parade.

All the prisoners turned their heads.

'Eyes front!' Kruger ordered.

'Who said "I did"?' Finch roared, his face puce with anger as he strained to look over the heads of the prisoners.

'Me, sergeant.'

'Who's me? What's your name? Where are you?'

'Leutnant Herbert Shultz. I am here.'

'Step forward that man,' Kruger called out.

A bedraggled, miserable looking creature shuffled forward. The prisoners quickly and willingly made a path for him through the parade.

'Who the hell are you!' Finch demanded, taking an involuntary step back when he caught a whiff of the new arrival.

'I'm Leutnant Herbert Shultz,' said Shultz, managing to muster a smile through his unkempt beard. 'It looks like we are all one big unhappy family again.'

*

Brenda unlocked the door of her sickbay, pushed it open and gave a gasp of surprise at the spectacle that confronted her.

There were toys everywhere. They were on her desk, on the filing cabinet, on the scales, and even on the couch. There were brightly painted little tanks, a glove puppet, a wooden soldier with a drum slung across his chest, a model train sitting on a circular track with a clockwork key sticking out of the top of the locomotive, and even a clock with toyland scenes painted on its face. The largest toy of all was a magnificent child's pedal-car that looked like a miniature version of Fleming's Bentley.

Hardly able to credit her senses, Brenda entered her Aladdin's Cave sickbay and picked up one of the toys. Four gaily coloured wooden chickens mounted on a table-tennis bat immediately started banging their beaks on the bat in time with a swinging weight suspended beneath the bat. She put the toy down and picked up a hand-painted Christmas card. It bore the inscription: 'To Stephen – wishing you a happy Christmas, a happy birthday, and a happy 1942. From all the prisoners at Grizedale Hall '

Brenda felt her legs threatening to collapse under her. She sat hurriedly down on her chair. Suddenly she was trembling violently and then she broke into a flood of anguished tears.

Fleming fell into step beside Kruger as the senior officer took his customary stroll around the grounds. 'That was a decent gesture, Otto,' he remarked. 'Making all those toys for Brenda's son.'

'Don't thank me, commander,' Kruger replied. 'Thank the officers who made them.'

'But you instigated it, Otto.'

'Perhaps.'

'I'm off back to London until the new year,' said

Fleming. 'I thought I'd wish you a happy Christmas before I left.'

'Thank you, commander. I wish you the same.'

The two men walked in silence for a few minutes. They reached the southern barbed wire perimeter fence. 'Have you thought about how much longer this war is going to last?' Fleming asked.

'I think of nothing else,' said Kruger. 'Four months? Six months perhaps? I don't know.'

'I think it will be longer than that, Otto. A lot longer.'

'What makes you so sure?'

'Everything has changed,' said Fleming. 'Hitler has just declared war on the United States.'

Kruger stopped walking and stared at Fleming. 'Are you sure?'

Fleming nodded. 'It'll be on the news within the hour.'

Kruger remained silent. He lit a cheroot and inhaled deeply. 'So . . . what will happen to us now?'

'Well . . . it looks as if you'll be here for at least another year.'

Kruger turned to face the wire.

Fleming waited for a minute but Kruger gave no indication that he was going to speak or that he wished for Fleming's company to continue. The British officer decided that there was no point in staying. He turned and walked away. Only when he reached the terrace steps did he look back.

Kruger had not moved. He was standing motionless, staring at the high barbed-wire fence. His greatcoat flapped in the wind and the flurries of driving snow sweeping down from the fells offered a bleak promise of a long, bitter winter to come.